ABOUT THE AUTHOR

Born in Belfast in 1962, Keith Reilly left to travel the world at 18, exploring Europe, India and South East Asia and meeting Dutch wife, Maryke, en route. Today they live in Dorset and have two grown up children. Keith focused on his career and became managing director of an international electronics firm. However, his creative side could not be ignored. Over the years he has published a number of artworks of Belfast and other cities, but more recently has turned to words for creative expression, from which emerged his debut novel, *Ahoy for Joy*.

Cover illustration from an oil painting entitled: "Belfast Shipyard from Pearl's house" by Keith Reilly

AHOY

for

JOY

Keith Reilly

Matador
9 Priory Business Park,
Wistow Road, Kibworth Beauchamp,
Leicestershire. LE8 0RX
Tel: (+44) 116 279 2299
Fax: (+44) 116 279 2277
Email: books@troubador.co.uk
Web: www.troubador.co.uk/matador

ISBN 978 1784622 084

British Library Cataloguing in Publication Data.
A catalogue record for this book is available from the British Library.

Printed and bound by CPI Group (UK) Ltd, Croydon, CR0 4YY
Typeset in 11pt Bembo by Troubador Publishing Ltd, Leicester, UK

Matador is an imprint of Troubador Publishing Ltd

www.ahoyforjoy.com

To my sister Jillian whose unique enthusiasm
breathed life into this story

To Jonathan.

Enjoy!

May 2021

Part I

Michael

CHAPTER 1

Morecambe, Lancashire, 1978

The three white minibuses arrived just before noon. A small, pale boy aged about thirteen with fair, roughly shorn hair, jumped out of the first and unlocked the rusty five bar gate to the farmer's field. Holding it open, he waved the vehicles through one at a time, before skipping enthusiastically ahead to a further gate a hundred yards up a steep incline and doing the same. The vehicles entered the large field and circled round a little before pulling to a halt together, roughly centrally and not far from the gate. Some men emerged from one of the minibuses, more from another along with boys, teenagers and then two women. The group stretched their legs. Some walked about the site surveying it thoughtfully, while others stood chatting in small groups. Some of the younger boys began chasing each other around in a rather haphazard fashion. There was a scream. Several of the boys had wrestled a small lad to the ground, shouting and giggling as they pulled his trousers to his ankles.

"Let him go, will you" shouted one of the men angrily. "There's work to be done."

The field sat atop a small mound that rose up from the outside of the town and sloped off into the distance toward the north. To the west, the sands of Morecambe Bay could be seen stretching away towards the far off headland. It was summer and warm. The wet sands fused into the shallow water without

3

contrast while the high sun sparkled on the Irish Sea beyond.

Then a van arrived followed by a large flatbed lorry which moved slowly up the hill. It was not of the very largest type, but was stacked high with all manner of awkward shapes, covered and held in place by a dirty green tarpaulin tied with rope. More men emerged and boys too. Before long there was a hubbub of activity where only moments earlier, the field had sat quiet with only the birdsong for company.

There were shouts for help and effort, punctuated with angry tones threatening discipline. The unloading began. Smaller items emerged from the van; boxes and cartons, some clinking with loose items, others packed tightly and tied with string. Spades, mallets of several different sizes and other tools emerged along with hurricane lamps, pots and pans, brooms and buckets.

One man in particular was in charge. He was a stout man in his mid-fifties, with an air of command about him and wore freshly creased dark blue trousers and a white open-necked shirt, like he was used to sporting a tie but had discarded it for the day's activities. He stood largely stationary near the truck, rotating in different directions while shouting instructions, identifying items and directing them to different places in the field. Groups of boys helped, pulling and hauling, sometimes without the most refined of methods. A number of them could be seen dragging cartons across the grass, hauling and straining. One cardboard box burst open and large cans of baked beans and vegetables spilled out, rolling in all directions across the grass to be rescued by the hapless young labourers, who stacked them untidily alongside the other equipment that was piling up nearby.

The flatbed was untied; a lengthy process that involved the

slow disentanglement of ropes and ties before the tarpaulin was removed and larger items unloaded. Trestle tables, chairs and benches, three kitchen cookers, of the regular gas type found in any kitchen, were carefully lowered to the ground. Half a dozen large gas bottles, several plastic water containers, four big industrial stainless steel sinks and two hot water urns, like those found in a church for serving tea or coffee to large groups, were all carefully unloaded.

Big heavy poles were handed down from the vehicle, some enormous, made of rough wood, cracked and splintered and painted in a light red colour that had faded with time. On one of them was written, in large letters; "Belfast Battalion." Dozens of hanks and coils of rope were thrown to the ground, followed by several large un-shapely bags tied at one end with small lengths of coarse string.

Everything was carried and placed in various locations around the camp at the direction of one they called the *Adjutant* who rushed around shouting and pointing. He was the second in command, aged around fifty and dressed more casually wearing jeans and a bright checked lumberjack shirt with the long sleeves rolled up to just below his elbows. He fulfilled a kind of mobile version of the central commander and watching the two working together, it was clear this was a well-practised routine. After the poles came large rolls of white canvas which were again carried around the field. Some took three or four to carry, other larger ones required, six, seven or even eight people to move.

Finally, tied tightly to the stanchion at the front of the truck, just behind the cab was a small bellow-operated church organ of the foot pedal type. It was built of polished mahogany, about the width of a standard piano, but a little deeper and stouter in nature. Once untied, it was carefully slid across the flat surface of the truck by several of the older boys. Then two large wooden poles were pushed through dedicated holes in the main body towards the bottom of the unit enabling it to be lifted stably by four people. Ushering it to the edge, four men each gripped a pole end and then taking up the weight, it was lowered slowly to the ground, before being carried to the main area where most of the other items now stood.

Once the flatbed was empty, the driver jumped once more into the cab, reversed a little and engaged gear. Rolling down the window, he leaned out and shouted,

"See you in a week," and with that he was gone. It was hot and with the unloading complete, one of the ladies ran around handing out cans of soft drinks as well as sandwiches and biscuits.

Michael Coglan didn't much care for Boys' Brigade camp. It was just organised bullying from his point of view. Instead of the usual two-hour harassments and minor beatings of a Monday parade night, the week would be more or less a constant barrage of youthful abuse, verbal and physical, that everyone liked to describe as *banter* or *horseplay*. The adults justified it with noble terms like *character building* or the process of *turning boys into honest young men*. Michael saw it as a kind of mildly sadistic abuse that his and everyone else's characters would build just fine without. Still, he never complained and it was a week away; a change of scene.

"Tours of the black hole, tours of the black hole," a voice rang out. Michael knew what that meant. Despite his reservations and complaints, he came every year and was familiar with the expression used for the series of ditches that would be dug at the edge of the camping ground for use as makeshift urinals. These would then be covered over again at the end of the week, quickly returning the farmland to soil and grass.

"Come on Michael; take these shovels and a couple of the younger lads. Your tent can dig the hole this year."

His mind protested, but he made no noise. Instead, he lowered his head and his eyes focussed on a clump of clover in the grass as he wondered if a four leaf might be among them.

"Come on now, dig the black hole and you'll at least know your way around in the dark!" The officer laughed openly at his own wisdom. "Look, go over there, as far as you can get, close to that hedge. The wind should blow mostly from the coast, so we should at least be spared the smell." Michael grudgingly took the four shovels and handed three to some of the smaller boys that were loitering nearby. He met their innocent eyes with a solemn nod to follow. *Welcome to camp lads. Tours of the black hole*, he sighed to himself.

"At least a foot deep, mind," shouted the officer at their backs.

Meanwhile, in the centre of the pitch, a huge canvas was being unrolled. It was opened out, placed and rotated several times under the direction of the Adjutant, as he carefully surveyed the sun's position and wind direction. Two of the largest poles were then carried over and while the edge of the main canvas was lifted slightly, the end of one of the poles was guided by a small boy who crawled underneath like a mouse beneath a rug.

Suddenly, to the sound of giggling bystanders, a large, fat boy jumped forward and belly flopped on the unsuspecting mite crawling underneath in the dark, causing a loud shriek followed by a slow, sorrowful murmur.

"Stop messing around" shouted the Adjutant angrily. At last the boy began moving again, inching forward and at the direction of the Adjutant, finally located the iron rod on the end of the pole into the sewn brass eyelet at the top of the first apex of the tent. The same process was carried out with the second pole and the small boy emerged looking red and bothered to a pat on the back from one of the officers and a small burst of applause from the now slightly more sympathetic onlookers. One of the canvas bags was then untied and dozens of tent pegs fell out. Some were rough wood with battered, frayed ends from years of mallet action, while others were works of art, eccentric designs complete with names and places engraved like; Willie Best, Prestatyn '73 or James Montgomery, Isle of Cumbrae '71. The annual tent peg carving competition had been generating a reliable source of high quality new tent pegs for many years.

The Adjutant then produced a tape measure and carefully measured a distance of forty-two feet between the bases of the two poles before selecting several of the better looking pegs and hammering them into the ground at the base of each pole providing horizontal purchase against the grassy surface. Four ropes were then attached by loops onto the pins, now poking through the brass eyelets on the top but shielded by little canopies to stop the rain seeping in at the top, and laid out flat on the grass on either side.

The guy ropes were already attached to the lower edges of the marquee roof and the Adjutant, along with another officer, ushered boys of all sizes into place on either side and on the ends too. Each was given a line to hold.

"When it reaches the top, take up the tension," he said again and again as he checked everyone's position, "*Don't* pull, *just* take up the tension," he emphasised. Finally, two officers one side and two of the bigger boys on the other took hold of the long ropes attached to the top pins and on one side, pulled the ropes tight to take the strain.

"OK, ready. At my command," said the Adjutant with confident authority, "take the strain…and…" he looked around checking "p u l l."

The huge white canvas flew into the air, bellowing and flapping like the giant sails of a yacht facing into the wind, their power still unharnessed, awaiting the control of the sailor. When the poles reached vertical, the forces of the lifting side were reduced and the two boys on the other side stepped and struggled to maintain their balance as they took the strain.

"Jackie, move that way, a little to the left, otherwise the poles will fall towards each other," shouted the Adjutant confidently. In seconds a balance had been reached. The smaller boys held the guy ropes firm around the perimeter leaving the great white canvas roof floating on the two main upright poles.

"Hold tight, hold tight. Perfect, everyone. Don't pull, don't pull, just take the strain, take the strain." The Adjutant stopped and smiled for a moment, his hand on his hip, as everyone held their positions. He hadn't missed a camp in 30 years and had hoisted many marquees in all conditions from pelting rain to high winds. This one had been easy. He marched to the position of one of the boys holding a main guy rope connected to the pole end, now some 20 feet in the air and taking a large mallet from the pile, he hammered a stout peg into the ground nearby. Then quickly, he took the rope and hooking it over the peg, adjusted the wooden tensioner to balance the strain. In moments, he had done all four. The older boys and officers, now relieved of their hoisting duties, then ran around the tent, hammering pegs, carefully aligned to run with the seams of the canvas, maybe ten or twelve feet from the edge. Then, methodically, relieving opposite boys in turn of their duties, they hooked the shorter guy ropes in position, again adjusting each one to balance the strain. Finally, the four main lifting guys were unhooked from the pegs and with a quick flick, the adjutant sent a wave through the ropes causing them to jump off the apexes at both ends.

Within minutes the canvas sat still in the air without the need for human aid, contrasting majestically with the blue sky above and the flourishing high trees that edged the site. Some, like the Adjutant, had done this many times before, while for others, it was their first camp, or at least their first mission with the advance party that would set up the tents before most of the boys arrived later in the day. Instinctively, everyone stopped briefly at this stage, without command or direction and admired the grandeur of the great white cape floating apparently unaided above the ground; the sun's rays lighting its shape and creating a kind of mystical vision, like an instant cathedral had suddenly appeared before them.

When Michael arrived back, the walls were being hooked in place and pinned to the ground with smaller pegs cordoning off the interior from the outside. His arrival was met with the departure of another group who loped off towards the *black hole* where a rough wood sign indicating the same had already been sited beside where Michael and his party had dug the ditches. The new group carried small green canvases and large tin buckets with wooden toilet seats for the construction of the individual tent cubicles or *latrines* as they were called, for more solid waste. Not that Michael would use them much due to the usual fear of having the tent suddenly removed by giggling youths leaving him exposed and with dirty bottom, sitting atop 30 lbs of chemically neutralised waste, to the gaze and puerile mockery of anyone interested enough to take notice.

With the main marquee built, the focus moved to the other tents required for the camp. Two groups of four boys went about raising the bell tents that would provide the sleeping accommodation for the boys. The principle was much the same as for the marquee, only that there was just one central post in the middle and the sides of the tent remained attached to the main roofing sheet, but they were raised in the same way. This was not quite as easy with the bell tents, due to the tent being round, as it could tend to 'rotate' slightly if any of the ropes were even slightly out of line, pulling one way or the other. It was important to get this right as this lining of the guys and seams was an important element of the camp inspection that would take place each morning. The bell tents were large enough to sleep up to ten boys, but usually eight was considered optimum, with heads at the sides and feet all pointing towards the pole in the middle. This allowed for a little personal space at the head end, but left the feet kicking each other by the central pole.

The female officers, who also served in the Boys' Brigade, would mainly manage the kitchen tent headed by Miriam, the Captain's wife. She was a harsh looking woman who managed to conceal the sympathetic side of her personality with as much success as she revealed her uncompromising commitment to the high standards of performance and respect she expected from the boys. This made her a formidable and feared defender of all things central to the camp, the preparation of food being the most important (in her opinion) and the serving and consumption of it being the second most important.

The northern edge of the marquee was the business end

with the entrance just on the adjacent wall to the east and away from the coastal draughts. This would stay open at all times save for very poor weather and the marquee when not in use for formal meetings, consumption of food and religious praise was an open, accessible and central meeting point at all times of the day. The kitchen tent was situated just behind the main north wall, so that food could easily be carried around and through the main entrance for serving of the meals.

Finally, those who had completed their tasks already, were put to work carrying the trestle tables, benches and chairs into the marquee before setting about preparing it for use. The tables were all placed parallel to the north wall, such that the benches were facing either, towards the front or back and these would be the boys' seats, with those facing the back being required to turn one hundred and eighty degrees during praise or when the Captain or other officers were addressing the camp. The officers' tables were positioned at the front. These were of the same trestle design but they had conventional chairs and all faced towards the centre of the marquee, such that they could watch the boys as they ate. The tables were then covered with woven plastic tablecloths of a red gingham design and clipped at the sides to prevent them from being blown away should the wind rise up, the marquee walls being of only partial protection. Finally, the last item to be located was the organ which was diligently carried over and carefully placed at a forty-five degree angle to the perpendicular opposite the main entrance.

Once fully set up, a Boys' Brigade camp of the late 1970s was quite a sight to see. Years of experience and military precision, designed and commanded by men, but largely carried out by boys had turned the farmer's field into a living, working camp capable of surviving weather of every kind as well as just about every other occurrence likely to happen where over eighty people of vastly dissimilar ages and backgrounds, set about living for a week under canvas on the north west coast of England.

At around 5.00pm, a coach liveried *Marlor of Lancaster*, arrived with a further fifty or so boys on board. These were mostly younger children, who had taken a more leisurely route to camp and stopped off for some sightseeing on the way, together with a few more officers who had supervised the travel. They alighted the coach, one by one carrying all sorts of personal belongings before dragging their far-too-heavy suitcases to their allocated tents. After a while, they emerged, dressed in their smart Boys' Brigade uniforms. These consisted of a dark blazer (usually their school jackets sufficed) white laundered haversack with a diagonal strap about two inches wide that attached to a tiny pouch with a brass button that sat just below a leather belt around the waist. The belt bore a shiny brass buckle at the front embossed with the Boys' Brigade symbol, of an anchor, and motto; "Sure and Steadfast," and was worn tightly over the jacket holding the haversack in place. The uniform was completed with a blue cap, best described by the boys themselves as a 'Thunderbirds' cap due to its similarity to those worn in the television series of that name that was popular at the time. The officers wore uniforms too, of dark blue suits with Boys' Brigade emblems on the collars.

"Where is Michael Coglan?" shouted the Adjutant as he rushed around, "where is Michael Coglan?" Michael moved forward. "Ah, Michael, would you like to be the bugle caller this year?"

Michael looked confused, his eyes almost meeting those of the busy officer.

"Come on, you know. Sammy usually does it, but he's left now. You have to sound the calls for camp, assembly, reveille and that."

Michael stared. "Hello, hello. For God's sake Michael, why won't you ever speak?"

Michael shuffled nervously. "Is there no one else who can do it?"

His words sounded awkward and stifled in his ears like they were not his but those of an imposter seeking to take on his persona towards dubious ends. How he hated BB camp. Here there was no hiding in the calm of solitude where his mind could wander toward placid lakes. Instead this would be a week of pressured babbles of incoherent conversation and unwelcome incursions into the only peace he knew which lay within.

"Michael, if I could get someone else to do it, I wouldn't be asking *you*, now would I?" He smiled encouragingly, leaving a short pause he knew instinctively would yield agreement from the young lad.

"Seriously though," he went on, "it is pretty important and I need someone I know I can rely on."

Everyone was different and the Adjutant was adept at understanding every boy in the company and the required process for acquiescence which he customised to perfection. But Michael was a different challenge. He had never met anyone so nervous and withdrawn, or anyone who looked so pained that he might burst into tears at the sound of authority.

"Come on. Here, tie this to your bugle." He handed Michael an elaborately woven rope of burgundy and maroon, which Michael looped in place, pulling the cord tight around the body and leaving the tassels dangling. The bugle had been in the company for many years and handed down from boy to boy as were aspects of the uniform such as the belt and haversack. Michael's Dad had seen to it that the bugle was polished to perfection prior to the trip and with the battalion colours attached and the warm summer sun glinting on the shining brass, it did indeed look like a very fine instrument.

"OK then, let's hear it. Call assembly."

Michael slowly lifted the bugle to his mouth and pursing his lips carefully, sounded the familiar notes that could be heard throughout the camp. Michael had seen Sammy do this many times before, heard it sounded many times more and responded to the very same call at every camp he had attended. Still, he was surprised as boys and officers too, hurried towards him from every direction, filing past and into the marquee for the formal opening of camp.

Michael stood fast and as they passed by and a rather unsuspecting sense of pride came over him. He did look smart with his uniform, perfectly turned out as always, the gleaming instrument in his hand, adorned with colours and tassels. They were his notes everyone had responded too. It was he who had commanded camp just now.

"I am the Trumpet Major," he muttered to himself. "Well the bugle Lance-Corporal at least." He looked across the valley towards the town and out to sea. He looked at the high trees behind, at the town below and at the cottages in the distance to the north. It was indeed a fine sight to see.

"The Trumpet what?" asked a voice breaking his solitary thought. It was Fred, a skinny boy about a year younger than Michael, who persisted in attempts to engage the quiet boy in conversation and was one of the few with whom he interacted at all.

"The Trumpet Major. It's a novel by Thomas Hardy. We're

15

reading it at school. It's about this girl, Anne Garland, she's called, who can't decide which bloke she fancies." He stopped talking and paused, his mind drifting as he looked around once more at the surrounding countryside; *She could be out there right now looking up at us setting up our camp like the soldiers in the book. She could be out there looking up at me, with my smart uniform and my shiny bugle glinting in the sun, flashing random reflections over the meadows.*

"Any good?" asked Fred, interrupting Michael's thoughts once more.

"Pretty sedate really. It's set in Dorset during the Napoleonic wars." He stopped once more, musing to himself, rather surprised, more at the positive flicker in his mind than his sudden willingness to share the literature he spent so much time reading, "he does really bring the Dorset countryside to life though."

"Is this Dorset then?"

Michael smiled. "No, this is Lancashire I think. Dorset is down in the South."

"What, the South of *Ireland*?" Exclaimed Fred vexed.

"No, not the South of *Ireland*, the South of *England,*" replied Michael exasperated. "Dorset is in the South of *England.*"

"Alright, alright! I just didn't want you reading about everyone chasing after some wee *taig* from the South"

Michael shrugged. He could see Fred's slow thought process was evolving.

"Napoleon, he was the French guy, right?"

"Yes he was. Invaded most of Europe, 'till Wellington defeated him at Waterloo. You wouldn't have liked him though. He was definitely a *Fenian!*"

"Waterloo, like the Abba song?"

"The very same!" said Michael, "Come on, we better head inside."

Michael and Fred took two of the last seats in the back row, shunting the boys along the bench to make room.

The Adjutant sat at the organ and pedalled. With a creak and a grunt, the bellows filled, the first chord was sounded and the Boys' Brigade camp of Morecambe 1978 burst into song:

> Will your anchor hold in the storms of life,
> When the clouds unfold their wings of strife?
> When the strong tides lift, and the cables strain,
> Will your anchor drift or firm remain?
>
> We have an anchor that keeps the soul
> Steadfast and sure while the billows roll,
> Fastened to the Rock which cannot move,
> Grounded firm and deep in the Saviour's love.

While they were singing and unnoticed by any in the marquee, the five bar gate opened once more and two rather overladen, small cars drove through. The occupants gazed briefly at the white tents and could hardly have missed the sounds of the organ and singing, before turning left and heading down hill to the far end of the long field.

Four young men, aged around 18 or 19, got out of the first car. They had long hair and wore blue jeans and T-shirts with bright slogans and images printed on them. Two more boys similarly dressed emerged from the second car, quickly followed by two girls, younger than the others. For the second time that day, a bewildering array of goods emerged from inside and on top of vehicles and before long, a second camp had been struck in the farmer's field overlooking Morecambe Bay.

CHAPTER 2

Foreign Visitors

The night time, just after *lights out* in the boys' tents, was always a mixture between torment and chaos, especially the first night of camp when spirits were high from travel and the boys still well slept from the relative serenity of home life. For the younger boys the experience was closer to torment. Activities such as *blacking*, the application of shoe polish to various parts of the anatomy, or *whiting*, the equivalent but with toothpaste which if gotten into the eyes, was quite seriously distressing for the victim, were popular. In between there were of course the thumps and punches, often over zealously applied to aid capitulation and all of course carried out with the unreasonable odds of the many upon the one. More usually, the process was carried out in near silence for shouts and screams were the equivalent of *grassing* to the officers, a crime which was bound to carry a much greater punishment to be meted out later in the week.

Invariably the youngest boys at their first camp would be left sobbing into their pillows, begging for their mothers' arms. For the older boys the choices were to participate in the bullying, a kind of perverted revenge for the assaults received themselves in younger years, or to just lie back and snooze, feigning disinterest hoping that they would avoid becoming the victim of a concerted attack, perhaps where personal resentments that had built over time were settled.

Such resentments did exist, for besides the usual arguments and disagreements, BB members came from all different backgrounds and in terms of social class, almost every group was represented. The church from which the company mainly recruited was situated in an area where the demographics were changing fast. The families of some members had been attending for generations and were drawn from the affluent classes of merchants, factory owners and managerial professionals that used to live in the large residences close to the city centre. These people had long since deserted the area and moved to the leafy suburbs with more modern housing, improved law and order and the calmness and serenity of tree lined avenues, neatly trimmed hedges and flowers and shrubs blooming in the gardens. But traditions hang heavy in Belfast and many would still travel across town to attend church, offering generous financial support in return for Christian witness and perhaps an element of stability in an uncertain world.

By the late 1970s, the area surrounding the church had become further run down and ravaged by sectarian violence and social unrest. Many houses were empty. Some were grand ornate residences of yesteryear that now stood still and silent, their windows boarded, now home only to a town fox or two. Others were squatters' pads, occupied more by drunks and outcasts than Bohemians and revolutionaries where the muffled sounds of nonsense chatter could still be heard in the dead of night. The shops in the area were now mainly of a specialist nature, selling car parts or second hand furniture and there was also a huge cinema, the subject of a bomb blast several years earlier, that stood on the corner of the main road, a burnt out shell, like a giant monument to a society that had gone horribly wrong.

There was only one shop, a general store, that served the local community in any way and it sat grey and lonely with dim lights inside and windows protected with huge mesh trellises, more resembling an army barracks than a retail outlet. While a stoic working class still existed, the area was now predominantly home to the downtrodden of society, those without the means to move out or to others, underperformers, social misfits, or those who just sought low cost housing. Unemployment was high, prospects dire and the streets dangerous. Still the church persevered with an unwavering resolve, a combination of Christian commitment and dogged determination not to let the gangland culture win. As a result new members were found from amongst these groups. For many young men of the day, the Boys' Brigade represented a perilously thin line between a life of honest endeavour, albeit a challenging one and one of misplaced political action, or just good old fashioned crime and punishment.

This lead to a diverse membership, almost irrational in its range, from the privileged elite of Belfast society who would go on to attend the top universities throughout the British Isles, with the prospects such an education offered to others whose life opportunities would be limited to humble occupations, or more often unemployment. This fractious mix of society would meet and function on a weekly basis pursuing activities including regimented drill, team games (volleyball was popular) and badge classes.

Michael had never been that sure where he might fit in such a diverse group, but he did know he was different, quite different from most or even all of the boys there. His tacit intellect and thoughtful sensitivity was like a red rag to the rougher kids more adept at functioning in high spirited, streetwise environments, who considered him privileged and accused him of pretending he was *better* than them. This was far from the truth for while he had won a scholarship to a good school and his family had enjoyed some past wealth, such affluence was a distant notion of which Michael had no memory. Today, while he hailed from a loving home, the financial pressures were if anything more severe than for others in the Company. As well as this, he was a deeply troubled young man whose personal motivation in all aspects of life seemed somehow to have become lost in a shady past he understood more through feelings and emotions rather than relationships and events. He was awkward, insular and his ability to function socially, rather limited.

Tonight however, as he lay awake in his sleeping bag listening to the stifled squeals of the victims and the sadistic sniggers of the tormentors, he was left alone. Maybe it was his age; he had just turned sixteen and was really now one of the older boys. Perhaps it was some new, subconscious authority his bugle provided with its polished brass form, now adorned with the grandeur of the battalion colours and the clear sharp tones of command that had echoed throughout the camp earlier in the day. Or, maybe the others had just become bored with beating on the quiet boy who never fought back and had turned their attentions to the more animated squeals of the new quarries that the camp supplied each year. He turned his face to the pillow. *Perhaps he should intervene.* No one had *ever* intervened, not really, perhaps for fear of the wrath of the group. But for Michael, whatever his circumstances, he never found peace of mind. He felt shame. He wasn't sure why, but he felt it all the same. Shame, loathing, *self*-loathing were constantly dominant in his mind, but he just didn't have the courage even to comment or plead for restraint. Fear pervaded his senses, and an abject sickness swelled in the pit of his stomach bringing tears to his eyes. Finally, he curled up and eventually went off to sleep.

Michael woke early the next morning, much earlier than the others. Indeed, he had slept well, and he almost chuckled to himself as he set about checking the guy ropes. The sky was a deep blue once more and the sun rose behind the trees to the east promising a fine summer's day ahead. He sucked in the cool, early morning air, his lungs keenly absorbing the oxygen, waking his body and his mind. The birds sang in the trees and the scent of wild flowers wafted across the silence of the camp seeking his nostrils like they had a message for him. *Maybe this year's camp would be better.* He felt an emotion, almost new to him. *An unfamiliar feeling.* He felt wary of it and at first pushed it from his mind, the way he had always done. For as long as he could remember, he had crushed any positive emotion with an ardent resolve for reasons he neither knew nor challenged. Today however, it returned, persisting like a seedling, pushing through the soil and feeling the warmth of the sun's rays for the very first time. Michael felt positive, hopeful even.

BB camp was a regimented affair with a set timetable throughout the day consisting of sports, games, sightseeing and competitions. Breakfast and evening meals were always held in the marquee and included a sprinkle of religious worship, usually a hymn and a prayer, but evenings were mostly free.

However, the day always started with camp inspection. This involved the comprehensive cleaning and tidying of the tent interior and providing the weather was fine, would include the rolling of the brailing. To do this, the sides of the bell tent were unhooked from the ground, then neatly rolled and tied with cotton strings to the underside edges of the great canvas roof. This allowed the tent to be brushed out and all the bodily smells of youth to disperse quickly into the surrounding air, a welcome cleansing in preparation for the coming night. Once complete, with no visible sides, this made the canopies look like they were floating on air, like giant Chinese lanterns rising from the heat of the land. The white canvases set against the multi-coloured hues of the countryside with rows of well turned out youngsters ready for inspection in their dark uniforms with glinting adornments to their apparel, was a distinct source of pride to the officers who gave their time freely in the guidance of the young.

As the second oldest in the tent, Michael was de facto second in command. The tent leader was Derek, an affable young man when it suited him, but dim witted and harsh towards those smaller and weaker than himself. He was a year older than Michael, and had left school already having been fortunate enough to secure an apprenticeship with a plumber in the city. Michael's father had also started out as a plumber's mate, so they had perhaps something in common, though he had never thought to mention it.

Derek was ambitious to see that his tent would win the coveted inspection prize this year, but despite Michael's cooperation, he did have his work cut out for him. There were always one or two boys in the company that no one seemed to really know where they came from. *Little squirrels*, Derek called them. They attended irregularly, were always filthy and stank, not entirely of the body odour of poor personal hygiene, but of a wretched, abject neglect. Uniforms were never cleaned, brass was tarnished and shoes went unpolished. On Mondays one of the officers, who should surely be admired for sheer dedication, would pick them up for parade night activities from their broken homes in unsafe parts of town where parents were often absent or drunk. Sometimes a woman in pyjamas would greet the officer with a cigarette dangling from her mouth, quickly ushering the child out of the door. Other times, some aggressive, burly bloke could tell him to 'eff off', causing a brief glint of concern for his personal safety. For these children, abuse of every sort was part of their daily lives and where they lived terror organisations ruled the streets, feeding their finances from the local community and recruiting vulnerable youngsters to fight for their *cause*.

For these boys, who always appeared younger than their years, looked thinner than the other boys and for whom the simplest of tasks always seemed a struggle, the abuses of BB camp held no fear and the tent leader's threats had little effect in raising standards. One such boy in Michael's tent was called Johnny. Michael showed him how to fold his sleeping bag. Folded, then folded again into four, he demonstrated. On top would be placed the towel, again carefully folded, then the bible on top of that. Johnny's towel was filthy and the bible absent, so Michael sent him to the marquee, to see Miriam, the Captain's wife to ask if he could *borrow* (Michael had emphasised) a bible for the inspection. In the meantime, he opened his can of *Duraglit* and sat down to polish the boy's brass belt and haversack button, buffing both quickly to a smart shine. Moments later, the lad arrived back, bible in hand and Michael laid it carefully on top of the towel.

"We'll try and get that towel washed for tomorrow, eh?" he sighed, looking at the child's blank expression. "Here, look, I've done your belt. Are those the only shoes you have?" He looked down despairingly at the lad's dirty trainers. Johnny nodded. "OK, don't know what we can do about that." With that Derek entered;

"Jesus, you really stink, get out of the friggin' tent" he shouted kicking the boy hard on the rear end as he scurried for the exit. "Bloody miracle if we win, with him in the team." Michael went outside with the boy's worn jacket in his hand, frayed at the edges and a few sizes too small.

"Here, get this on," he sighed, holding the garment open, revealing the lining ripped and torn inside. In moments, Michael had him dressed with dirty haversack and filthy jacket complete with gleaming brass button and belt buckle. *Not sure that's an improvement* thought Michael thinking the contrast only emphasised the dirt.

The boys lined up, the older ones straight to attention, the younger ones suddenly afflicted by shakes and itches and little Johnny on the end, seemingly unable to even stand with his toes aligned with the others in the group. The Captain walked past slowly, standing before each boy, checking him up and down and making the occasional comment. He paused by Johnny, smiled warmly and moved on.

At last the command came:

"*Stand at ease*" and a short moment later, "*stand easy.*" The tent groups relaxed. Derek looked over at Michael and nodded, indicating behind him,

"What are those tents doing down there then? I thought this was supposed to be our site."

Michael turned and gazed down the long field. There was indeed a little collection of blue tents in a group at the far north end of the field beneath a giant oak tree that grew out of the hedgerow like a great colossus watching over the land. It cast a welcome shadow over the site delaying the rapid rise in temperature that would make further sleep for the inhabitants impossible once the morning sun hit the canvas unhindered.

"Don't know. I guess the farmer was offered a few more quid by someone. I don't suppose they're doing any harm. They are quite far away."

Derek didn't look convinced. He viewed everyone with suspicion, a caution his life experience had taught him and one that he rarely ignored.

"As long as they don't come nicking our stuff while we're away. Fred says he saw one of them up at the black hole last night. Seems he'd been having a shit in one of our latrines," he went on. "Bloody nerve. Claimed it was OK. Said he had brought his own toilet paper! Hey Fred," he called out towards the next tent, "What's with the hippy types down the bottom of the field?"

Fred walked over nonchalantly. "Foreign" he said.

"What do you mean by *foreign*?"

"Just foreign. They talk funny."

"Funny, like not *English* funny?"

"Yes, like not English funny, like European or something. They don't speak English that well."

"So, you talked to them then?" enquired Derek further.

"Yeah, I saw one of them in the bog, like I told you. Then again, two of them were coming through the gate last night." He nodded towards the main entrance to the field. "Looked like they had a carry out or something. They, nodded and said; *we have de fiss en chips.* Guess they'd been to that chippy down the road. Bloody hell! Fish and chips. I'd love that, instead of the crap Miriam serves up here."

Two of the mini busses started up and pulled over next to the marquee. "If you're playing in the football team against the Blackpool squad, get in the bus," barked the adjutant.

CHAPTER 3

An Unexpected Liaison

While the days were crammed with sports, visits and competitions, the evenings were largely kept free. The boys were allowed to go into the nearby town of Morecambe where the main attraction was the fun fair with its roller coasters and slot machines. There was of course a curfew, but other than that the only real rule was that the groups should stay together. It was on the third day, when money was running a little short and the officers hadn't yet released the second half of the children's spending money from the makeshift 'bank' they operated, that the group of boys Michael had tagged along with, returned to camp early. The flashing lights of the fair had lost some of their lustre, now that they were mainly observers rather than participants in the fun. Michael had been lost in his thoughts all day and had gone along as much out of habit as for want of anything better to do, rather tailing on the end of the group and moving from one activity to another according to the others' wishes.

As usual, they approached the camp through the outer field, but tonight some people had built a small fire and were patiently cooking sausages speared on the ends of long sticks. They sweated with oil and sizzled enthusiastically releasing a familiar aroma that wafted around the field, stimulating the taste buds and enticing the boys' interest. Fred immediately recognised them as being the foreign people who had pitched their small camp in the far corner of the BB field. One of them called over to Fred,

"Farmer said we could light a fire here. Not in the big field, but OK here he said." Most of the BB group headed on back to camp, but Fred, Michael and Lorrie, another boy of similar age remained, chatting politely, if a little awkwardly, with their new acquaintances. They seemed friendly enough and spoke in a kind of accented, broken English, punctuated with pauses, nonsense and mispronunciations. While conversation didn't exactly flow, communication was successful. There were six of them in all, perhaps a little older than Michael. It turned out they were from Holland or the Netherlands as they tended to say, alternating between the two terms perhaps intending to maximise the chances of being understood but this mostly just left the BB boys wondering if it was the same country or not. They had clearly spent some time earlier in the day gathering up sticks and branches from around the field and adjoining meadows as a considerable pile of wood still remained to one side of the fire which raged enthusiastically in the warm, early evening air, flickering a homely light on the faces of the bystanders.

Generously, as they had surely not been expecting company, they shared the sizzling sausages, wrapping them in soft baps and covering them with copious amounts of mustard squirted from a large plastic bottle, before handing them around to their new friends. Fred sniffed the mustard cautiously and inspected the bottle, which bore an unfamiliar brand name and indecipherable text before scraping the yellow sauce off and dropping it on the grass. He then crammed most of the snack into his mouth in one go, scoffing it down eagerly. Michael on the other hand, chewed gratefully, nodding and smiling approval as he ate. Some of the older boys drank beer, which they offered to Fred, Michael and Lorrie, who politely declined – the consumption of alcohol being among the most severe offences that could be committed while on BB camp. In the end, they talked for some time, laughing and joking.

The Dutch boys were particularly amused by the BB camp, with the uniforms, inspections and bugle calls as well as the hymns and praise, all of which they had been observing from afar. One of them, an older boy or young man really with fair hair and a brisk face of unkempt whiskers, introduced himself as Geert. He jovially complained about being awoken at 7.00am to bugle calls as the camp came to life in the morning. This was a point Michael timidly admitted responsibility for, before rather shamefully undertaking to blow his bugle *quieter* the next morning. This caused a few laughs among the now assembled international group and even through his awkwardness, Michael felt the sides of his lips jerk upward slightly into a nervous grin few had seen before.

There were five more besides Geert whose name with a soft 'G' at the beginning required a throat clearing exercise for proper pronunciation. The BB boys struggled to say it without spitting, much to the amusement of their new friends. There were also two brothers, Alex and Stan, who were both a little younger and still at school. They described the school as HAVO which provided for both academic development and vocational preparation. Alex hoped to become an electrician and Stan wanted to study nursing, an occupational choice the Irish boys found rather bizarre, though they nodded approval politely.

Michael was interested in the education system and rather out of character, found himself asking questions. It seemed the Dutch had a selective system divided into three categories according to the child's interests as well as, of course, their intellectual potential. The HAVO school most of the boys attended, offered a wide range of academic instruction including; Maths, Dutch, History and the sciences as well as English, of course, but there was also a more vocational school with advanced education in practical skills such as wood and metal working, art, design and craft. For the more academically minded, there was also a school specialising in what Michael concluded as being a more classical education, including subjects like Latin and Greek, like what might be found in a Grammar school similar to the one he attended. This, they referred to as a *Gymnasium*, an amusing term in the context, more associated with sport and exercise in the English language. It seemed Geert's sister, Anna and her friend Grietje, whose name they also couldn't pronounce, attended such a school and were also with them in the camp.

On this news, the Irish boys, in a slightly comic synchronisation, looked around the small field, as if bemused that they hadn't noticed the female attendance. This caused Alex to laugh out loud, explaining that they were back at the tents, reading or something. Michael liked the new boys friendly, foreign – their strange accents, eccentric clothes and casual mannerisms amused him and they seemed to be able to have long hair without looking like thugs. One of them, called Hans, wore a kind of necklace that would surely be considered effeminate back at home and another, perhaps the oldest and de facto leader of the group, called Loek wore a red bandana around his head like a cross between the tennis start Björn Borg and a Cuban guerrilla.

For conversation, football seemed to be the most successful subject and with the World Cup Championship taking place later in the summer, hope and expectation was high. Holland had been in the final in 1974 and the lads seemed to think they had a chance again this time. Northern Ireland, like England, had failed to qualify, but was not as invisible on the international stage as they might have imagined as everyone knew George Best, whose talent and antics were almost as newsworthy in Holland as they were in the English press or back in his Belfast homeland. Scotland, while a rank outsider, was however enthusiastically supported, but the Dutch boys reckoned that with Johan Cruyff and company, they had a serious chance.

Eventually, the fire died down and the evening could easily have finished there with the BB boys returning to their camp and their new friends returning to theirs. But Alex suggested they might like to see the Dutch set up and with the tantalising prospect of some female company, Fred and Lorrie, who it turned out had noticed the girls before from a distance, were keen for an introduction. Michael saw no reason to retire and followed on behind, an unfamiliar motivation beating its way to consciousness in his mind.

The tents were of a more modern style made from thin, lightweight, blue nylon fabric and were fairly large for this more domestic style of tent, each being capable of sleeping at least three or even four in reasonable comfort. There were three tents in all, pitched such that the front entrances were facing each other with an open space to allow the campers to come and go. This provided some privacy as well as creating a natural communal outdoor space. A folding table and a few chairs had been set up in this area where there were also the remains of carry out food packs and soft drink cans as well as some other rubbish awaiting disposal.

They were introduced to the two girls, who were a little

younger than the boys. The first, and older looking of the two, was Grietje. She had long, reddish brown hair and engaging hazel eyes that flickered teasingly as she shook the hands of the Irish boys. The second introduced herself as Anna and smiled bashfully as the boys jockeyed for attention. She had curly blond hair, not long, but voluminous that sat untidily, dishevelled even with side locks that dangled across her face, that she habitually pushed away from time to time. Her deep blue eyes, soft pale skin and freckly face made her look more childlike than beautiful. Michael gazed warmly at her. She wore a checked shirt, a little too large for her slender frame and skin tight trousers, perhaps of cotton with an eccentric multi-coloured pattern of an eastern looking design and no socks on her feet. Michael liked her at once.

It turned out, Anna was Geert's sister and the other girl, Grietje was her friend who had clearly come along as company. From what Michael could tell, it looked like Geert taking his younger sister on holiday had been a condition the parents had stipulated on granting permission for him to go. However, Michael, perhaps more sensitive to such things, had seen a warm affection between the two siblings as he was introduced and he quickly discovered the benefit Anna offered as despite being the youngest in the group, her English was rather better than any of the others. What did seem strange to him though, was that they all seemed awfully young to be there, abroad, in a foreign country with a foreign language, unsupervised and far from home. What amazed Michael more was the casual attitude the older boys had towards the two girls. None of them seemed in any way protective towards them, or mistrustful of their new friends who clearly found the girls very engaging company.

In time the Dutch boys elected to go off to the pub and

while the invitation was extended to Michael and his friends, it was politely declined, leaving the three of them following the girls into one of the tents. Inside they scrambled for position. Michael, without any particular agenda, but perhaps by reverse intention or maybe even Anna's design, found himself directly opposite her, sitting cross legged in the cramped surroundings. Around them were strewn sleeping bags, pillows, clothes, toiletries and the various other paraphernalia required to make life in a tent as comfortable as possible. Michael stared at her intently, absorbing her image in his mind, this being perhaps physically the closest he had ever been to a female of his peer group. In time, all were more properly introduced. The girls seemed to find Fred's name amusing, which they pronounced 'Freet' with the long vowel sound their accent afforded and the hard 'd' at the end.

"It means *chips* in our language" giggled Anna, referring to the Patat Frites, smothered in mayonnaise, she would buy occasionally when out with friends at home. Michael could have looked at her forever and never become tired. She smiled openly, engaging him with her eyes. "Anna" he mused, not *Anne*, but Anna. *Close though*, he thought. *Maybe this was his Anne Garland after all*, but what struck him most was that unusually, quite unusually, she seemed interested in him. Normally, he would always hold back while the other more gregarious lads would make all the running, preferring or at least feeling his place was on the side lines, in the background. Now, tonight, suddenly it was he who seemed to be the centre of the conversation. And, indeed it was, for Grietje hardly spoke and in any case her English was fairly limited, but she laughed openly at the humour and more so at the confusion and misunderstandings that often ensued.

To the bemusement of his BB friends, and even his own surprise, instead of reverting to his usual disinterested silence, Michael found himself working hard to keep the conversation going, adding to her comments and politely correcting her English, something the other boys would not perhaps have had the interest or knowledge to do. Soon, Michael asked to learn some of her language and the little group laughed and joked as his poor efforts became the centre of attention. Her English was better than any of the others including the older boys and Michael took to watching her intently. She would listen to what he said; a question or comment, then look away, shyly towards the ground or towards an irrelevant object at the side of the tent. Then she would bite her lip once more, before her gaze shone on him again and the properly constructed sentence would be stated with carefully studied accent and diction. He soon realised that the long pauses were for thought and admired how wonderfully she had mastered her skill. Of course, she had a strong accent, which made him laugh and her giggle when her speech went wrong and Michael would interject, apologising and smiling at the same time, as he detailed the correct sentence construction or pronunciation of the words.

"English is so awkward" she said smiling. "*Though, rough, bough*. How can they all be spelled the same, but pronounced so different?"

Michael hadn't especially thought about it, but yes, he could see the problem.

"Isn't it like that in your language, in Dutch?" He had asked, but no, it seemed, despite the well-known English euphemism of Double Dutch for a complicated language, everything was very uniform.

"If you can read it, you can say it," replied Anna.

Michael was elated. She didn't want to talk about football all night. Not only was she beautiful, she was charming, interesting and he was sure, if he dared be sure, she liked him! How could she ever like him? No one had ever liked him before. Suddenly he clutched urgently for reason, for a stability of thought, a datum point in his mind to relate to. Quickly he knew he was floating in an unfamiliar current of warm air over which he had no control. Was he imagining it? Was it real? Could it be real? He glanced over at the others. They seemed quite bored, just sitting there while he and Anna traded comments and ditties of fact across the language and cultural boundaries that offered a world in which he felt able to comment.

Eventually, they moved on to music and the seal of mutual interest came to a head, for most people Michael knew were interested in the top 20 music hit parade with its plastic actors singing songs by commercial songwriters of shallow intellectual value. Anna was much more interested in album tracks by singer songwriters with profound messages to send. For Michael too, it was all about people like; Bob Dylan, Leonard Cohen and Neil Young, where the lyrics were not just rhyming nonsense, but poignant, touching stories of sorrow or triumph or political statements and observation of the changing world.

Michael had been listening to such music for several years by then, but had barely even had the shortest of verbal exchange with anyone of a similar mind in his life. Now suddenly this beautiful girl engaged completely as they each mentioned favourite songs and albums. Anna ventured questions or comments on lyrics, which she somehow expected Michael to immediately be able to clarify as if his mother tongue was also the fountain of literary understanding. He did try to explain the analogies contained in Dylan's Blowing in the Wind and they both speculated if the lyrics were just an observation of life, as Dylan himself had claimed, or part of a subtle theme of political change. They both liked Neil Young and fellow Canadian Joni Mitchell whose haunting lyrics of love and relationships seemed to speak to them separately and together, joining them now at this moment in time as if the same songs offered a constancy of understanding like the sun or the moon. Anna had laughed and of course agreed that nobody could decipher the words of Procol Harum's Whiter Shade of Pale and speculated that they were probably inspired by some form of substance or alcohol abuse. On the other hand, American Pie, the only song by Don McClean they rated, clearly had clandestine messages that would keep the music speculators busy for a long while yet.

"It might be," Michael offered, "that some messages, we just have to enjoy not understanding." Anna smiled, her white teeth showing quickly before she once again bit her lip,

"Don't you think the new Dylan song, Forever Young, is one of his best?"

"Perhaps the very best," agreed Michael, looking into her eyes and thinking of the lyrics he knew by heart. "Nothing political in that," he said at last, "just maybe the most perfect ode to youth ever written." Suddenly Michael seemed able to express himself. After years of near silence, at last he seemed able to say what he wanted, as if a door in his mind had suddenly opened. Anna smiled once again. Engaging, warm, open. He could have looked at that face forever. It was, *she* was, sublime in every sense. He watched intently as her gaze left him bashfully during the short, silent interludes in the conversation, before returning, engaging him once more and breaking into an open smile. As the evening wore on, and the pace slowed, Michael took only to watching her, like he wanted to absorb everything about her into his mind, through his pores and his being like this was Brigadoon and tomorrow she would disappear from his life for a hundred years. He reeled at the thought.

At last, Fred looked at his watch.

"Hey, shit!" He exclaimed, "We've got to go. We should have been back twenty minutes ago." Lorrie jumped up and crawled for the exit, causing Grietje to fall over as the pressure in the blow up bed that had been their seat rose, and suddenly fell. Fred quickly followed, crawling head first through the door, but Michael stayed put.

"Hey Michael, aren't you coming?" shouted Fred.

"I'll be along in a minute."

"You'll be along in a minute? You'll be in trouble. You'll lose points for your team." Michael looked back at Anna. She laughed.

"Points for your team?" she questioned, grinning. Michael blushed. This was indeed true, he would lose points for his team, for while the boys could earn points for all sorts of activities, like good inspection results or winning games or even individual tasks like the tent peg carving or orienteering competitions or kite construction, they could also lose them for lateness or any other misdemeanour. Michael tried to explain how it worked, but suddenly, it all seemed so silly, so childish, so crass. He whimpered with embarrassment, reddening as he spoke, revealing vulnerability that unknown to him, Anna, who just sat there smiling and amused, rather liked. Suddenly, he had nothing to say. He just looked at her. Then, Grietje cleared her throat and said something in Dutch, before grabbing what looked to be a soap bag, pulling up the zipper once more and leaving the tent.

They were alone. This should have been his opportunity, but his mind was suddenly as empty as a liar's promise. He tried to recapture the subjects of the last hour or so, but nothing seemed appropriate. Anna just sat there, looking at him, then looking away when the gaze became too much and focusing once more on an imaginary object at the side of the tent, biting her lip, then looking back at him again and again. Michael just watched, perhaps in a curious premonition, recording her image in his mind, like he might need it again, forever young. At last there was an angry shout from outside.

"Is Michael Coglan in there?" Michael jumped. It sounded like the Adjutant.

"Yes, OK, OK, I'm coming," he shouted back, entirely failing to conceal his irritation.

"Well, get up to camp at once boy, or you'll be touring the black hole all week! I don't want to have to come down here again," and perhaps with some sympathy for the lad's situation, he walked off. They both listened intently as the steps faded and Michael was just about to launch into explaining what the black hole was, when Anna saved him from himself. She put her hand on his, her palm atop his knuckles and softly wrapped her fingers around, squeezing gently. Her touch felt electric, spiritual, sublime, transcendent.

"You have to go," she said.

CHAPTER 4

Desire – the Mother of Poetry!

Michael slept uneasily that night, his unfamiliar elation not lending itself to a gentle slumber and by the morning bugle call, the one he had undertaken to do 'quietly' the night before, the endorphins in his mind had begun to transmit a rather mixed bunch of messages. He was really quite troubled. *How could he see her again?*

It was Wednesday and today was the eagerly awaited trip to Blackpool Pleasure Beach and England's largest Big Dipper, as well as an endless host of other attractions whose principle objective was to relieve children of their money. They wouldn't return until evening. *Perhaps he could see her then.* Suddenly a chilling thought surged through his mind; *What if she was gone by then?* He had no idea what her plans were, if they were to stay until the weekend or when they would leave. Fear took hold and suddenly he became convinced that Anna would be just the shortest of fleeting encounters that would simply fade into the past like a fond memory of no consequence. He wondered if he could feign illness or injury and stay behind with the women officers.

While the others were preparing for tent inspection, he found a few moments and slipped away, heading down towards the Dutch camp. He called Anna's name quietly outside her tent, but there was no reply. He didn't feel he could quite burst in, so instead went over to one of the boys' tents, unzipped the door and crawled in, waking its inhabitants who seemed to have been undisturbed by the bugle call that morning. Geert sat up, perhaps at last a little fearful for his sister's virtue and exclaimed,

"Man, have you been here all night?"

Michael was quick to reassure him that all was indeed well and he had slept in his own tent at the BB camp, but that he would be gone all day and wanted to see perhaps if they might meet up again later that evening. Geert rubbed the sleep from his eyes but Michael's fears were not without foundation for the Dutch group were indeed set to leave that very morning.

Michael arrived back at the main marquee as breakfast preparations were underway. He was distraught. His mind was in chaos as he struggled to find a way forward that he felt he could live with. He ignored his team's activities for tent inspection and sat silently, head in hands, in the empty marquee as Miriam and the others milled around getting everything ready. At last, Danny, one of the younger officers, a thoughtful and sympathetic sort, who Michael remembered had been one of the older boys when he first joined the company, sat down on the bench beside him. He didn't speak. Instead, he just sat there quietly, his hands clasped on the table. Michael tried hard to ignore him, but at last, his presence irritated him sufficiently and Michael turned towards him revealing a face, red and swollen with pain and anguish.

"What do you want?" he barked quickly.

Danny smiled back warm heartedly, but didn't rush to reply. Eventually he said,

"I'm just here to see if I'm needed." Michael scowled back. "Do you want to tell me about it?" Danny went on, his voice soft, considerate. "Girl?" he questioned.

There was no girl. No *girl*. Michael's thoughts raged. Maybe he wanted there to be a girl, a relationship, something, but there wasn't. It had just been a fleeting moment, a mirage, a dream that could never be. A sickness rose in his stomach. Anna had probably forgotten him already. Why hadn't he just let himself be? He had been fine, he got up, went to school, he went home, watched TV, he slept. Life had been fine, now a giant anvil had fallen from the sky and his fragile demeanour lay crushed and distorted in a way he hardly understood.

"See, Michael," he went on, "you don't look great. You're upset and you're upset maybe because it's something important to you. That's fine." Danny paused, thinking a while, taking care over his words. "Look, I probably can't help. I admit that, but you might feel better after talking about it. If you tell me about it, maybe you'll get an idea. An epiphany!"

Michael smiled inside at the use of the word, *epiphany*, but prevented it showing.

"Look, you're an intelligent boy, but at this moment in time, are you really using all your grey matter? No you're not. You're simply lost, wallowing in your own self-pity. Maybe you need to raise your game a bit. Maybe you're short of time. Maybe you need to think fast. Don't let things get you down, confuse your mind. There are some outcomes you can't control, but you can control your own actions."

There was logic in his words and Michael sought to confide in the friendly young man. He even opened his mouth to speak, but emotion came over him and he had to bite his lip hard to maintain composure, clasping his face once more to conceal the distress in his eyes. Danny sat patiently. It was a busy time in the morning and he too, like the boys had various duties to carry out, but still he sat allowing his responsibilities to fall by the wayside as a greater priority, sat in abject misery beside him. Eventually Michael composed himself.

"Well, it's nothing really," he explained at last. Danny raised his eyebrows. "Well, just…" His voice tailed off. "Well, there was this girl and I though we got on so well and probably she didn't really like me anyway and she's foreign and I would probably never have seen her again anyway and now she's going, like right now this morning, like while we are away and that will be that. Oh God, why do I feel so utterly…" He paused and his red eyes met Danny's for the first time, "so utterly, well lost, miserable?"

Danny smiled, once again, maintaining the eye contact that he saw as a victory, sympathetic for the boy whose very dignity he had trodden on to get to the nub of the issue.

"Sounds like you're in love," he ventured at last. It wasn't the right thing to say.

"In love? *In love*? How can I be in love? I only just met the girl. There was nothing. Look nothing, you know. Nothing happened. I wanted it to, but it didn't. It just didn't, now it never will." Michael slumped forward, his head once more in his hands and now resting on the trestle table in front.

"Well, has she *actually* left yet?"

Michael didn't answer, but Danny went on anyway.

"Well, why not leave her a note and ask her to write to you, or even just to send you a postcard from her home town or something. Or just give her your address and see what happens." Michael knew it wasn't a bad idea, but the mood of grief and desolation in his mind was still very much in play and he rejected the notion lamenting sorrowfully,

"She'd never write. Why would she write to me? She'll forget me. She probably has already," but the more he went on, the more reasons he presented dismissing this as a plan, the better it sounded.

It seemed such a poor compromise though. He wanted to *see* her again, but it also seemed the only way forward. *But what if she never wrote to him? What if she just left his note tucked deep in her bag but never retrieved it, never wrote?* Every step forward in his life, however small, always involved a whole wider scope for new fears and terrors, worse than the last, that would occupy his mind and eat at his soul. At home, he spent most of his time alone in his bedroom. It was easier that way; simple, undemanding. In solitude he appeased his vulnerability, a sense he found so debilitating, now he had adopted the greatest vulnerability of all.

Oh the joy of love could never be worth the pain of loss, he lamented silently. But there was also a new sense he felt inside too; a logic, a consideration, a reality. Perhaps one day he would have to stand up and accept these human emotions that he crushed from his consciousness with a zeal that had left him alone, silent, friendless and all but invisible to those around him. *Perhaps, this was not right?*

He presented this notional challenge to himself that moment on that bench, in the camp marquee, Danny by his side, for the very first time in his life. Perhaps he had found a prize worth fighting for and his default setting of disinvolvement with everyone around him may actually be a bigger problem than he had considered. He shuddered. Perhaps today was the day when he would finally have to confront reality and accept that his state of mind; his solitude and his withdrawal, was not a true state, not a natural state. His mother had always worried about his quiet nature, his apparent social ineptitude and awkwardness. In truth, it had never really worried Michael, not until then that was. But by now he did know that love was in his mind and in his heart. He also knew that if he was to move on, then he would have to invite once more, another, more familiar emotion, one that had tormented him, bullied him into silence and detachment for as long as he could remember. He would have to welcome fear as willingly as he sought love for he knew that without the fear of loss, there could be no love.

And fear chilled him to the core. Fear was all he had known for as long as he could remember. Fear was the predominant emotion in a mind complicated by a murky past and a disturbed present. Tentatively at first, but quickly a confidence grew in him and although a fear did rise inside, it was not quite a negative fear, a debilitating fear in the way he knew it, but a fear that focused his senses and stimulated his mind. Suddenly, Michael knew that if he got the next hour or so of his life right, he would change it forever. He knew if he got on that bus for Blackpool without taking the right action, the emotion that he at last realised he wanted to share would remain buried in him and Anna would disappear from him forever, like an illusion, a fantasy that never was.

Politely, he thanked Danny for his help, excused himself from the table and went to his tent. Rummaging in his suitcase, he found some sheets of paper he had brought with him to write to his parents. Derek shouted at him to help with the inspection preparations, but he hopped out of the tent again, oblivious to the abuse directed at him and returned to the marquee taking up the same position at the trestle table. Then, with pen in hand, he settled himself down to write.

However, before long, breakfast was ready to be served and the boys quickly appeared, milling in around him. It was not the best environment for so important a task, but he was obliged to be there and couldn't really be anywhere else. In any case, this was the only horizontal surface available. So, to the sound of further complaints at his failure to prepare the tent for inspection and as the table moved and shook as the others constantly pushed and shoved, arguing over the milk, sugar and cornflakes, Michael wrote.

While he wrote, the others poked and prodded him and each other and mocked and ridiculed and tried to wrestle the sheet from his hand, but he resisted, his introverted nature adept at shutting out confusion. He had just finished, and was writing his address at the bottom when one of the boys snatched it from him and pretended to read. Michael lurched at him but he quickly passed it on to the next boy and from him to the next, along the bench. Distraught, Michael jumped up from his seat, knocking the arm of a boy behind who emptied his spoonful of cereal onto his lap, before retaliating with a hard thump. He ran around, after the note as it was passed, thrown and tossed from boy to boy. Every so often, one would hold it just almost within reach, then pull it away suddenly as he made a lunge to catch it. After a while, some took to reading bits of it before bursting into fits of laughter, then handing it on to another, or throwing it across the table. Michael was hysterical. A cocktail of rage, fury, embarrassment and humiliation ran through his veins as he danced to everyone's tune, desperate to get his note back. At last, Jackson, a boy a year or so younger than Michael with a quick wit and a cheeky grin the girls back home rather liked, jumped to the centre of the marquee.

"Shall I read it?" he said, egging a response as he ran around the Marquee dancing, holding the paper in the air while Michael begged for it back. Once or twice, he almost grabbed it, but Jackson was too quick for him. Michael struggled to hold back the tears welling in his eyes. He could take the mocking and the humiliation; these were prices he was willing to pay, but he wanted his note back. Then, one of the larger boys who had rotated his position on the bench to watch Jackson's performance in the middle of the marquee, grabbed the unfortunate Michael from behind, pinning his arms helplessly to his sides before pulling him down and holding him tight upon his lap. The shrieking faces of onlookers laughed and leered at him from both sides, from before him and behind, their heads turning to look and laugh like he was some kind of nineteenth century freak show. Michael struggled in desperation, swooning from the heat, the exertion, the attention. "Don't you *want* me to read it?" Jackson jeered, inviting a response. Michael struggled once more, but his breath was short from the strong arms surrounding his torso and he whimpered, a response so pathetic, it only added to the fun.

The adjutant, now startled at the commotion shouted angrily,

"Will someone please give that boy whatever it is belongs to him," before going back to eating his breakfast and continuing to try to hear the conversation with the others at the officers table. Seeing Michael now pinned down, his challenge mollified, Jackson filled his chest. There was something of the performer about the young man and he confidently set to address the room, the paper in his right hand with his left gesturing for emphasis and effect.

"To Anna," he began,

> Last night I met a friend but now
> I find that you're to go

So here's a note to get your goat
And maybe even though

You live abroad so far away
Beyond the lough and sea
I hope the most that you will post
A note addressed to me

He stopped, pausing for effect amid hoots of laughter. "This is bollocks" he retorted, before reading on silently, "Hold on, it's getting better."

And if you do, I'll sit and scribe
A verse to send you back
One set in time or rhyming slang
Of jolly wit and craic

So please do get the time to write
And speedy letter send
A little think with pen and ink
To me your new pen friend

Michael struggled and cursed, his energy quickly sapping away as the big lad's grip, firm and resolute, held him fast. His face grew red with desperation as the endless humiliation showed no sign of abating. At last, Danny rose from his seat and grabbed Jackson roughly by the hair and tightening his grip slowly to the sounds of shrieks and protests withdrew the paper from his grasp. He then handed it to Michael, who had just now been released by his co-tormentor who had been astute enough to see the situation change.

"The coach is here already. You have ten minutes to get this to wherever it's going," he said.

Michael grabbed the letter, his face red with anger and stress, his composure long since gone and ran full pelt from the marquee to the sounds of further jeers and whistles. Outside he folded it quickly and placed it in the envelop he had planned to use for his parents letter and wrote 'Anna' on the outside.

He ran down the hill, his trembling legs feeling like they might give way at any time. By the time he reached the tents of the Dutch visitors, he was quite out of breath and could hardly call her name. At first there was no reply from inside but at last he heard the reassuring sound of the zip un-fastening and Grietje stuck her head out. She didn't look at all pleased to see him.

"She's not here." she said. "She's gone to get the breakfast with Geert. He's not that happy with you. Thinks you spent the night here."

"Ok, ok," said Michael at last. "Well can you give this to her?" He produced the envelope from his pocket. Grietje's face lit up at once as she put her hand out from inside the entrance.

"Ah" she smiled, "that looks a lot like a letter! How very *interesting*."

"Can you give it to her? *Please*," Michael implored, the serious look on his face leaving her little room to doubt his resolve. Grietje giggled rather aware of the strength of her position but without any gain she felt able to lever from the situation, she agreed. Michael handed over the letter and thanked her gratefully and got up to go. He stopped suddenly. "Did she mention me at all?" he asked. She shrugged and smiled once more.

"I'll see she gets it" she added reassuringly.

In the distance Michael could hear the diesel engine of the large coach ticking over and the logistical commotion of getting more than 50 unruly boys on board. He was just about to leave when Fred arrived, he too out of breath.

"Ah Mr Chips!" smiled Grietje playfully. Fred didn't respond;

"You've got to come. Adjutant's pretty pissed off."

With that the two boys headed, running once more up the hill to the main camp. The bus was almost full and Fred arrived first, jumping on quickly and taking one of the few remaining seats. Michael entered to more jeers and whistles, although there were also a few claps, the meaning of which he was unsure. He looked around for an empty seat but the only one he could see was next to little Johnny. The lad looked expectantly at Michael as he sat down, his face still red and swollen from the emotion and stress of the last hour or two.

The little words of encouragement that people receive from time to time. The little comments that make us feel okay about ourselves and our decisions sometimes come from quite unexpected sources. Life can be like that, just when we doubt ourselves the most, when our fears have invaded our consciousness, when our limitations seem to have been breached and our thoughts are at their lowest ebb, a little light shines. Michael didn't want to talk but he could feel little Johnny's eyes piercing a hole in the side of his cheek. Eventually he looked over. The little chap who turned up infrequently with no explanation of previous absences, sometimes bruised, emaciated, a sad little wretch who seemingly had nothing at all to offer the world looked back at him.

"Them words you wrote," he paused. "Thems the bestest words I ever heard."

Michael glimmered a smile. He sat back in his seat and relaxed a little. *Yes, they were quite good weren't they,* he thought to himself. He had to pull himself together. He hoped she'd write, but even if she didn't he had given it his best shot. He had done everything he could. He could do no more. There was satisfaction in that.

He looked over again at the young boy who was now busy gazing out of the window. His hair was matted at the back and his tiny shoulder blades made sharp little humps in his shirt. Who was he to whimper of his sorrow when others lived so tough a life, hardly knowing the warmth of a mother's love or the firm guidance of a father's hand? He thought back to Anna once more and suddenly, unexpectedly, felt his heart lift. Maybe there was a good side to love. Maybe there was a salvation in the mental motivation he could now feel. Maybe he *was* worthy. Maybe she felt it too. Maybe she *would* write. He lingered on the positive possibility and tried to banish the negative fear from his mind, but it wouldn't go. So, he nodded to himself in acceptance once more. Fear would indeed have to be his bedfellow for now, but he would banish it. Or at least he would tame its power. He felt resolve in his mind. One way or another, he would prevail. Already he felt it weakening. The grip it had had on his life was not as frim, not as resolute, not as uncompromising as it had been and a chink of light, the first he could remember, shone in Michael's dark mind.

CHAPTER 5

Return to Belfast

The remainder of the camp passed unremarkably and by the end Michael's unusual foray into the world of girlfriends had mostly been forgotten. Later when the officers were scouting around for stories, jokes and of course accounts of the usual holiday romances for inclusion in the camp publication, Michael declined to comment claiming to have forgotten the girl. For some reason, Fred said he couldn't remember her name, perhaps confusing her with Grietje.

"Just some foreign name" he couldn't recall, he had maintained. In the end there was no lasting record of the meeting at all, apart from Fred's new nickname of *Chips* that lasted the holiday out.

The warm weather that the North West of England had enjoyed for most of the week was just fading when they left Lancashire and as the Heysham boat docked back in Belfast, Michael could see the reason why. Heavy rainfall was already soaking the county Antrim coast and outside, the raindrops danced on the pavements before wicked squalls once more whipped the rain into frenzied swirls before drenching the streets once more.

Somehow the weather seemed to mirror Michael's state of mind for, following his incursion into a more elevated emotional condition, his sensitivity was now heightened. The sight of the grey city with its patrolling soldiers, security searches, barbed wire and road blocks suddenly seemed more foreboding than it had done before. He thought back to the camp with its choirs of birds and rustling leaves, dappled sunlight and spongy grass below his feet. He thought back to the great white tents, the basic food, the hymns and praise and even the boisterous interaction with the other boys. He smiled briefly, his heart elsewhere as he looked out through the rainy wet window of the minibus, but there was no escape. He was home. He scanned the ominous dark buildings surrounded by high walls topped with glass shards set in cement that sought to cordon off the passenger terminal waiting zone. He thought back to the Dutch visitors, their different ways and casual warmth and to Anna, whose image had hardly left his mind since they met. Suddenly it all seemed a long time ago.

Outside the terminal, groups of parents stood already awaiting their children's return. Some greeted them with a matter of fact 'hello' while others enthusiastically hugged their sons, relieved to have them safely home again in the darkness of those uncertain days. Some of the smaller children had already resolved *never* to go to BB camp again and shyness would in no sense impede the bliss of the mother's arms they had fantasised about since the first day away. But, time has a way of healing and development at that age is rapid. Despite the abuse and the bullying, for most, forward steps had been taken on the sometimes challenging path as childhood prepares slowly for adulthood. Many would still return the following year and perhaps for a few, one summer in the future, they too would have a *good* camp that would define their lives.

Michael's life had changed and permanently. The camp had a way of forcing interaction between individuals. People who would never normally become involved with each other were placed in positions where cooperation was a necessity, not an option. It was like a university team exercise, building a raft or planning a fictional village fete and such a model was a specific part of the purpose of the Boys' Brigade. For Michael Coglan, this was anathema, yet he had survived and had to some extent enjoyed himself. He had spoken and functioned socially with the others around him more in the last week than he had done in the entirety of the last twelve months. His little flirt with the Dutch girl had shone a light in his life and it still flickered in the background waiting for a letter to fall through the front door and fan the flames of a love that was currently holding its breath.

Michael returned home, the way he left, in the minibus driven by Danny, but first a number of other boys had to be dropped off. When they arrived at little Johnny's house, the place was in darkness, the blackness of the windows, somehow blacker than the night itself. Danny approached the door, his arm around the young boy and knocked, but there was no answer. It took several further knocks before a light appeared upstairs and to the sound of shouts and curses, the front door was finally unbolted. The small boy, held his wide eyed gaze on Danny's as long as he could, but was finally ushered inside. Not a word was spoken.

It was late at night when Michael was finally delivered back to the little house where he lived with his parents in the north of the city. It was in an area of council housing where the residents would always have been of poor stock. In the early part of the 20th century, as traders and factory owners established their businesses, it would have been populated with busy workers and noisy children. Today, it was mostly populated by the workless, the workshy and those of dubious intent, but the noisy children were still present and roamed the streets in small intimidating groups.

The building was in an only adequate state of repair with a slate roof and red bricks of the Victorian era, many of which had been affected by water freezing in the pores causing the faces to crumble and fall away, leaving concave shapes missing in the walls. At the back was a small walled in yard which the previous inhabitants had covered with corrugated plastic panels providing a sheltered outdoor area. Here bicycles and other paraphernalia, which the Coglans had previously stored in the garage of their old house, were kept clear of the rain. It did have a small bay window at the front though, with a little garden stocked with a variety of small bushes and shrubs that Michael's mother tended together with flowers and herbs she planted in spring each year. Her efforts jollied up the appearance of the street but sadly, these were often trampled or pulled out and tossed in the street, a pointless act by vandals who can surely not have considered the sadness it caused Michael's mother, Susan. The plot, if such a term can be used for so small a terraced property, sloped upwards a little from front to back, so there were two steps that rose to the entrance making the street appear a little more grand than the others nearby, where the front doors opened literally onto the footpath. To one side of the door, and extending underneath the bay and up the wall between the neighbour's house was a hawthorn bush. With its sturdy branches and razor sharp thorns, it grew stronger every year and was never troubled by the vandal's incursions. But, for Michael, it was home.

Before the minibus had even stopped the front door was thrown open and a dark haired woman with a light blue ribbon in her hair, whose tired appearance hardly concealed her attractive features, launched out onto the pavement. She threw her arms wide and her smile teamed with a mother's love. She hugged him warmly causing jeers from those remaining in the vehicle and while she knew her embrace caused him some mild upset, her relief to have her only child safely back at home was always too much to thwart the impulse. As the front door closed, the minibus drove off, splashing through a puddle, providing an unexpected extra watering for the little flowerbeds at the front of the house. The BB camp of 1978 was over.

CHAPTER 6

Family Life in a Fractured Society

Michael's parents' relationship was what is known in Northern Ireland as a *mixed marriage*. His father Brendan or Branny as he was known, was a Roman Catholic, while his mother, Susan a Methodist Protestant. In other societies in the world, a mixed marriage may perhaps mean a greater diversity in terms of culture and religion or even race. In Belfast, even in the relative calm of the 1950s when they met, there was no diversity greater than that between the two Christian denominations that made up the vast majority of the population.

Branny had left school aged fifteen and been apprenticed to a plumber, who taught him well. He completed his training in the scheduled four years without bother, but the bustle of the city recovering from the hardship of the war offered much interest and excitement for the young man, and he became more interested in his social life than mastering his craft. He quickly took to participating in Belfast's lively nightlife, drinking beer and courting girls. He was a good-looking young man whose subtle wit and easy charm made socialising easy and friends abundant.

In those days there was still a good degree of segregation between Belfast's religious groups. Although there was little in the way of actual trouble and people did mix, it was still a small community and everyone did know who each other were, or more accurately, *what* they were. Most people preferred to keep to their own sort finding comfort and security in that familiarity, but for Branny the *other side*, for want of a better term, offered an array of intrigue and fascination he couldn't quite find amongst his own people.

So Branny took to heading south in the evenings and courting the more adventurous girls from the leafy suburbs of Stranmillis and Malone. He was charmed by their orderly culture, the posh schools they attended, hockey games, ballet lessons and the like. Maybe it was the differences, maybe it was the tacit danger, maybe it was the guilty pleasure he felt in the betrayal of his own kind or his slightly unwelcome incursion into this other world. He didn't really know for sure and was not disposed to consider particularly, but he found a thrill there that he couldn't quite find back at home in the narrow cobbled streets of Belfast's Catholic heartland. Although he was sometimes looked at with suspicion, for he never made particular quiet of his own background, he was adept at getting people on side and had honed and adapted his charm, cleverly disarming scepticism with flattery and wit. He knew when to talk, when to smile and importantly when to stay silent.

It was around this time that he met Susan. She was the youngest of three daughters of a solicitor in the town. She was cultured, educated and accustomed to the finer things of life. To her, Branny was a good old rough diamond. For sure, she never meant to fall in love with him. He was just a bit of risky entertainment, to show her friends she could be adventurous or perhaps he represented a slightly rebellious reaction against the staid conformity of the life her parents had planned for her. But, fall in love she did. While always problematic, these relationships were not that uncommon and she hoped her parents would grow to love Branny as she did. They were not particularly understanding and campaigned for a breakup in the relationship, but rather predictably, the more they campaigned the more resolute the young couple became about their feelings.

In 1955 they were married at a little Methodist church just outside of Belfast. There were few guests. Susan's father attended, but bizarrely declined to give his daughter away, a compromise he and Susan's mother had negotiated that ended up being more hurtful than his absence might have been. Both Susan's older sisters now lived in Australia. One had married a soldier she met while working in France as a nurse in 1944. The other had simply upped sticks and gone to a new life and the opportunities the new world offered. Neither had particularly kept in touch with Susan although irregular letters were exchanged with her parents. While both sisters had been invited to the wedding, neither had elected to come, citing the high cost of travel from Australia.

Branny was in still less contact with his family. His father had died in the Easter Tuesday air raid of 1941 and his mother died soon after of tuberculosis, a problem aggravated by the poor living conditions that were still rife in those days. Branny's two older brothers had also died this way. A sister and another brother had emigrated to Canada or the US, Branny wasn't quite sure which. That left only Branny and his youngest sister to be raised by their Grandmother. The sister did come to the wedding and seemed altogether fine with the event, but they quickly grew apart and when she later married a staunch Republican, all contact between them ceased.

Still, the marriage was a happy one and they rented a small house on the outskirts of town, where there was less sectarian segregation. They were a popular couple, involved socially and intellectually with those around them but in the meantime, Branny's occupation had had something of a reality check. His pay as a plumber's mate might have been enough for a decent social life for a single man, but it would hardly provide for a wife and the children they hoped for. Also, having lost touch with his plumbing skills a little he now took to doing more basic labourer's jobs, moving from site to site, from job to job, taking on various little tasks. However, he did manage to buy a small van and invariably would be sent to the builders' yard or hardware store to pick up bits and pieces, always receiving payment for the goods; a bit for his time and a bit more for his petrol.

Branny cottoned on to this and started to carry various useful tools and other items in demand in his van on an on-going basis. Standard plumbing connectors and joints he carried all the time. They always needed them. Then the carpenters needed screws. 1 ¼ No.8 woodscrews were by far the most common in use, yet they continually ran out of them, so Branny always kept a few boxes on hand. He bought a selection of small tools, hammers, trowels, buckets, saws, chisels, screwdrivers and the like and could supply these instantly when required for a small mark up. Before long, Branny's little van was crammed to the gunnels with every small item a builder, plumber, carpenter, plasterer or ground worker could want. As his jobbing work diminished, he spent more and more time going from site to site, checking what was required. Before long, he had developed a price list and negotiated wholesale rates from the suppliers. By the time the swinging sixties arrived, life was looking pretty sweet for Branny and Susan Coglan.

In the spring of 1962, Michael was born. They had always

planned to have children, but for years nothing had happened, so Michael was in the end quite a surprise. By this time, they had been married for over seven years and while contact with Branny's family had mostly been lost, they did see Susan's parents, albeit irregularly.

Neither Susan nor Branny attended church any longer. Early in their marriage they had sat down together and decided they wouldn't involve themselves in any organised religious activity outside of accepting any particular invitation they might receive to events such as baptisms and weddings. Susan's mother had been appalled by the decision, rather unusually claiming that even Catholicism would be better than nothing at all. However, when the baby Michael came along, the whole issue came to the forefront once more. In the end, Susan's mother asked that she should be allowed to bring the child to church on Sundays so that he would have the benefit of Christian instruction and could then make his own decision from an informed point of view once older. It was a valid argument and both Susan and Branny agreed.

So, baby Michael was baptised into the Methodist church, one in the north of Belfast where Susan's mother had grown up and where she still attended. Susan's father never saw the child. In late 1960, he developed lung cancer and was given only months to live. He made his peace with his estranged, now pregnant daughter in the way that dying people do and living people should, but despite his best efforts passed away only a few weeks before Michael was born.

By then, the van deliveries were doing great business and together with a loan from Susan's mother, they opened a shop in the north of the city called HARDWARE by Branny Coglan. The business was a great success. Branny redeveloped the van deliveries with their small stock, and the drivers took orders for larger items for delivery the following day. By the mid-sixties, Branny had five vans running and fifteen staff in total. The shop was never empty and there were up to eight staff serving at any one time, providing just about everything the building trade needed.

The family moved to a large detached house flanked by a glorious garden full of rose beds and apple trees. Susan could often be seen, secateurs in hand, pruning the roses or weeding the beds. When it became time for Michael to attend school, he was enrolled in a fee paying prep school in a glorious setting in the outskirts of the city.

But in Northern Ireland, all was not well and the nineteen sixties had prompted unusual change in many aspects of life. Throughout the world, people had become increasingly concerned with their own positions in the societies in which they lived and progressively sought change and improvement to their lot. In Northern Ireland, the two historic communities that had always lived uneasily side by side began more and more to look on each other with suspicion and resentment. Those who felt left out, sought change and improvement, while those who feared losing out to such change resisted. As the pressures rose, each sought refuge in their own community, their own type, their own culture. And the deep rooted embers of resentment that had smouldered beneath the surface for centuries, glowed once more. And the voices of the past and of the present both near and far, breathed on the embers and the embers flickered to life, lighting fires: Fires of dissatisfaction, fires of discontent, fires of distrust and fires of hate. And in 1969 Belfast burned.

War, violence and political upheaval are not usually good for the local economy and Branny's little business was no exception. He had always found it easy to operate in both communities, but increasingly this became difficult. Unconnected sectarian incidents became reasons to move business away and the building trade became even more segregated than it had been in the past. There was also the rise of a mafia style protection racket operated by the terror groups that effectively taxed Branny's operation. With the descent into lawlessness, vans were often broken into or vandalised. Threats to drivers and even physical attacks on them were not uncommon and every incident set the business back a little more.

In the turmoil, margins were squeezed and one crisis led to another. Branny tried to keep staff, but the financial pressures grew. Adept at building the business, Branny found himself wanting in contracting it. While he had made every decision in advance of its needs as the business expanded, he made every decision just a little too late in contraction. He kept too many vans too long. He kept too many staff too long. He found himself horribly over committed in a falling market.

Eventually, the debts piled up at a rate that astonished even Branny and in November 1971, as the building trade contracted for the winter months, it became clear that the business would be unable to service its debts. The receivers were called in and the business closed. To make matters worse, once the dust settled and Branny and Susan had had a chance to check on their own personal finances, they realised they would have to sell their home having re-mortgaged it to supply working capital for the business. But the troubles had not been kind to property values in the province and there was still a considerable shortfall. It was early in 1972 when Branny met with his accountant who maintained that he had no choice but to declare himself personally bankrupt and be released from his obligations to his creditors. Branny resisted and sought instead an *individual voluntary agreement* which would allow him protection from his creditors while paying them off at a rate he could afford through a legally approved intermediary. This would have the advantage of assuaging the humiliation of his predicament and would also leave him free to start a business again in the future without the fetters and restraints on his activity that a personal bankruptcy would involve. All he needed was a job with a decent salary for a few years and he would be free.

In Northern Ireland in the 1970s work in private industry had become increasingly scarce in an economy that had become in practical terms dysfunctional. Former mighty employers like the shipyard became dependent on government aid in one form or another and despite efforts to revitalise the economy with generous subsidies for foreign direct investment, jobs were few and far between.

However, there was still one employer, larger than all the others who were expanding its activities in the city. With every tragedy, every bomb detonated, every misery and every slight, the security services manned a thin line between chaos and anarchy. The most notable of these was the police who, provided you had no criminal record and could successfully pass the fairly rigorous training, could offer a rewarding career, as well as an attractive salary. Branny saw this as a viable option. From Susan's point of view, it was no option at all.

"They'll kill you," she had screamed when Branny broached the subject. "They'll booby trap your car, they'll bomb your home, our home, they'll shoot you in the street and leave you to die. You'll never sleep a good night's sleep again."

Branny had rather felt she was over exaggerating the situation, hugging her closely and reassuring her that he wouldn't make any move she would not support, but deep down, he knew there were not too many other options. It was only weeks later, when still jobless and the pressures of life without any more than unemployment benefit sat on the hall table in the form of red utility demands, when Branny came home one evening, brimming with a new idea.

"The prison service," he had said at last. "I'm going to join the prison service." It made sense of course. The prison service offered many of the benefits of the police, but the dangers inside a prison could hardly be the same as for a policeman operating in the shadows of the streets of West Belfast in the dead of night. Of course, instinctively Susan was as hostile to this as she had been to the Police idea, but she too had seen the red utility bills sitting on the hall table and knew she would have to compromise at some point. The following day, Branny applied to join. The job would involve the supervision of those convicted of crimes both relating to the conflict as well as the regular criminal element; a feature of any society.

And so, Branny started his new job. He had been dreading it, but the training was thorough and after a short time, he settled down to his new role, supervising prisoners during various activities; eating, leisure, exercise etc., as well as escorting them from one place in the prison to another. Most activities passed without incident and most of the prisoners were relatively friendly and courteous having settled down to do their time and wanting as little hassle as possible.

In time, Branny became a well-liked guard, if such a thing could exist. Awkward or aggressive prisoners could smell fear at a hundred yards and Branny showed none. He was respected for his position, but known to be fair and even-handed. There was verbal abuse of course, especially from those who felt he had betrayed his Catholic roots, but Branny hardly noticed. There was also a fairly continuous stream, of shouts and taunts from some of the more colourful inmates who would question everything from your sexuality to the legitimacy of your children. In truth it was entertainment as much as anything and didn't trouble Branny at all.

So Branny settled down to his new working life, not one he had imagined, but it was OK. He paid regularly into the account for his creditors and looked forward to receiving the monthly statements showing progress. But for Michael, who was now nine years old, this change in circumstances and the events that followed would have a profound effect on his psyche that would last until and beyond his meeting with Anna, seven years later.

CHAPTER 7

A Riddle or Two

Grietje didn't turn out to be the most reliable of messengers as she had quite forgotten the important little envelope she held in her purse. It was not until they were back in Holland and Anna happened to mention the brief encounter with the shy, slightly troubled young man that her rather embarrassed friend unexpectedly pulled the letter from her purse.

She was most apologetic for her oversight as she handed it to her friend and at the same time quickly noted how its recipient lit up as she inspected the little envelope. Anna opened it carefully and slowly unfolded the crumpled paper that had been so tersely thrown around the marquee a week or so earlier, remarking that it looked like it had already seen some adventure! Grietje watched intently as Anna started to read the little poem, frowning and squinting where she couldn't understand and smiling at the funny words and phrases he used. At last she raised her eyebrows, before silently folding the pages once more, replacing them inside the envelope and then carefully into her bag.

"Well?" asked Grietje inquiringly, her eyes wide in expectation. Anna paused, then smiled. It was a wide, open smile. It was the smile people sometimes smile when things have gone rather the way that was wanted, without having made any particular effort to make it so.

"He wants me to write to him."

Now, it was Grietje's turn to smile.

"And?"

"Well, yes, I think I shall!"

The two girls giggled together and hugged.

Later that evening, Anna read the little poem once more. It was simple and charming, but what was so very special was that this wasn't a classic text by a well-known poet, like those she studied at school. This was a real message, an invitation written for and addressed personally to her. She found it thrilling and her heart skipped a little as she mused the lines of text once more.

There were of course a few words she didn't understand, so she reached for her little pocket Dutch/English, English/Dutch dictionary that she always kept in the canvas bag she used to carry her other school books. She confirmed the translation of some of the words, while others were entirely new to her and she sought the definitions, noting to herself to use the new vocabulary at the next opportunity. However, there were two words she couldn't find as neither *lough* nor *craic* were listed. This rankled her rather proper nature, but she still chuckled at the challenge.

The next day she took the note with her to school. Her English teacher was able to help with the word *lough* and invited her to accompany him to the school library where he opened the big atlas and laid it out on a study table. The map of Ireland was littered with the word *lough*. There was Belfast Lough of course, but also Strangford Lough, Lough Neagh, Lough Erne, Lough Ree and Lough Derg.

"It means lake or estuary," the teacher remarked, watching intently as Anna broke into a broad smile. "But can you pronounce it?"

Anna tittered engagingly, "Oh no, not another *o-u-g-h*!" she exclaimed.

"It certainly is," said the teacher. Anna took a breath.

"Well, it could be like rough, so *luff*. Or it could be like though, so *low*. It could even be like bough, so *bow*, but rhyming with cow! Oh dear, how can you tell?"

"Well," said the teacher, "I can tell you this. It's none of these!" He stopped to let the girl think, enjoying the interest she was showing in his subject. It was students like Anna who made teaching worthwhile for him and he always experienced a little vocational thrill when someone became involved over and above the standard curriculum.

"I'll give you a hint. The same word is used in Scotland, but they spell it differently there. Have you heard of *Loch* Ness?"

"Like the Loch Ness Monster?" Anna had read a short story about the legendary creature just last year.

"Yes, yes indeed, so Lough is pronounced like Loch? Yes, yes, yes, now I've got it!" He couldn't help with *craic* though, but suggested that it too may be of Irish origin or else some form of colloquial slang.

And so, Anna did write. A few days later a letter with a stamp marked *Nederland* arrived at the Coglan home. Michael thought his heart would stop as he opened it and Anna's enthusiastic text, full of joy and light lit his heart once more. She *loved* his poem and maybe one day she would love *him* too. He read the chatty text with its natural rhythm and casual tone and saw her face once more in his mind's eye. For Michael who instinctively mistrusted his own emotions, there was now at least an objective validity in letting himself feel for her. Fear took another knock as love pushed its way a little further into his mind.

A regular correspondence quickly developed between the two young people. Each, communicated in their own way with Michael, buoyed by the success of his first poem, writing further texts, sometimes interlinked with clandestine messages, puns or plays on the language. Anna loved reading his work, deciphering the words and phrases, which was in no sense easy, English not being her first language. This was a fact for which Michael made little allowance. But she applied herself and would write back with questions or suggestions about what he might mean. Sometimes Michael would confirm her thoughts, other times he would gently tell her to think again.

After a while there was a steady flow of poetry coming from the pen of Michael Coglan. Letters usually arrived on Tuesdays or Wednesdays, having been posted at the weekend. Anna would arrive home from school and take the envelope to her room before opening it excitedly and reading the new contents. He made her feel wonderful, she being the exclusive recipient of his work. There were poems covering diverse aspects of life, everything from the glories of the Irish countryside that he brought to life in her bedroom to the perils of riding a bicycle in the city. Some were serious and thoughtful pieces, while others were full of subtle humour, sarcasm and irony. He wrote other short texts, intense descriptions of mundane activities like men working on the road, using words to create the slouches and mannerisms of the workers he had observed over many hours.

One was a fascinating, if haunting piece, about a little bird, a starling, that had built her nest in the hawthorn bush in the small garden at the front of his home. He had watched her incubate her eggs, then care for the chicks, feeding and tending to them diligently from hatching through to preparation for their first flight. He would check progress every day after school and had even set a small stool at the base of the shrub, so that he could raise himself up the extra height required for a direct view right through the branches and into the nest. The hawthorn bush provided the perfect cover and protection for the chicks with its strong, slim branches, too flexible to support the weight of a cat. With its razor sharp spikes, the defence it offered was as good, or better than the great rings of darnet wire the army favoured for their own security.

He spoke of the privilege he felt at the ringside seat he had on the natural world and concerned himself that he may scare the bird, with his large head periodically gazing inside, only inches from the mother hen and her chicks. Still, he set aside the bird's fears deeming them unwarranted and watched closely until one day the three chicks were finally ready for their first flight.

Breathless, he watched as the first launched itself from the nest, but it failed to gain enough lift and despite some flapping landed in the little garden below, horribly exposed to the local cat, which lost no time in slaying the defenceless creature. Then, in horror he watched as the predator, clearly considering the possibility of siblings, lay in wait beneath the nest in patient expectation of another little feathered creature falling from the sky with which to entertain itself.

It didn't have to wait long and presently, the second little bird launched from the nest with all the hope of any creature starting out in life. With enthusiastic flapping it was just gaining enough height to keep clear of the grass below, when the cat raised its paw and hit the hapless chick while it was still in the air, stunning it and leaving it flailing on the ground.

The third fared no better and in just a few moments, the

product of a mother's love, care and diligent effort lay in three tiny, feathered clumps on the grass beneath. The work culminated in a poignant description of the frenzied flight of the distraught mother, squawking desperately as she searched for her lost chicks, something he described as a desperate grief as real as any human emotion. Anna had cried over this one.

He had written another wonderful poem called *In search of Cadmium Yellow*. It seemed he had spent the day trying to find all the colours in an artist's pallet. They had wonderful names such as yellow ochre and burnt umber, cerulean blue, sienna sap and alizarin crimson. Most he seemed to have been able to find without too much trouble, but one in particular, *cadmium yellow* had left him most exasperated. He described it as being a yellow of *primary shade of form and tone.*

Anna couldn't understand the problem, the countryside was surely littered with yellow flowers at the time of year. Everything was available from Dandelion to Foxglove, but it seemed that none would do, for he declared it was *plant* he sought not flower. Anna was confused and couldn't think of a yellow plant and it all seemed a little gloomy until the final verse. Then at last, he mounted a ridge and triumphantly Samson and Goliath came into view, quickly ending both his search and the poem.

Anna couldn't understand the biblical reference but had taken up the challenge, reading her old testament fervently, searching for any reference to these two giants that might associate either with yellow of the cadmium hue or indeed any shade. She could find none. Giving up, she had asked him for hints and help, but he had provided none, other than his assurance that she *would* find out one day.

Everything seemed to come to life in his texts and she would laugh and cry as she read, reaching occasionally for her dictionary for definition or clarification of his meaning. Increasingly she used an English dictionary providing descriptive meanings rather than just translation examples of similar meaning words in Dutch. Her command of the English language improved dramatically over these months and at home she modelled her speech on the spoken words of the sub-titled English serials and costume dramas that were popular on Dutch television at the time.

However, Michael never wrote of his personal life. This troubled her at first. She had asked about brothers and sisters, friends, the school he attended, his parents and so on, but he had just said there was not much to tell. When pushed, he had written a little; that he was an only child and described his home in some detail, with the steps at the front and the little garden, a description which had sounded rather quaint and attractive to Anna.

He did write about his school a little, something of the subjects he was taking, but never really elaborated much and the text was staid, awkward and impersonal. In the following letter, there was nothing more which had disappointed her. She knew she was falling for the young man, and wanted to know more about him, but in the end, she settled for his poems and stories and eventually, let the issue drop. After all, she didn't write poems for him.

Anna wrote mostly of her own life, her family, her friends and school. She was the youngest of four children, the three older all being boys, so she was a little spoiled and occupied a unique position in everyone's affections in the family. Her letters were mostly accounts of her experiences more or less as they happened, but as time went on she became more adventurous and began to write extensive accounts of her family history and the community where she lived.

CHAPTER 8

Michael's Pledge

Anna lived in a small town in the east of the
Netherlands situated between Utrecht and Arnhem
called Pijpersbos (pronounced Pipersboss and
meaning *Piper's wood*). The name was derived from the small
wooded area which surrounded the town on two sides and
mostly defined its boundaries. Despite the ravages of World War
Two it had survived fairly intact and represented a rather quaint
example of a small Dutch country town. It had an old town of
modest neo-gothic buildings, a central open square and
residential areas with rows of attractive houses placed in small
terraces along cobblestoned streets.

The town lay about 50km from the German border and in
the late nineteen seventies, it was already relatively affluent as
the economy of the Netherlands had grown rapidly in the post
war years. The Dutch had discovered copious supplies of natural
gas both off shore and in the Northern provinces which they
used to fuel their economy. Outstanding language skills and a
long tradition of trading and export served them well in a
Europe that, through the European Economic Community
(EEC), was increasingly open for business. The Port of
Rotterdam was the biggest in the world and one of the major
entrances to the continent from the West. Foreign organisations
flocked to the area to set up trading or communications hubs
in Europe and the well educated population who seemed able

to transcend almost every cultural boundary were quick to exploit their skills. Despite this, the village of Pijpersbos was still out of the way of the heavy industry and trading centres of the *Randstad*, the triangle joining Rotterdam, Amsterdam and The Hague where most of the business and commerce of the Netherlands was centralised. In many ways, life was slow, a little old fashioned and quite idyllic.

Anna's family home was a single dwelling cottage not far from the town centre, built over 150 years ago and preserved as part of the cultural heritage of the town. While small, it was set back from the road and accessed via a little humped wooden bridge that crossed a small waterway that ran the length of the road and beyond. Although the villagers referred to it as a *Gracht*, or canal, it was really a small stream of slow moving water that fed into the river below, the village being situated in a slightly hilly area of a nation rather renowned for its flat landscape.

The quaint little building was set over three floors and constructed of the small, reddish brown bricks, common in the area, with a steeply pitched roof of terracotta tiles that angled over the top two floors. The gable end faced the road, with the edge of the roof trimmed with pristine white barge boards. The upper floors had small, white framed windows flanked with shutters painted in a dark olive green shade that matched with the paintwork of the front door and many of the other houses in the street. Anna's father kept the house in perfect condition, regularly painting the window frames and shutters as well as the little bridge which bore a small sign reading; *van der Vliet,* the family name of Anna's parents' household.

The main living area was fronted by a large, square picture window that faced the cobbled street. There were no curtains and Anna's mother had adorned it with crocheted screens at the top and plants on the sill that provided some privacy from the gaze of passers-by in the street outside as well as the warm reassurance of house proud residents. Inside, the floors were of polished hardwood and the carpet was more in the form of rugs that lay centrally in the rooms, rather than the wall to wall fitting that was more usual in the larger towns and cities. This was more of a style decision than an economic one and there was a general feeling in the house of a strong connection with the past. It was quaint, old fashioned and homely.

It had been a struggle bringing up the family in such a small house. There were three bedrooms in all; two on the floor above and a large attic accessed by a precariously steep staircase that spiralled from the landing, claiming almost no floor space at all. The three brothers had shared this room, but Anna, being the only girl had a bedroom to herself on the middle floor beside her parents' room. Perhaps they might have moved from there, but the quality of life was high and the house was rented and once relinquished, they would never be able to get it back again.

Two of Anna's older brothers had already left home, so there was now more room in the house and it was only Geert who was a full five years older and had taken Anna to England, who still lived in the house besides her parents. The oldest, Jan had gone to live in Amsterdam and married there a few years back. The family saw him only occasionally, for birthdays and other family events. The second brother, Piet had gone travelling, when Anna was just eleven and would send postcards and letters from all sorts of interesting and exotic places in the world. Currently, he was in South America, but nobody knew where exactly. Whatever his plans, they had always changed by the time the next postcard arrived and he would be in a different country and usually with different people. Now and again, he would find himself in Europe once more and stop by the family home, often unannounced, but never stay for more than a few days at a time.

The Gymnasium school Anna attended was situated in the larger town of Veenendal and Anna would travel by bicycle each day, rain, hail or snow the 11km in each direction to attend classes. She was a bright and popular girl who participated enthusiastically in all aspects of school life. It was a co-educational establishment and by the age of fourteen or fifteen her soft features and relaxed disposition had already attracted some attention from the boys in class. However, she responded little to the advances she received. This may have been initially as she hadn't felt ready for any form of relationship, but as the months went by and her friendship with Michael developed, she increasingly came to feel more unavailable than uninterested.

She never considered herself beautiful, apart from perhaps one summer evening when she was in front of the bathroom mirror, preparing to go out with some friends and the sunlight caught her loose hair and reflected in her blue eyes. She smiled approvingly for a moment to herself, but this was not a thought that would linger. As she got older, she came to wear a little shadow around her eyes when she was going out in the evening as well as some lipstick of a shade so close to her natural colouring, that it was almost invisible. This was really only a sop to her friends, a gesture to fit in, rather than any personal wish to enhance her beauty or serve her vanity. However, she was quite beautiful, but her beauty was natural, innate and existed in her whole aura and not just in her physical appearance.

Anna wrote extensively about her family and her parents.

Her mother, Adrie had lived on Anna's grandparent's farm in the East of the Netherlands, not far from the current home of the van der Vliet family. Anna's father had originally been from the province of South Holland, close to the sea and when they had married, had joined his wife in her community, rather than she joining him in his. The family had lived in Pijpersbos ever since.

The farm was situated not far from the German border and in 1940, when the invasion took place, Adrie was just fifteen years old. It was a horrific period, but really rather short lived in itself and the family quickly accustomed themselves to a life under occupation. It would not be until 1944 that the true horrors of war would pass close by as the world's superpowers of the day faced each other in bloody conflict.

It was just after dawn one day in late 1944 and Adrie was out feeding the chickens in the yard when she saw a man walking across the field, his form silhouetted against the rising sun. She watched him for some time but his progress was so slow that she eventually picked up a pitchfork and ventured out onto the field herself taking cover behind a bale of hay. At first she looked on with apprehension, but as he came closer she gained a better view. He was bearded with neglect and emaciated, limping slightly, his short paces hardly hastening him to his destination.

At last he had advanced level with her and she called out softly. At first he didn't respond, but she raised her voice a little louder and he quickly turned towards her, startled and in fear. These were dangerous days and that part of Holland was still under occupation, but he seemed harmless and unarmed, so she decided to reveal herself and stepped out from behind the bale. Facing him she could see the look of desperation in his narrow eyes. He looked to be maybe in his late twenties with skin reddened from exposure and gaunt with hunger. He wore brown canvas trousers that hung limply off his hips with hems trailing that caught on the grass stubble below. At last she motioned towards him, but he fell to the ground even before she arrived.

She rushed over and knelt by his side. At first he spoke in a kind of broken German, but she quickly realised he was Dutch. She brought him back to the house where she fed him coffee and potatoes. He seemed disorientated and thought he was still in Germany. Adrie concluded that he must have escaped from the Nazis and simply headed west. He stayed at the farm for several weeks, gaining strength each day, before transporting back to his home in South Holland to see what was left of the life he had left behind. However, he promised to return once he had found his feet and thank the family properly.

When the war was over, he did return, now healthy and rested. He came bearing gifts and stayed several days, once more enjoying the hospitality of the farm. He was just about to leave and tearful goodbyes were being said all around when Adrie surprised herself and everyone else by asking him to stay longer. The couple were married in 1947. After thirty years Anna's mother had still never learned of how or why he came to be walking across her field that day.

For those who survived World War II, their experiences will have been influenced entirely by their personal situations. For much of the British population and that of the free allies, the war was a period of unity and purpose, of bravery and heroics punctuated by grief and horror. These were the inevitable side effects of a heroic struggle of good against evil. However, for many in the Nazi occupied territories, such as the Netherlands, the experiences were more of degradation and humiliation, of unpalatable choices forced by unreasonable captors and of shame and desperation. For some peacetime never managed to countenance the past and everyone sought to deal with their own experiences as best they could. For some who survived, the war would never truly be over.

Anna's father never spoke of his experience of the war, or the *occupation* as he called it. Neither she, nor as far as she knew, her mother or any of her brothers, knew anything of where he had lived, if he had spent any time in Holland or been interned in Germany to work in their factories. They didn't know if he had fought in any way or otherwise what he had done or indeed had done to him. There were no stories, no tales of gallantry and intrigue or even fear and incarceration. Nothing. Instead, there was just a great big burden of hatred for the German nation and people that he carried around with him everywhere he went. Sometimes it would exist as a passive emotion, but other times, usually stimulated by a small event, a comment or newspaper story, he would become agitated and animated and his burden would become apparent to those around him. Anna was troubled by her father's past and especially by his present day attitude to it and she had confided her thoughts on the subject more than once in her letters to Michael;

"Oh Michael. Please say you'll always forgive. Please do say you will, for hatred is a burden to carry, heavier than any weight known to God or man. My father cannot see through the hatred in his eyes. It is eating him up, consuming him. The Germans don't care. They're sorry anyway. I'm quite sure they are, but even if they aren't what good is it doing him? None! He's just sending himself to an early grave while the Germans rebuild their economy and worry about the Russians invading. They have forgotten him or whatever they did to him a long time ago. He causes them no harm. The only one he hurts is himself."

He wouldn't buy a German car, or any other goods from Germany, nor would he have them in the house. This was increasingly a challenge, for trade between the two nations was brisk and the Germans were adept at producing quality manufactured goods that most homes wanted. She feared for him, but there was no talking about that particular subject. It was just something they never did. In truth, she hadn't ever tried. She assumed her brothers may have asked questions some years ago, but as her years of teenage consciousness developed, she grew to feel more and more the burden he bore. It was in the way he walked, he stooped. She described it, "like someone is tearing the pages of history from a book and they are landing on his back, slowly piling up, crushing him with their message. He carries the weight of his past and every day a new page of history lands, crushing him ever deeper into the mire of hatred that permeates his soul."

In his mind, Michael had reflected on the conflict in his own society that he had at first thought quite unique, but Anna's words had made him confront more consciously the legacy Ireland has always left its children. He realised that without forgiveness, history was set to repeat itself again and again. Whatever the transgressions of the past, however foul, however severe, however evil, there would never be peace without forgiveness. Forgiveness was essential.

He had written back, quite unusually outside of his usual prose, expressing himself now rather, formally and promising a firm undertaking on his part to forgive others for any transgression against him. He made no conditions, like demanding remorse or expecting his own absolution in return. His statement had been plain, succinct and unambiguous. A pledge from which there was no escape. This had pleased Anna, for she saw this as a fundamental instrument of life, one not to be diluted or compromised. Furthermore, if the pages of history had been landing on her father's back consuming him with hate, the petals of love had been falling on her for a while, each one stopping to kiss her on the face or hair or shoulders before accumulating around her in an emotion she felt less and less inclined to temper.

However, there was a kind of fascination with English culture and tradition in the van der Vliet home. The *Island* people, as her Dad often referred to them, describing them as perhaps the most foreign of other Europeans, or even not European at all. He would comment on their polite ways and sense of fair play, the queuing, the pin-striped suits and bowler hats her mother was convinced everyone still wore. These were the characteristics of civility and decency they clung to. Even if the news from across the North Sea was entirely contrary, with stories of a failing economy, political strikes, power cuts and an unsettled population, for Anna's Mum and Dad, the England of old was the one they believed in and a few news stories weren't going to change that.

When Geert had suggested he and some friends make a car trip to England, the idea had been met with approval or even some enthusiasm by the parents. Anna's father had even been perhaps a little envious, for despite everything, he had never been to England. The children had all been on school trips to London already, but for one reason or another, neither he nor Adrie had visited and perhaps in deference to that had suggested

Anna go too. Geert had not been enthusiastic. Anna was quite a few years younger than he and her agenda would be quite different, but some gentle persuasion and a little financial subsidy had helped, so the trip was arranged.

When Anna returned, she announced before long that she had a new pen pal, a boy. Her mother hadn't thought much about it and had simply assumed he was English, having never been told any different. It wasn't until once when Anna left her letter to Michael on the counter ready for posting that her mother noticed, *Northern Ireland* written on the envelope. She had been a little bothered by that and had questioned her daughter. After all, the news from there was not of people striking for a pay increase, it was rather more severe. This was a dangerous place. There were bombs and bullets, rioting and civil unrest. But Anna had assured her that all was fine and that these events were happening far from Michael and the life he lived.

And that was what Anna believed. Michael never mentioned such things and she never sought to bring them up. Before long, she put such thoughts out of her mind and paid them no heed. Occasionally when the news was on and there was some awful report of explosions or rioting, she would ponder a little and wonder about Michael, but come Tuesday, Wednesday at the latest each week, his new letter would arrive. In time, it ceased to be an issue.

And so their little romance developed. Michael had been in love from the start. For Anna it took a little longer, but she was charmed a little more by each letter and Michael seldom put a foot wrong. His letters would be laced with little rhymes and verses, poetry and prose. He always wrote well and she liked that. The truth was despite the awkward ways she remembered from their sole meeting; he was a deep, sensitive, thoughtful young man. Before long, she knew he was the one for her.

Michael thrived in the uncomplicated world of written correspondence and could carefully filter his texts, tuning them cleverly to the messages he wanted to send. In the written word, he could shield his vulnerabilities and keep his fears under control. In all the time the two young people corresponded, Michael never once mentioned the *Troubles* as they were called. They were happening all around him every day, but like Anna's father, he chose not to speak. Like Anna's father, his scars lay obscured in a silent horror. Like Anna's father, he feigned normality. Michael may not have been mired in hatred, but his life was marred all the same by his experiences, the people around him and the world in which he lived.

CHAPTER 9

Sectarian Children

Michael Coglan could not remember anything from before about his 10th birthday.

His early days had been idyllic, living in the big house in the leafy suburbs and attending a private school which specialised in the development of all aspects of its young charges. Here academic work mingled flawlessly with nature walks in the hills nearby and a healthy dose of sport and games to whet a competitive spirit and instil a sense of fair play. When the Troubles arrived, few could have been more insulated from the harsh realities of sectarian conflict.

Times had been good and Michael was very much a normal outgoing, gregarious young boy. He was intelligent, quick witted and charming interjecting conversation with a cheeky grin or even a sly wink which he would use to build up funny little parallel relationships with adults as well as other children. Indeed, his parents' friends would comment, *oh, he's just like his father*, and Susan would smile and look fondly at her husband, proud of the product of their marriage.

"We'll have to watch him when he gets older, for that's a ladies' man if ever I saw one," said one neighbour as the little seven year old boy who had just complimented her appearance ran off into the garden with a jump and a skip.

In his peer group, Michael was popular too. At school, he participated fully in classes interacting with the teachers and other pupils and developing understanding of the academic subjects as well as the world around him. Outside of school he also made friends readily often playing in the neighbourhood, climbing trees and getting up to mischief with the other children in the area.

He had one friend in particular, called Paul, who lived a few doors away. Paul attended a different school, but in the afternoons the two would play together endlessly, slipping in and out of each other's houses, playing games, building dens and riding their bicycles in the nearby park. One might have assumed they would remain friends for life and when Michael's family moved to the rental home following the collapse of Branny's business, both sets of parents made every effort to see that the two children maintained regular contact.

Every Saturday, either Michael was delivered to his old residential area, a trip Susan still found very difficult, or Paul would be delivered to play in Michael's new stomping ground. The latter troubled Paul's mother a little, but it offered new opportunities for exploration for the young boys and generally Susan kept them well supervised.

This worked well for a while, but Paul, like Michael's father was a Roman Catholic. This was a point hardly noted at all in their old neighbourhood but Michael's new home was in a staunchly Protestant working class district of rented housing. At first, the two boys mostly kept themselves to themselves, playing happily in the small garden or in the streets outside Michael's home. However, as time went by, they strayed further afield to the local park where there was a playground with swings and roundabouts.

It was one day when they visited the park that the two youngsters, both not yet ten years old, were approached by a group of bigger boys. They were a little older and Michael knew some of them a little having seen them around the streets or at the local shops. They were a rough looking bunch, with shaven heads his mother maintained was to keep the nits away and jeans too short that left skinny white ankles on view. Still, Michael knew they were to be taken seriously.

At first they chatted amicably, but they were suspicious of Paul and began milling around him in an increasingly intimidating fashion. His name could easily pass on both sides of the religious divide, but they wanted to know what school he went to, a fact that would immediately reveal his religion.

"The same school as me," Michael had maintained, "sure we're in the same football team."

Michael could see they were unconvinced and felt the situation deteriorating. The two friends made several attempts to leave, wishing the others well and motioning to go. But someone always stood in the way, each time with increasing menace and then once with a sharp push that caught Paul square on the shoulder shoving him firmly towards the centre of the group. Both boys looked around for an escape route, but there were five of them, bigger and faster and making a run for it seemed less and less of an option.

What might have started as mischief with no real agenda, quickly turned into fairly threatening behaviour with the five larger boys surrounding the two frightened young friends. Tacitly it became apparent that Michael, the relative newcomer to the area, didn't quite know the rules and had brought his little *fenian* friend along to play. Strangely, this was a point they failed to mention, nor an accusation they openly made. Instead, they rather campaigned from a veiled agenda, seeking some *truth* from Michael, the off-loading of a burden on his mind, or some admission of guilt that could then be considered reasonably and objectively.

The game was sophisticated far beyond the years of its players and certainly beyond the intellectual capacity one might have imagined such youngsters might possess. They weren't explicit in their accusations, but said things like; *no one would bring a Catholic here to play* and describing the beating that *anyone* who did would receive, but that *Michael would be fine, because he would never do that.* No Michael was an okay guy, they knew Michael. *Michael* would never do that.

It became like a mantra. *You would never do that, sure you wouldn't* they were saying to him, one after another. Poor Paul was petrified and Michael distraught, his eyes wide, staring like a rabbit, comatose in fear as the inevitable set to unfold.

Suddenly, the mood changed to a more conciliatory tone. It was really all the more sinister, but the voices were less jeering and feigned sympathy. *People do make mistakes.* Then one of the older boys put his hands on Michael's shoulders and stood square before him. He was pale and gaunt, with a gold earing in one ear and just above his left eye was a scar that slanted upwards making him look slightly Chinese in appearance.

"Hey, we're all human after all." He said softly. Michael wasn't convinced of that, but he listened to what was said. "But sometimes, if we make a wee mistake, it's better to just admit it. Get things over and done with. You know?" He raised his eyebrows, looking expectantly at the young boy who was very much aware that the shaking of his body could easily be felt through the hands laid upon him.

"Hey, we all make mistakes," he went on. "Listen, Michael," the lad leaned over close to him and whispered in his ear. Michael could smell the cigarette smoke on his breath. "You know what it's like at home when you've done something wrong." He paused. Michael nodded. "Sometimes, it's just better to own up if you've done something wrong, rather than spinning the thing out. Makes it all the more unpleasant for everyone."

Michael could feel the sweat form between his shoulder blades, and he shivered as it trickled down the line of his spine.

"Now, you see my Da. If I lie to him, he takes the big belt, not the little belt, but the big belt, the one with the big brass buckle with the red hand of Ulster on it and he beats me with that."

The boy undid the belt of his own jeans to reveal a wide scar on his hip, that had clearly been caused by a serious gash some time back, "that's what that belt did to me. That's what I got for being a dirty little liar."

In his mind, Michael could feel the pain of such a belt hitting him, not the cracking slap of a leather belt or a cane, an honest punishment for deeds done, but the raw thud of a blunt metal object struck in anger with such force that it broke through the skin. The poor boy stood motionless, his mind no longer in control of his shaking body.

"Now," he went on. "Now, I tell the truth. There is respect for the truth. We all make mistakes. From time to time, we all need to be punished, that's fair, but no one likes a dirty little liar." He paused, "are you a dirty little liar Michael?"

The tears burst in Michael and began streaming down his face, "no, no, no, I'm not. No, please I'm not," he sobbed.

With that, an older boy, perhaps the oldest in the group, who had thus far not really participated too fully in the activities, approached. "Leave him alone," he said sternly to the other boy. "You're scaring him. Can't you see he's upset?"

He put his arm around Michael's shoulder, causing him to shudder once more and led him off towards a nearby park bench, leaving Paul with the others who were now laughing and joking once more. Paul backed off a little, but was held in check by the gaze of one who said, "where do you think you're going, just when we are all getting along so well? You thought you would just slip away. Why's that then? Why's that I wonder! What reason could you have for wanting to slip away?"

Paul stopped in his tracks. He made no noise, but his composure broke and his rosy cheeks of childhood innocence streamed wet with tears of terror. The boy smiled once more and the others burst into a fit of laughter, seemingly amused by the look on Paul's face.

Meanwhile, the good cop in the group who had clearly developed a sophisticated understanding of such an interrogation method, had sat on the bench, lit a cigarette and was chatting casually to Michael.

At last he said to him, "Look here Michael. See, if it was up to me, I would just let you go, and your little friend with you. Well, doesn't make any difference to me really, but you see some of the other lads, they worry that if people keep bringing *fenians* in here, the next we know, there'll be loads of them. Then what'll we do?"

The question was really asked rhetorically, but Michael shook his head. The older boy smiled, "well, we don't want that now do we?" Michael shook his head once more.

"The thing is," he went on, taking a deep drag from his cigarette, "the others are being well behaved, but they're only doing that because they're afraid of me. Now, Michael, listen carefully. Very, very carefully." He breathed the last of the smoke from his lungs which caught Michael in the face, causing his eyes to sting, "we know your Dad's a *taig*, but he's all right. Yes, he's all right." He sat down on the bench.

Michael was flabbergasted. *No one knew that about his father. Did they?* It had been a closely guarded secret in the family since they moved to the area. Anyway, they were *allowed* to be there. Even the 9 year old Michael knew that when mixed marriages were housed, the clerk would usually seek a sort of unofficial approval from one or two influential people in the neighbourhood, even before offering the house to people on the list.

"Here, look. Here, sit," he said patting the bench beside him. Michael sat down nervously, taking care to leave as much space between him as he was able to without seeming to be rejecting whatever friendship or comfort might be on offer.

"Look, Michael. All we want to know is the truth. We know anyway, about your little friend. We've always known. Well, he's not kicking with the same foot as you and me, now is he Michael?"

Michael stared. The tears were building once more in his eyes. Indeed, their presence may have even indicated a small depletion of the terror he felt, as tears show remorse and relief while terror is hard and cold.

"Look, Michael, if you tell me the truth…" He stopped briefly. "Look at me," he said, still softly and lifting the child's tiny chin higher with his hand, forcing their eyes to meet. Michael looked up at the boy, right in his eyes. He knew he was evil. Evil in a soft voice.

"If you tell me the truth, I'll see that nothing happens to you. Look, you grew up elsewhere, with the posh kids and whatever. That's fine. Doesn't matter to me. Maybe things weren't as rough there, but, well, you're here now aren't you.

You have to get on with us, but you're young. It's alright to make mistakes when you're young. What age are you Michael?

"Nine," whimpered Michael.

"Look, who can expect a nine year old, not to make mistakes. Hey," he smiled menacingly, "I thought you were older. Look, for God's sake, everyone has to be allowed to make a mistake."

The boy sat, looking at the ground in front of the bench and Michael followed his gaze. The grass was worn from the endless fidgeting of its users. He dragged deep once more on the last of his cigarette before flicking it skilfully into a waste bin that sat nearby.

"What do you say, we go over to the others together. Look, I'll hold your hand. It'll be all right. I'll be with you. Just tell the truth. If you tell the truth, I'll see that no one will lay a finger on you. Is it a deal?"

Michael found himself nodding, but already he knew what would happen.

The older boy got up from the bench and beckoned Michael to follow. Michael stood up and the boy put his arm around his shoulder once more. They walked together towards the waiting group, but stopped just short.

"You won't make a fool of me will you Michael? You won't make me look like a fool in front of everyone now will you?"

Michael shook his head. Seeing them approach, the waiting group now stopped their chat and looked expectantly at the pair.

The other boy, the one with the belt buckle scar, had taken to sitting on a low wall that edged the grassy area in the park, stood up when he saw them approach.

"Well?" he asked.

Michael felt the firm support of the boys arm around his shoulder. It squeezed him gently, then pushed him forward softly.

"Well?" he said again.

Paul's eyes met Michael's only briefly, before the pain of the contact became too much and he looked at the floor once more. He knew what he was going to do.

"He's a Fenian," said Michael at once, failing to look but pointing at his friend.

There was a sort of relieved sound in the group, not quite a round of applause, but mutters of approval. For a moment it seemed like the tension had dropped, but of course that was a lie, for the wickedness of the foreplay had come to an end and the main event was about to begin.

"There look. That wasn't so difficult now was it," said the older boy soothingly. Michael raised his eyes but the sting of his friends gaze was just too much and he dropped them once more."

"Ok you can go then."

Michael just stood there as if the whole thing was just some kind of pointless anti-climax and in a minute he and Paul would run off home and each get a glass of milk and a currant bun.

"Michael. It's okay. You can go. You did well. Very well indeed."

"What about him?" Asked Michael nodding towards his friend.

"Oh he'll be along in a minute. We just want to talk to him. Don't worry. Run along now."

Michael paused.

"GO!" the bigger boy shouted at last and Michael took off, his little legs wilting with terror, struggling to carry the weight of his body. Tears streamed down his face and felt cold as the moisture evaporated in the evening air. Cold tears of betrayal. Cold tears of denial. Cold, cold tears.

It might have been sensible to go home at that point and raise the alarm, but home was still some way off. Instead, Michael stopped around the corner. Despite the terror of his ordeal and the humiliation of his betrayal, he couldn't go. Instead he took refuge behind some bins in the street with a clear view of the playground where the group had now gathered around little Paul. They were jeering and pushing and chanting and spitting. Five boys, their limbs tense, their fists clenched and one little boy quivering with fear among them.

At last the fists raged and the blows fell on the child's slim little body. His crime? Ireland's shame. The odds, if it could be imagined that there were any, of five to one, could have been five hundred to one and they would have been no less equal. The fists raged, pummelling him to the floor before the feet were raised kicking and stamping and spitting on the child's huddled body curled in pain and torment, his screams fading as his strength and will petered to quiet murmurs.

The tears streamed down Michael's face, his fear only tempered by shame.

At last, the group pulled back a little and Michael could see his bloody friend whimpering softly in the clearing. There were shouts and screams as the boys lit off in two or three directions, the two older ones together, patting each other in a kind of buddy bonding exercise, slapping their palms in joyous celebration. Michael was just about to rush over to help his friend, when suddenly the two older boys, turned around and quickly returned to the whimpering body on the floor.

The one with the buckle scar knelt beside little Paul and

grasping his curly brown hair tightly in his hand, lifted the bloodied little head off the floor. Meanwhile his friend, the good cop, carefully took aim with his foot before wielding a mighty kick to the boy's already bloodied face. Paul whimpered no more.

It was only moments before the ambulance arrived, closely followed by two police Land Rovers, apparently having been alerted by a neighbour who had seen nothing. Michael had only just gotten to his friend's side and knelt crying and shaking by the still body. A police woman gently put her arm around him ushering him towards one of the police vehicles.

"The paramedics will look after him now," she said. "I'm sure he'll be fine. These things usually look much worse than they are."

Paul spent the next three weeks in hospital with severe concussion and a number of wounds, mostly superficial, but the force of the final kick to his face had been so powerful, it had smashed his eyeball. The surgeon's efforts to save the sight in his left eye were in vain. In time, he recovered and set about his life within the limitations his partial blindness imposed. His parents were distraught and although there was never any plan or discussion, the two children never played together again.

The group at the playground had not touched a hair on Michael's body, but of the two, he was the more injured. The terrible screams and yelps of his friend's pain echoed day and night in his mind until his own personal terror would no longer sustain reasoned thought. In time, the only relief he could find was to crush every memory of his friend from his mind. He became subdued, perhaps in the way it might be reasonable to expect, but he never really seemed to recover. He didn't play outside any more. In any case his parents didn't want him to, but his friend was gone and he didn't look like making any new ones where they were now living.

Quickly, the subject of the beating became taboo in the household and wasn't discussed. It was not until over a year later when Susan just happened to mentioned Paul's name one day that Michael didn't appear to know who she was talking about. This had perturbed her and she had questioned him more. Before long it became apparent that, not only could Michael not remember the beating, but he couldn't remember his best friend either, nor anything at all of his early life. Not his schooling, not his Grandmother, Susan's mother, who had died a few years back. Not their old home in the suburbs, nothing. It was like his whole history had been deleted.

Susan took him to the doctor who did some examination and concluded as Branny and Susan had already established themselves that Michael was suffering from some form of amnesia, presumably brought on by the trauma of witnessing the beating of his friend. Despite this, Michael didn't seem to have any trouble remembering more recent events and was himself not particularly concerned by the diagnosis. He showed no signs of valuing anything he couldn't remember.

However, Michael never had a friend again. The subconscious self-protection mechanism of his mind fended off any form of familiarity and his more subdued personality didn't invite others readily into his life. Over the years that followed, he became more and more solitary. At times he seemed intense, but mostly he just seemed disinterested in what was going on around him. By the age of twelve, his parents were the only people he had any real involvement with and even that was confined mostly to the practicalities of life, like what was for dinner, or tidying his room.

Susan in particular found all this difficult to take. Michael knew little of the upset this caused his parents, but one evening he heard them shouting at each other downstairs. An argument was in full flow. Susan was yelling, "they beat his little friend black and blue, they stole his memory, they stole his personality, bastards, bastards, *bastards*." Branny was trying to soothe her, but plainly not doing a good job, "get me away from here, get him away from here, get us away from here," she was screaming.

"We owe money, we owe money," his father was shouting back.

"Then tell them to get lost. Forget your bloody morals, don't pay your debts. What debt are we owed? What have these people ever done for you?" she yelled, "I want my son back, I want my son back."

The outburst was so severe that Michael had gone down stairs and tried to comfort his mother. She hugged him closely, weeping and sobbing openly, her tears wetting the back of his shirt.

This was the first understanding Michael had that things were not quite right with him. He did try to make an effort, if only to please his mother. He tried to get on better at school and indeed, he was a bright child. He had passed the 11+ and gained a scholarship to the local grammar school. He joined the Boys' Brigade at the church he had attended with his Grandmother when he was younger. One of the officers would call and collect him each week, then bring him home after. He would do badge work and learned to play the bugle, but Michael hated it and the rough and tumble and frequent bullying his timid personality invited, terrified him.

By the age of fourteen, Michael's life had settled into a not unusual existence. He was just one of the quiet boys. Every school had them. Everyone is different and he didn't cause too much consternation. He was seen as an underperformer by his teachers. One or two took interest in him from time to time, and academically, there was the occasional glimpse of brilliance, especially in English. One teacher noted how he would have to harass the child into producing homework and he would sit in class without making a sound. Then, when pushed could suddenly make statements of profound clarity, seeming to identify underlying notes and themes within literary works the teacher himself had not considered.

But, it would always stop there. Somehow, despite these little glimmers, Michael would always settle back to a sort of dream state and no one ever seemed to know or understand what he was thinking.

CHAPTER 10

An Ardent Invitation

Anna and Michael had been exchanging letters for over a year and a half and during that time, Anna had been feeling a warmer and stronger connection with him with every week that passed. It was now January of 1980, the month of her birthday. She would soon be sixteen years old and perhaps with that particular milestone on her mind or perhaps as part of the natural building of their relationship, she began to acknowledge quite openly to herself the love she felt for him.

She was not an over ambitious child in this respect and had never had any particularly extravagant romantic view of her future life, but she had always considered and expected even, that she might fall in love one day, just as her parents had done before her. She had looked forward to the possibility of the strong feelings of friendship and oneness with another human being that were part of a relationship, maybe even a marriage and a future together. She had of course never considered that her love might be for a boy from far away, abroad and in another land, another culture, but it had happened that way and she was not sorry about it.

But did Michael feel the same? *Yes, yes*, she answered to herself. Deep down, she knew he loved her. Perhaps, he had never said it explicitly, but implicitly, it was woven into everything he wrote. The intense descriptions and romantic prose about nature and the world around him were always written to her and for her. She knew that much and felt confident about him in that respect. She was still troubled that he remained so insular in his approach, but she settled this in her mind simply believing him to be perhaps excessively shy. Gradually she took to considering this as a slightly negative characteristic she might be able to help with in the future and imagined the two of them in company, with her nudging him playfully in the ribs urging him to join in the chat.

However, this particular problem was exacerbated by the great physical distance between them and increasingly she wanted a closer involvement with him. If he didn't want to talk, she wanted to hug him, to encourage him, to confront the barriers. Increasingly she became no longer happy to just accept this aspect of his nature as the way he was. Once, she had asked him simply what his father did for a living and the question had been completely ignored. She wanted to challenge this and had written down her dissatisfaction in a letter to him, but had declined to send it, instead once more reverting to diary entries and stories of her own life that was her usual offering. But deep down, she wanted to have the argument, even a row if one was necessary, but she just didn't feel it could be done by mail and in the case of Michael, the flowery texts were in this sense a barrier.

He had never asked her to visit Northern Ireland. Already she knew so much about the place and was inspired by the visions in her mind of jocular characters and endless rolling hills. She was also not unduly put off by the negative press the small province received, but there had been no invite. She had of course thought to ask him to visit Holland, but was somehow waiting for him to make a move, or send some other explicit sign. But she acknowledged as well that he had really made all the running in the relationship, so this next stage was perhaps required to be her initiative. This played on her mind a little and on further consideration, she wondered if he resented that he had always had to push things forward, while she just relaxed and allowed things to progress in a way that suited her, with little conscious effort or exposure of her emotions.

She had taken to talking to Grietje and her other friends about Michael, indicating playfully that there might be more to the relationship than just pen friends. Generally, they had been encouraging, engaging in the romantic excitement of a love conducted from afar. *Enchantment by mail*, one friend had described it, where elaborate poems disarmed the girl's defences leaving her swooning in the wake of his charm. This was not so far from the truth, and Anna saw no reason to resist, but considered her friend's enthusiastic encouragement as potentially unreliable. They were after all like her, young and prone to romantic notions and emotional overreactions. In the end, she felt her mother to be a more sober confidante.

She did feel awkward though. Neither her mother, nor father had met Michael. All they knew in a first-hand sense was the writing on the envelopes that arrived every week. Anna herself had only ever met him that one time in Morecambe and she felt just a little vulnerable about this. *How could you form a relationship with someone you had met only once?* But, she felt she could answer that. It was all about the letters. Not that she was volunteering to let either parent actually read them for they always seemed so personal to her, but at the same time, she couldn't really see a reason why they shouldn't, aside from the fact she felt indisposed to let them. There was however, nothing incriminating in them, even overtly personal. They had been key in the development of the relationship, but the letters did not express love, or at least not specific love. Love was in everything he wrote, but it was never aimed directly at her.

She longed to tell him how she felt. She longed to look into his eyes and to utter those words, so personal and so divine. She longed to speak of that which would trade the deepest senses of her own vulnerability for her trust in him. But, more than anything, more than the sparkle of the highest stars or the glories of heaven, she longed to hear those words herself. She longed to hear his declaration of love for her. She longed for him to validate her own amorous emotions. She longed to drift into that reciprocal state of mutual devotion, no more as friends, but now as lovers in whom each could depend. With each letter, that arrived, it was that simple message of love that she awaited with increasingly earnest expectation.

Adrie had been a little surprised by Anna's sudden confession of love, which she described quite bluntly. She knew of course that the two young people were quite involved with each other through their correspondence, but hadn't progressed the thought much in her own mind. She was however much more enthusiastic about the prospect of Michael visiting than Anna had envisaged. Anna had described the invitation and the visit she hoped would follow, rather unemotionally as an opportunity to see if there was a long term future for their affections and her mother agreed entirely with this sentiment. Besides, she, Anna's mother, was now interested to meet the young man herself. After all, her daughter was not like her sons, who had leapt with enthusiasm, sometimes at the most unlikely of life's opportunities. Anna was different. Despite her young years, Adrie greatly respected her daughter's judgement and understood quickly that she saw something quite wonderful in the Irish boy. Furthermore, she had described her planned invitation in an almost formal and business-like fashion. This was her way and she had carefully and unemotionally explained the situation, but she had also lit up when asked to tell a little more about him. She smiled and the pale blue eyes her mother had looked upon since she was born flickered and sparkled as she described the poems and texts.

Words, like *quiet* and *thoughtful* were not hostile to a mother's wishes for her daughter's significant other, so she saw Michael already in a positive light. However, she had insisted that Anna would talk to her father as well, but in principle, she agreed that the young man should be invited to come.

Anna's father was a taxi driver and always worked nights, preferring the peace, solitude and quiet to the busy traffic and congestion of the daylight hours. With his early morning finishes, breakfast had become the most important meal of the day as this was often the only time the family would all eat together.

Typically he would arrive home at around 6.00am complete with fresh bread from the bakers, still warm from the ovens, which he would place in a basket in the centre of the kitchen table. It would emit a warm, homely aroma that would quickly fill the small house. For the rest of the family, the smell was a subtle but familiar alarm call, waking them to the new day. Then he would peel fresh fruit slicing apples and oranges, peaches and grapefruits and placing the pieces into individual bowls for the family members.

The fresh fruit emitted another aroma milder than the first, but one that sweetened the scent wafting around the house. For any family members who happened to venture by the kitchen during preparation, the smell of the fruit was indeed an indication that the clock was ticking and the day was beginning.

He would then carefully lay the table, placing a selection of cured meats and cheeses on wooden platters, together with a large jug of yoghurt to compliment the fruit.

Finally, he would place a handful of coffee beans of a variable quantity, reflecting his mood, into the grinder and press the start button. With its grating noise and the familiar pungent aroma released from the crushed beans, any in the household not yet arisen from their slumbers by the milder previous wake up calls would immediately recognise that they were late and would now start the day entirely on the wrong foot.

This particular morning, it was Anna's sixteenth birthday and her spirits were high. It was mid-January and outside a heavy frost had settled on the cobbled streets. The frozen condensation had decked the trees and shrubs outside which were now lit by a pale blue glow from the last of the moonlight and the occasional street lamp that kept the winter darkness at bay. A few tracks already ran across the road surface, including those of Anna's father's car, but there were also foot prints and the narrower lines of cycle tyres which criss-crossed each other back and forth in elongated figures of eight as the riders sought stability at the start of their journeys.

Inside it was *Gezellig*, (beginning and ending with the soft 'G') a word commonly used in the Dutch language that can most directly be translated as *warm and cosy*, but also contains elements of homeliness, friendliness, relaxation and peace. Anna and Geert, together with their parents gathered together to eat, as they did every morning. On this occasion, cards and presents were also handed over to the smiling girl who her father quietly observed, was fast becoming an attractive young woman. She seemed in buoyant mood and having discussed Michael with her mother the previous evening, and as she in particular was the centre of attention, it seemed as good a time as any to announce that there was increasingly a significant other in her life.

Geert was the only family member, besides Anna who had met Michael. His opinion of the young man was mostly indifferent, but the eager look on his sister's face encouraged him to enthuse a little and he described Michael as a polite and interesting youngster. He described the BB camp with a little colour and jocular charm, mildly mocking the eccentric rituals, but emphasising too that it seemed a credible Christian organisation that had no doubt supported the healthy upbringing of the young men. Geert was in any case, not unhappy about his sister's liaison considering that it seemed far more likely to be a relationship of value than just youngsters experimenting with intimacy for the first time.

However, it was Geert who had emphasised a fact their parents had quite missed for Anna had also been affected by Michael in a more pragmatic way. This was not simply in the very positive demeanour she had been displaying in recent months, but also that her command of the English language which had, almost from the beginning, been superior to his own, was now quite exemplary. He had noted this himself recently, while during a trip they had made together to the local supermarket. They had met an English couple, just some tourists visiting the area, who sought some advice about what cheeses to buy. Anna's vocabulary and diction was now so very perfect, that the couple had asked if she was indeed English herself.

Anna's father was perhaps the most reticent; the natural protective instinct of the patriarch coming to the fore, but this too was mild. He wanted to know where Michael would sleep and what they would do all day during the long summer recess, for

Anna's request was that he should stay not just for one or two days, but for a matter of weeks if possible. He did note though, that his daughter, who really asked for very little from him, studied diligently at school and of whom he was as proud as any father could be, had everything really rather worked out. He concluded that whatever misgivings he might have, he knew the only course he could reasonably follow was to give the idea his blessing.

With the formalities over, the family split from the table, each to follow the day's activities they had in store. Anna's father would now sit outside, reading a book and smoking his pipe in the small veranda at the back of the property, enjoying his 'evening' while her mother and Geert headed off to work. Anna set her cards on display on the mantelpiece and with the small pile of presents in her arms she returned to her room, quietly satisfied that her little mission had been accomplished without too much fuss.

She settled at her desk and read through the pages of the latest letter she had already written but left uncompleted. To this Anna added a further short paragraph.

"Dear Michael," she began for the second time in the same letter, "this morning, I have been discussing you with my parents and of course with Geert, who you have met already. In view of my strong feelings for you and the way in which our relationship has been developing over the past eighteen months or so, I feel more and more that I would love to see you once more. Your letters and especially your poems are fine and exciting and tender and loving, but I yearn to see you again. I have asked my parents if you could stay here for a while during the summer, so that we can get to know each other properly. They have both agreed and are excited to meet you, so I do hope you will be able to come.

As always, I look forward to receiving your next letter, but this time with extra hope and expectation,

Love Anna."

There. She sat about considering her words carefully. She had used the word 'love' three times in the paragraph. Firstly, she would *love* to see him, depicting an enthusiastic prospect relating to him, using the potentially emotive word indirectly. Secondly, she had said his letters were *loving*, indicating the view she took that for his part, of course the letters were loving, but since they were sent to her, then there was in fact some emotion of that nature directed at her. Finally, she had written, *love* Anna, a general term of endearment of course and widely used, but it maintained the theme of quietly courting some declaration of emotion from him. Deep down, she felt he loved her, she knew he loved her, but she also wanted to be *told* he loved her. That was in any case part of the reason for the invitation; that their relationship might progress further in a way that such declarations might be made by both parties.

She read her words through again. She was satisfied. Yes, they were OK. They hit the mark. The invitation was there, not a hint nor just an idea, but a direct proposal requiring a response. She folded the pages, placed them in the envelope, licked the gum, placed the stamp and was ready to send as she had done every Monday for the past 18 months.

She left for school, a little early that morning and stopped by the post box on the end of her road, smiling as she dropped her letter into the box. Then off she cycled towards school, over the rough cobbled streets of the old town, leaving her own tracks behind. Her books and pencils and bits and pieces of school apparatus bounced joyfully in the basket in front like an eccentric dance of the emotion in her heart. She turned at last and headed northwards towards school along the smooth path through the wood on the edge of the town from which Pijpersbos took its name. The winter sun now shone low in the sky, flickering through the trees, casting dappled shadows with diamond sparkles on the frosty earth and glinting on the shiny spokes of her bicycle which flashed to a rhythm, the rhythm of a heart filled with love. The air smelled fresh and clean and the cool wind reddened her face and tousled her hair, like a lover running his fingers through her locks in ardent affection.

She was happy with her thoughts, her family and the choice of action she had taken. She thought of Michael as she rode along and her heart swelled with love for the young man, so far away, but who might soon come and see her once more face to face.

If Michael could have seen her then, riding along, the light flashing on the spokes of her bicycle like a cine film of years gone by, the embodiment of everything good in the world. If Michael could have seen her then, her heart full of love, pure, special and unique as love always is. If he could have seen that young girl, with the wind in her hair, the fresh cool air on her face and a heart the size of a pumpkin, he would have known there was nothing in this world that he would ever want that was not there that day.

And Michael may well have visited Pijpersbos that summer. And he might well have returned. He might even have stayed, learned the language and settled down in that little village, far from the darkness of Belfast's streets. Far from the tensions, the resentment, the tears and the madness, the grief and the revenge. He would surely have met once more with that young girl whose heart he had courted through his poems and discovered that her love for him was every bit as real, as serious, as lasting and as triumphant as his was for her. And he would have been welcome too in that small community for the young Anna was already warming a place for him there.

But the sounds of doom drummed in the distance like an inevitable discord from hell demanding its prize. And the devil schemed as he always has and already, as Anna cycled through the wood, his will had settled in the hearts of those whose confused rhetoric somehow justified their horrid means. But the devil cared little for such enterprise deeming it but a channel for his purpose. It was the gratification of loss to the world of this young love looking forward to life and a future together with such glorious expectation that he truly lusted. As he pondered lasciviously the prospect, he celebrated with a cocktail of Champagne and blood for no change of fortune could ever truly match the perfect loss of this love that would never be.

Michael Coglan would never see Pijpersbos.

CHAPTER 11

A Nervous Assassin

While the development of the relationship between the two young people had given Anna her first taste of love, for Michael the change had been altogether more profound. Firstly, he had found something of an inner peace and had begun to experience more progressive emotions such as hope and expectation about life. Externally, although he remained for the most part, solitary and painfully introverted, he had at last come to acknowledge that there was a problem. Gradually he attempted to interact with others in a more meaningful way.

Susan had been the first to notice. Somehow, he seemed more animated in his mannerisms and would smile more freely, though still not often. At the dinner table, he would chuckle at his father's stories from work, intrigued by the close proximity of the hopelessness of incarceration with the ever present casual humour, a characteristic Irish people of every creed and fortune have always shared. Or he would sometimes compliment his mother's cooking, perhaps with a little flattery, in the way she remembered from his early childhood. She noticed that he would comment more and without prompting, on television programmes or other inconsequential issues, sometimes awkwardly like he was attempting to practise a new skill he was learning but had not yet developed. This was of course true but while the long silences that had been a characteristic of his personality for so long still existed, they were no longer the fearful empty solitudes of a dull mind. Instead, inside his head, his senses fluttered with activity as the life few noticed he observed, transformed into random words and phrases that would quickly associate with each other. In time these would develop to become the ever more profound lines of poetry that Anna would read with excitement a week or so later.

There had been change at school too. His marks were still maintained diligently at a level one teacher described as being equidistant between expulsion and exasperation, but there were subtle developments taking place. Now, he would maintain eye contact from time to time, where previously he had always really just gazed at the floor. This was of course a characteristic not exclusive to Michael and not unfamiliar to the teachers either, but rude and cold all the same. He would make the occasional contribution in class, sometimes a little out of context or as if a parallel thought process had taken place, but there was at least some interaction. Generally the teachers and the other pupils in the class were sympathetic and sought to develop his points rather than dismiss them outright. At the end of the previous year, the school report had pointed this out to his very relieved mother, describing the change in his demeanour rather frankly as the first chink of light in a darkness they had all imagined to be permanent.

Despite this, things hadn't really changed that much socially. Michael had been a loner for so long that he knew no different and few sought to change that. Others had found, developed and settled in their own little groups of teenage friends and didn't really require newcomers. It was only with Anna that he maintained any form of social relationship. She would write extensively about music, asking if he knew the lyrics to one song or another, or what he thought was meant by the expressions they contained. This had inspired and developed his interest and he had taken to visiting one of the few music venues in the city that still persevered in those troubled days. There, in the dim light of anonymity he would listen intently to the various bands and singers practicing their talents and even enjoy a beer or two.

He was not really old enough to drink, but both Branny and Susan made no objection figuring that alcohol may even act as an antidote to his solitary nature and bring him out of himself a little. This was also not in any sense a problem for the police as they had more pressing priorities and the pursuit of underage drinkers was not high on the agendas of either the force or the communities they sought to serve. He always arrived alone and left alone and would stand to one side, his back to the wall to avoid shielding anyone else's view and watch and listen intently and in silence as the musicians played, save for clapping politely between songs.

The little club, despite being in a rough part of the city centre where conventional wisdom might have considered it unwise to go, carried little of the sectarian prejudice apparent elsewhere at the time and Michael felt relatively safe there. While he sought conversation with no one, the regulars did come to recognise him. The doorman was a lanky guy in his forties with long grey hair and a beard who Michael pictured as a modern day *Gandalf* from the *Lord of the Rings*, imagining he might suddenly don a cloak and send fireworks streaming through the night sky outside. He was actually an aging hippy who had never really accepted that the summer of love was over and the music scene offered his only refuge from a world that had become altogether too harsh for his liking. He always wore jeans and a T shirt, merchandising from a past gig of some sort, and as he came to recognise Michael, would offer a warm smile when he arrived.

The barman too would see him coming and pour Michael a pint of Smithwicks, [pronounced with a silent w] a beer of the bitter type that was brewed locally, sometimes even before he requested it. Michael's round was rather the simplest to provide and he would smile and raise his glass a little catching the eye of the tender as he handed over his money. The place could of course become boisterous at times and Michael would occasionally be bumped into or splashed with beer, but usually these events ran through without much commotion and he would smile or nod accepting the casual apologies on offer.

The club specialised in original music and Friday nights were characterised by an open mic policy. This featured a series of short sets by a variety of artists, mostly amateur and largely unknown outside of Northern Ireland. What was unique however was that cover versions; that is popular, well known songs by established artists, weren't allowed. This meant that all musicians had to either play their own work or work specifically written for them. Belfast had produced a long list of singer songwriters, some who had achieved international recognition, but many more who had never gained nor even sought fame outside of the area. Folk like this had entertained local people for decades and it was this tradition, the club owners sought to maintain.

Some of the little bands, duos and a few single artists were of course awful, while others could play well though their material was poor. But there were also some whose melodies were really quite beautiful, only the lyrics sounded staid and dull, as if they had been added as an afterthought. In time,

Michael got to know some of the tunes quite well, even putting his own words to the music in the quiet of his mind. He had flirted with the idea of offering his services, which unknown to him, several of the artists would have gratefully accepted, but shyness and the inner self doubt that pervaded his mind always got in the way. Still, his confidence was improving and who knows what might have happened if others in the city had not sought a different agenda for the events of this particular Friday evening.

Michael's past had been mired in fear and solitude, but what might his future have held? Little extrapolation would be required to see that his mental state was in a process of recovery. The illness that had plagued his life, brought on by the trauma he suffered from the beating of his young friend was now clearly in rapid retreat. It was already becoming apparent that those around him would soon see him develop into a fine and talented young man. He himself might not have been certain, but must surely have suspected that before long, he would have a very fine young woman by his side. His life may have been tough and painful, but at this point in time, the light of his future shone with a radiant brightness. Michael Coglan had everything to live for. Instead, he would be at the centre of a tragic story that would later make the evening news.

By 1980, much of the terror activity had become prescribed and methodical, targeted predominately, though not exclusively, against those seen as representing the state on the one hand and often simple sectarian retaliation on the other. The level of violence was not at the heights seen in the early nineteen seventies and journalists and commentators from time to time criticised the government and the security forces for having reached what they called an *acceptable level of violence*. However, it was, if anything, more organised and the fear of terror attacks loomed ever present over the city like kismetic clouds prophesying the people's fate. Every so often, that fear was entirely justified.

The terrorists developed hit lists of those to be targeted. In the bizarre public relations of a terror war, the proposed victims were of differing values and as security was stepped up, access to people like judges, politicians or senior police officers became more and more difficult. In time, the net was cast wider and softer targets, like junior prosecutors or the bobby on the beat joined the list as did the guardians of the convicted, prison officers.

The killings took different forms. Some would be caught in a hail of bullets perhaps as they left home or work. Individuals would often alter routines to disrupt any plans being made, but nothing was fool-proof. Others would have their cars booby trapped in the night with explosive devices set to activate when the car moved or when the brakes were applied. A popular method was for someone to simply call at the home of the target asking for him by name before shooting him down, sometimes in front of his wife and children. At the time, those who might consider themselves potential targets would have been reticent to open the door to strangers, especially after dark.

However, others in the household were considered to be relatively safe as the killing of someone's wife or child was akin to what the western military might call collateral damage and consequently had a profoundly negative impact in PR terms. So, it was usually the wives who would cautiously open the door to any unannounced callers. More often than not, these would of course be entirely innocent and genuine visitors. Where there was any doubt or cause for suspicion, she would simply state with regret that her husband was not home and would they like to leave a message.

In some instances, this worked well, but there were also occasions where the house was then stormed and the victim killed inside, in the kitchen or in front of the television. For all those who worked in these occupations, this fear was a part of everyday life and each dealt with it in their own way. All were entitled to be armed and most kept a gun at home. There was also usually an agreed process by which the door was opened. Some couples operated prearranged drills where the husband would take up position perhaps by an upstairs window while the wife opened the door. Code words were sometimes used. These were innocuous words that could easily be calmly included in the conversation, but would only be uttered under specific circumstances. It might be something like; he's gone over to see Malcolm, when in fact he knew no Malcolm. It was a dangerous game, for once uttered, such code words were the signal to fire. Some terrorists were killed this way.

However, Branny Coglan kept no gun. He had no interest in such things and could never imagine himself shooting another person. In any case, he feared too, the friendly fire shooting of an innocent and felt, perhaps naively, that being unarmed was some protection in the world of terrorist PR.

On this particular evening, Michael set out a little early for the walk to the main road where he would catch the bus into the city centre. The ground was wet from an earlier shower and the streets silent save for the occasional whining of an errant cat. Dim lights shone behind thick curtains inside those houses still occupied. It was a cold night and Michael was already well huddled into his dark grey duffle coat and engaged in his own thoughts when he passed two men, walking with some degree of purpose. One was much younger than the other, not much older than Michael but a little taller at around six feet. He wore a heavy black coat, fully buttoned up the front and despite it being dry, had the hood pulled right up over his head and his hands buried deep in the pockets. Their eyes contacted for a fleeting moment.

The other man was older, in his mid or late thirties and of a short, stocky build. He had long, black, lank hair that edged forward on his stooped head, obscuring his face from the sides. On his head was a small black woollen hat that clipped the tops of his ears. He wore a large sheepskin coat with the collar folded upwards such that only the edge of the cream fleece was in view. Michael didn't much like the look of the pair and hurried quickly by. He didn't recognise them, a point which was not in itself unusual, although since he had been going out more often, he would see the same faces of the older youths that still loitered in the area, some of which nodded and smiled at him in a confusing way, as if they knew him.

These men were not local though and the rough area was not one where strangers lurked uninvited. Furthermore, there was something else about the pair that troubled him. At first he couldn't put his finger on it, but as he walked it vexed his mind some more and he reluctantly turned and looked again. Just as they were about to turn the corner into his own street, it came to him. The sheepskin coat! It was too big. Not ill fitting, simply big. It was *far* too big. This man was not wearing his *own* coat. He was wearing someone else's coat, a much bigger coat and he was wearing it because he was concealing something inside it. A shiver ran down the young man's spine as his thoughts engaged, for suddenly he was quite sure he knew who they were and also suspected he knew what errand they were on.

With that he turned and hurried back towards home. There was no sign of the men and all seemed quiet. He went around to the back of the house, for he always entered and left that way and unlocked the door into the kitchen. Just as he entered, the bell rang at the front of the house. In the quiet intensity that had built in his mind, it sounded like the clang of a cathedral bell reverberating around the cloisters. At the end of the hallway, he saw his mother calmly reach for the latch of the front door. He ran forward silently, miming an almighty shout of alarm, a scream of terror, his arms waving and grabbing at his mother, but it was too late, the door was open.

Susan knew immediately she had made a mistake and they both froze in the doorway. The two men now had their faces covered with black balaclavas of the sort favoured by the terror groups at the time. An ominous sign. There would be no negotiation here. There would be no, *Branny's not home at the moment* this time. Only their eyes were visible through the rough holes cut in the material that left frayed edges to the irregular circles from which terror peered. Michael found himself imagining them sitting at home, cutting the holes with blunt scissors as they made their plans for his father's execution. They were just two men but at that moment, the sight was one of unbridled horror, like an encounter with Satan himself. Michael had seen similar images on the television, but face to face, they were the mirror of death, looking at life. They were a sight most hoped never to see, but they were here and Susan and Michael would have to figure out how to deal with them.

The older of the two men was Patrick (Paddy) Flannigan, a hardened operative and veteran of a number of similar schemes. His commitment to the cause was stoic. He was a cold blooded individual, who had little difficulty dehumanising his victims into simple aberrations and justifying his actions with simple political dogma that he never questioned.

"Is Branny in?" asked Flannigan calmly.

Susan just stood there frozen in terror, speechless, her tongue glued to the roof of her mouth. She could feel her heart pump adrenalin throughout her veins. Her limbs shook and a sudden blast of cold air from the silent street hit her adding to the foreboding of the events which were now clearly unfolding before her like it was a play at the theatre.

Michael stood behind his mother and had raised his hand and placed it on the top of her arm. He squeezed gently providing her with a welcome sensation of comfort and support, but this was not long lived. Quickly it evaporated into a realisation that the son she thought to be in the comparative safety of the city centre streets, now stood behind her, another actor in this awful play, his life too in danger.

Michael's gaze shifted from the coldness of Flannigan's eyes to the younger man. His name was Sean Bradley. This particular endeavour was his first serious foray into organised political violence. He had lost a brother a few years back in a sectarian killing. This type of incident was manna to the terrorist groups. On both sides, they had become adept at harnessing the rage of friends and relatives of victims and providing sympathy and support before mixing it with a sort of romantic notion of a new, better Ireland. A better Ireland that would of course have to be fought for. They had quickly recruited the grieving, teenage Bradley and groomed him over several years for action as a foot soldier in the armed struggle. Earlier that evening, Bradley had heard the name of Branny Coglan for the very first time.

Michael could see the fear in the young man's eyes and as

they each gazed at the other, the connection between the two was forever sealed. Bradley's eyes were not cold or empty, like Flannigan's, but brimming with trembling emotion as he looked upon Branny's son. Bradley didn't see a dehumanised victim before him, he saw his brother. In Susan he saw his own mother. He saw himself. His humanity was quickly compromising his effectiveness in the task for which he had volunteered.

Of the two, it was Michael who remained most calm. Perhaps he had lived with fear in his mind for so long that perceived danger and actual danger had simply fused into one. Now that a situation had arrived that truly warranted a nervous collapse, his senses had become so dulled that there was really little effect. Perhaps his subconscious still felt a guilt over the betrayal of his childhood friend and he sought this time to stand up to adversity. Perhaps it was just a natural, human instinct to protect his mother. For whatever reason, Michael felt his senses sharpen, his body straighten and his resolve stiffen.

But Bradley had not been affected in the same way. The courage he had felt earlier in the evening was quickly evaporating into the night sky. A nervous unpredictability invaded his senses and his hand sweated around the grip of the handgun in his pocket.

"He's not here, he's not here," cried Susan, desperate to mollify the situation.

With that, the agitated Bradley pulled the gun from his pocket and pointed it at the terrified woman who uttered a subdued scream. Michael had never seen a gun used to threaten in earnest before and it was a chilling sight. Cautiously, he stepped forward, pushing his mother behind him and shielding her slight frame almost entirely with his own body.

"Go, tell Branny we're here," said Flannigan. He leaned into the hallway, past the terrified woman "Branny," he shouted, "we've got your wife here. We're going to kill her," he shouted almost casually.

Michael stepped forward, pushing his mother further behind him. He wished she would take her chances and flee inside the hall.

"My father doesn't have a gun," he said calmly and clearly, wanting to ensure the assassins knew that this would be no gun fight, no shoot out between confronting soldiers. This would be a cold blooded killing of an unarmed victim. "My father has no argument with you. He wishes you no harm."

Bradley, now crazy with fear, was waving his gun erratically, wondering which of the words was the *code*. Was it *gun*? Was it *argument*? No it had to be something bland, innocent. Maybe it was just; *my father*. No, that would be no good, Mrs Coglan would also have to say it. His mind raced and he could feel the fear quickly engulfing him. His hands shook and his body flexed involuntarily. Already, he could feel the searing heat of a bullet, perhaps from an upstairs window or from the shadows nearby, enter his body as the hunter became the hunted. He could imagine it entering his head, blowing his brains out, an event perhaps only seconds away.

Bradley drew forward to protect himself from the bullets he was sure were about to rain on him. He was now face to face with Michael, so close that Michael could smell his breath. It was a familiar smell of something he must just have eaten. Mints of some sort! Perhaps polo mints. He had been eating polo mints! Michael dismissed the pointless incursion into his urgent mental state, tucked his mother further behind him, expanding his chest, as if to make his bodily defences bigger. He could see once more right into Bradley's eyes. Now they were flickering erratically, seemingly failing to focus on him. Michael could sense his fear and behind the darkness of the balaclava, the face of the young terrorist grimaced as if in pain. Michael stood his ground and for a brief moment, he wondered what road had led this young man to the doorway of his home that night, with gun in hand on such an evil errand, sent by those more powerful.

Meanwhile, Branny was in the back room wondering what to do. To run out, would be suicide, but for his wife to be slaughtered, maybe his son too, would end his life anyway. He had no gun. There was no plan. Now he wished he had both.

Flannigan stood fast, coldly watching and waiting, while Bradley became more and more agitated. Suddenly, there was a loud bang. The noise echoed throughout the empty neighbourhood, there being insufficient foliage in the area to absorb much of the sound. Bradley's eyes widened and he jumped at the blast, startled as he felt the recoil action punch at his palm quickly releasing the weapon from his shaky grip. It flew into the air before quickly disappearing behind the evergreen foliage of the hawthorn bush.

The sound of the gunshot, left Branny no choice and he ran screaming from the back room in a frenzied rage like a red Indian warrior, somehow hoping his yells would fend off the assault. Flannigan at last pushed his coat to one side revealing the sub-machine gun he had concealed throughout. He quickly lifted it horizontal and set off a swift hail of bullets ringing up the hallway towards the defenceless man. They caught him before he reached the door. The bullets punctured his body and the sudden collapse of blood pressure drained the strength from his legs leaving them collapsing beneath him. The kinetic momentum threw his body forward in a sharp jolt. Branny

Coglan finally settled at the entrance of his own home, his knees bent, his bottom in the air and his face on the doormat, balanced like a Muslim in prayer. Beneath his face, an expanding pool of his blood was gradually covering the word *welcome* on the mat.

"What the fuck did you do that for?" screamed Flannigan. "If you'd just shot in the air, the bastard would have come out." He quickly looked around. All was still. On the steps lay the bodies of Susan and Michael, their blood mingled into a common pool, the one bullet from Bradley's gun seeming to have assailed both mother and son.

"Where's the fucking gun," yelled the angry Flannigan. Bradley just stood there frozen and shaking, his face ashen, his own blood also having deserted his needs.

"Jesus, fuck," muttered Flannigan now to himself as much as to his accomplice. He looked again at Bradley, who beckoned at last towards the Hawthorn bush. Flannigan dropped his weapon on the little patch of grass and got down on his knees. It was dark and at first, he couldn't see the gun. He fished about in the branches, yelping and swearing as the thorns cut right through the glove on his hand and scratched at his outstretched forearm. Eventually, he found it but it was lodged firm between a fork in the branches, set deep inside the bush. He stretched his hand further and further inside but in the last year or two, the little bush had grown much stronger. Perhaps having failed to protect the little starling chicks, it defended the evidence it now held at its thorny heart with uncompromising valour. The thorns cut unreasonably at the terrorist's outstretched limbs and when Flannigan eventually gave up, there was a trail of his own blood left behind on the thorny branches.

Leaving the gun behind, he got to his feet again and lifted

the machine gun, stowing it once more out of sight beneath the bulk of his coat. He shoved Bradley hard, the force bringing the quivering young man quickly to his senses and the pair lit off into the dark night.

CHAPTER 12

An all too Familiar Scenario

The police were alerted by a neighbour who had seen nothing and within minutes of the departure of Bradley and Flannigan, several of the grey armoured Land Rovers, familiar in the city at the time, screeched to the scene. An ambulance quickly followed on their heels and the paramedics jumped from the vehicles, carrying green and red packs of drugs and other lifesaving equipment, each adorned with the white cross of medical emergency. These trained professionals went about their business seemingly unperturbed by the dangers they faced on a daily basis. As they worked, their eyes never left the job, their minds remained focused on their tasks and their senses closed to the hubbub of activity that surrounded them.

They tended to Branny first. His body was still warm, but there was no pulse. One tried desperately to revive him, while the other checked on Michael and Susan. Michael was unconscious and there was a severe wound to the side of his neck, quickly oozing blood onto the step, but there was a pulse and a sort of gurgling sound was coming from his mouth. He was still breathing. The assessment was swift and almost immediately, he was stretchered into the waiting ambulance, the doors closed, and the blue lights wailed *emergency* as the vehicle quickly accelerated from the scene.

Susan wasn't so lucky. The single bullet from Bradley's gun

had driven right through Michael's soft neck, plunged through her eye, and settled in her brain. She had died instantly. Meanwhile, a second ambulance had arrived, and more paramedics quickly jumped from the vehicle. Efforts to revive Branny were looking less and less hopeful. One paramedic was desperately trying to stem the flow of blood which was draining from several places in his flaccid body. Large pads were placed and tightened on to the wounds in his limbs. Presently, two more medics arrived and also knelt by the body, quickly locating key points in his groin, vainly applying pressure to keep what blood remained, inside his torso to serve his organs. That too had little effect as there was also a wound above his pelvis from which more of the clotting liquid now emerged. They took it in turn to massage his heart in the hope of stimulating it to beat once more, but experience told them they were just following a procedure that would yield nothing. Before long, they looked at each other and nodded. Branny, like Susan was pronounced dead at the scene.

The police milled around, looking and checking the area, then built cordons at the end of the street. Soon after the army arrived and set about checking the vicinity beyond. Road blocks were set up and within minutes, the Coglan family home had become the scene of yet another terrorist incident. Before long, the CID would arrive. Then there would be the TV cameras and the newspaper reporters. The next morning, the politicians would comment and the neighbours would say what a lovely family they were. Days after that, the funerals would be held and the people would weep. And the lives of the Irish people would go on as they had done before and would do so again.

Who knows why Branny was chosen. Some of the terror

groups claimed there was never any vendetta against any particular individual. Targets were chosen according to the potential for successful attack. Some speculated that it was because Branny was a Catholic working for the government services. Others said he was a soft target. They knew he had no gun. In the end, Branny and Susan Coglan would become statistics, recorded in the posterity of the province's relationship with its own people. However, at a hospital only a few miles away, Michael lay in intensive care, but he was still very much alive.

CHAPTER 13

Bernie O'Callaghan

Michael's mind was awash with confused information and perceptions. Images, flashing lights, gabbled voices crying and moaning in the background that would become louder and louder, reaching crescendos before falling back were also vying for attention. He could hear mutterings and whispers; *just tell the truth, just tell the truth*, they hissed and everything will be OK. He knew it was a lie. Then a voice would laugh, a heinous, high pitched laugh like a frenzied jackal in the night. Clouds would roll into his mind, then the sun would break through once more, dazzling and hurting his eyes.

A face appeared. It was a small face, a young face. It was a boy. He had brown curly hair and rosy cheeks. A big brown eye gazed at him and flickered eagerly. Michael didn't recognise him, but he smiled back warmly, beckoning him forward. Then it turned grey and distress showed in his features and he drifted off backwards from view.

He saw his mother in a garden, but it was not their garden. It was another garden with a beautiful lawn that sloped downwards, away from the house. It had enormous beds of roses, all in bloom. The glorious flowers swayed in the wind and there were vast arrays of fallen petals on the soil beneath so much so that it was almost covered. Michael's mother seemed younger than he remembered and had her dark hair tied back from her face with a pale blue ribbon that fluttered softly in the breeze like a little flag hoisted on the halyard of a yacht. Her skin was soft, pure and radiant and her cheeks shone with life, reflecting the colours of the roses she tended.

She was beautiful and looked up at him, smiling lovingly, her red lips expanding, captivating him with her gaze. "Come here Michael," she said softly. Michael felt himself start forward, but a small boy appeared, maybe six or seven years old. He wore short flannel trousers and a white shirt. On his feet were grey socks and brown leather sandals. As he approached she held out a large bloom for him to smell. The fragrance wafted willingly from the ripened blossom and invaded his nostrils with an intense scent. The boy smiled, his face radiant. His mother's love reflected in his eyes. She laughed playfully. *The smell of love*, thought Michael.

His mother looked up and Michael saw a man appear. He was in the drive, some way off and the evening sun was behind him silhouetting him with a halo all around. At first, Michael couldn't recognise him and squinted in the sharp light, but as he came closer he could see that it was his father, but he too looked different. He wore a smart tweed jacket with grey slacks and a tie. It was a bright blue tie with a large knot, but loosened slightly and the top button of his shirt was unfastened as if at the end of a hard day's work. In his jacket pocket, a pale blue handkerchief jauntily peaked out. It too fluttered in the wind like it was cut from the same cloth as Michael's mother's ribbon. On his head he wore a cloth cap that poorly matched the tweed of his jacket and the peak shadowed his eyes. Michael started to call out to him, but no sound came.

His father stopped by another rose bed and carefully broke away a stem, then carried it like a baby towards his wife and the boy. Susan giggled once more as she received it, holding it carefully to her nose, and inhaling the scent herself. She smiled and nodded approvingly, looking over the blossom with big cow eyes towards her husband. Michael could now clearly see the face of his father who smiled broadly as he engaged his wife's ardent gaze. They looked at each other with such warmth, intensity and sublime delight in a way only those who truly love each other can. Michael gasped at the sight. *The look of love*, he thought. Then his father got down before the boy, his eyes alight with life. "What did you do at school today, Michael?" Michael smiled bashfully, but it was the boy on the lawn who spoke. "I got a gold star in my report," he answered.

Then Branny smiled, a confidant young smile, Michael had never seen before and put a hand to the young boy's ear and quickly snapped his fingers. A bright red apple suddenly appeared which he handed to his smiling son. The boy eagerly bit from the apple, the white flesh breaking away with a distinct crack. *The taste of love* thought Michael. Then he plucked the boy effortlessly from the lawn and lifted him high into the air, twirling him around, above his head. Michael took a sharp intake of breath as he prepared for flight, but the boy just smiled delightedly as he rose up and flew through the air, safe in his father's grip, his face surrounded by the blue sky behind. He didn't feel afraid, he felt safe, held firm. *The strength of love*, thought Michael, watching.

Then he could hear the gentle tones of the chimes as the door of the conservatory at the back of the house opened and a woman walked out onto the veranda. She was much older and wore a multi-coloured scarf on her head, with grey locks escaping at the front. Her blouse was prim, ironed and of a crisp, pink gingham check and she wore a pinny around her waist.

Michael didn't recognise her, but the boy cried, "Granny, Granny." He let go of his father's grip, and ran up towards the woman, the apple still in his hand. She hurriedly bent down and hugged him fondly.

Granny? That's my Granny!

Then the older woman turned once more to look at the door. "Look who's here", she said. Another small boy appeared, his curly brown hair was ruffled and his sleeves rolled up. He wore a pair of brown canvas shorts and underneath his left arm lodged a football. It was a brown leather football, scuffed and scruffy, like the boy who smiled enthusiastically, his rosy cheeks shining as he called out. Michael couldn't hear what he said, but still drew in his breath to reply. No sound came. Then he saw the little Michael run towards his friend, smiling and laughing as the grown-ups watched the two disappear behind the house, dribbling the ball between them. *My friend? The boy must be my friend.*

The dream came and went with interludes of more confusion, clouds and shrieking noises. Michael would long to see the garden again, mentally pushing the fear, torment and confusion from his mind to make way for the new images. It took effort to return, but once there he would feel peace for a time. The order of events changed and sometimes Michael would watch intently from close by, absorbing the smiles and the flickers from the actors' eyes that seemed so alive with life. He would walk between them, even right up close where he could smell his mother's scent or gaze closely at her white skin and the fine hairs on her neck and arms.

He walked freely around the garden feeling the soft bounce of the healthy lawn and breathing in the scent of the roses. The garden was awash with noise as the boys played and Granny hurried around bringing juice drinks with ice cubes loudly clinking in the glasses. Birds tweeted in the air and the flies and wasps buzzed around. Then his father took his mother by the arm, raising her to her feet and hugging her closely against him, his palm pressed firmly into the small of her back pressing her body close to his. Their eyes sat intent on each other, radiating love like there was an eternal supply. Then Susan and Branny turned and looked at him and their smiles faded slowly. Now they looked more like the parents he knew. It was Susan who spoke:

"We're sorry you missed it Michael."

She leaned forward and raised her height on her toes before gently kissing him on the cheek. Then, the couple turned and his father's arm still around his mother's waist, they slowly walked off. Michael would have liked to have watched for longer, but another voice was calling him. He turned sharply.

"Michael, Michael! Can you hear me?"

The voice sounded distorted, but nearby and he felt his senses alter towards a more troubled state as he sought to find its owner.

"I think he's coming round. Check the drip."

Then, he was aware of more people near him. The sounds from the garden had faded and he could no longer see his parents. The smell of the roses now seemed acrid and stale and new sharp scents emerged that he didn't recognise.

"Michael, if you can hear me, just nod. OK?"

A man in a white coat was staring at him intently. A white light hit his eyes making him blink, but it didn't last long and disappeared with a soft click.

"Pupils dilating OK. Good, good. Blood pressure, stabilising."

Michael's eyes focused and met the doctor's gaze. He smiled reassuringly.

"I think we have you back in the land of the living young man," he said.

Gradually the blurry group subsided as his eyes focused and only the doctor remained, with one other, a woman, still holding his hand. Michael turned his head a little to see her. His neck was tightly bandaged and his movement restricted, but he did make out the blue and white uniform of a nurse. She looked softly at him. She was in her late forties with warm dark eyes, practised in sympathy, looking out of a plain face. Her black hair was intermingled with occasional grey strands and cut unflatteringly, encircling her face on three sides, like a bowl had been used as a guide.

"I'm Bernie," she said at last smiling, and leaned over the bed a little to aid his view. A tiny clock dangled from a button on her pinafore. It swayed back and forth like a hypnotist's watch on too short a chain. Michael tried to focus on it.

He struggled to speak, opening his mouth once or twice before engaging his vocal chords. There was a sharp pain, but he went on anyway.

"It's upside down," he said at last.

"What's upside down?" asked Bernie slowly, leaning forward and looking intently at him. "Michael. What's upside down?"

"The clock." He nodded towards her lapel.

Bernie smiled. "It's so I can see it easily. Look," she demonstrated, lifting the dangling watch and tilting it up towards her face.

"It's 3.30," she said. "3.30pm."

The doctor chuckled.

"Oh, I think this young man is going to be just fine."

132

He lifted the clip board and scribbled a few more notes, before dropping it with a clang in the steel holder at the end of the bed and walking off. Bernie sat beside him, watching him intently. She took his hand in hers and gripped it firmly.

"Pain?" she asked at last.

"A little," he replied. "It's okay."

"Pain is something we take very seriously. Let me give you something for that."

Gently, she set his hand back on the bed and went off. Michael looked around. He was now alone in the room. Behind him he could hear the gentle whirr of the cooling fans of various pieces of electronic equipment and a soft beeping that he guessed might be in time with his heart. A strap held two tubes up his nostrils and a catheter had been inserted into a vein in the back of his hand. It hurt a little when he moved and he could see the vein stretch and strain as the tube that dangled from the drip moved as he shuffled to aid his comfort.

The window blind was down, but some light still penetrated and the room felt rather bright and airy despite the hospital smells he would become used to in the coming weeks. Bernie returned with a glass filled with a blue liquid bubbling with a pale aqua effervescent foam on top.

"Here, drink this," she said.

Michael bent his head forward and took a sip. There was a sharp stinging as he swallowed.

"Drink it all. The pain will subside very quickly."

It did too and shortly, as if by magic, he felt the twinges and pangs in his throat and neck become more manageable and finally disappear altogether.

"Can you remember anything?" asked Bernie. Her dark eyes focused intently on him.

Michael thought for a bit, trying to separate the hallucinogenic sounds and dreamy images that had been filling his mind from the hospital bed that he suspected might be reality. He saw the face of the small boy again. Now he recognised him. This was his friend, but he couldn't understand the associated fear he saw in him. Then he saw his mother and father, young and attractive as in his dreams, but a haunting chill invaded his thoughts. He was confused.

"It's not good, is it," he replied at last.

Bernie sat for a few moments, gathering the words for her reply, but discarded them before she spoke again, "No, it's not good," she said at last. "Someone is going to come and talk to you shortly. If you feel up to it that is?"

Michael didn't reply. *It's not good though*. He spoke again to himself.

"Take it easy. Rest. If you need anything, just pull this cord. Look, see." She demonstrated, pulling a plastic handle that dangled from a red string connected to a box in the ceiling. A light went on above the bed. "See, look," she gestured upwards with her hand. "The string also sounds a buzzer outside to alert us. Now, try to relax."

Michael faded off into a snooze once more aided by the sedative nature of the drugs being applied intravenously through the catheter in his hand. His dreams came and went. Memories from an ancient mist, the imaginary, the spiritual, the fictional all crammed into the same chaotic space, each fighting for a position in his mind. He longed for the garden between the howling cries of despair that also seemed to invade his senses, not solely for its tranquillity, but also for its reality. The subconscious in his mind had already begun to re-construct his own history and make it once more accessible in his thoughts.

It was the next morning when he woke again and Michael took his first opportunity to look around the room. There were four beds, but his was the only one occupied. The walls were painted in a shiny cream colour and the floor was of polished concrete with tiny red and grey specks that fused to a single shade in the further reaches of the room. Without lifting his head, he could just see the end of the stark hospital bed with its construction of grey tubular steel that gave it a discomfiting, clinical feel. Bernie was standing by the door talking to a doctor and the pair looked over at him several times as they spoke, leading Michael to believe he may be the subject of their conversation.

At last Bernie noticed the staring of his wide eyes and came over, "how are we this morning?" she asked smiling sympathetically. Michael didn't answer.

She checked a few of the whirring machines behind him which emitted sporadic pips and toots while their little green monitors flickered digits or messages and graphs with fuzzy lines on their screens. Once more, she sat on the bed beside him.

"Look, there's someone you need to talk to."

Michael didn't react.

"You don't have to if you don't feel up to it. It can wait. You are my number one priority. It's you we are concerned about. Getting you better." She smiled. Her smile was kind and reassuring, but not broad enough to show a tooth. Her disposition immediately engendered a sense of trust in Michael and he felt every inclination to take whatever direction she proposed.

"Who?" He asked at last.

"He's a man from the Northern Ireland office. He needs to talk to you about your parents." She paused briefly, her dark eyes gazing at him intently as she tried to measure his level of understanding. "Ok?"

"OK," replied Michael. The tears built in his eyes. He was seventeen years old and almost a man, but yet still a child. Emotionally at that moment, he was as a tiny toddler who yearned more than anything for the warmth of his mother's embrace. He looked around, noting her absence.

"I'll be here too. All the time." She squeezed his hand once more, taking care to avoid snagging the catheter. "OK?" she asked once more.

"OK," replied Michael.

Bernie upped herself from her perch and walked swiftly off towards the door. She returned a few moments later with two men. One was the doctor, he remembered from the previous day. The other was a man in his fifties who wore a grey suit with neatly trimmed brown hair and a moustache shaved rather too far above his lip. His mannerisms were courteous and pleasant but could not disguise the cold air of the establishment that he represented. It was the doctor who spoke first.

"You've been badly injured, Michael. Do you remember what happened?"

He didn't wait for a reply and Michael offered none.

"You were shot in the neck. You've been out for a while. You woke up yesterday and we did some checks. Then we sedated you overnight. We operated twice. It was a nasty wound. A lot of blood was lost, but we've stabilised you and it looks like you should be OK. The next day or two matter, but we do have some bad news. "Can you remember anything?" he asked once again hoping Michael would help him out by delivering at least some of the news himself.

Besides the dreams, Michael did have a hazy recollection of

the confrontation, but he had no idea of the outcome. He didn't remember the gunshots or the tragic events that followed.

The man in the grey suit leaned forward. "Michael, I am from the Northern Ireland office. Do you know what that is?"

He nodded.

"Look, there was a shooting. You were shot, as you know." He paused a little, thinking. "The wound in your neck is a gunshot wound." Michael lifted his hand and touched the bandage on his neck with the back of his knuckles. "The thing is," the man went on, "both your mother and father were shot in the same incident."

The news seemed to take Michael by surprise. Suddenly it became clear to him. When he woke, there was no Mum, no Dad, no hugs and kisses from a loving family, just some nurse. He looked bitterly at Bernie, her sympathetic face suddenly offensive to him for the surrogate role he now saw she sought to play.

"Well are they all right?" he demanded, the force of his voice straining at the still fragile wound that had grazed his oesophagus, causing him to cough uncomfortably. Bernie lurched quickly forward, steadying him on the bed, holding him firmly on the shoulder and connecting his eyes with her own penetrating gaze. Michael pushed her away roughly.

"Michael, I'm sorry, really I am. I'm sorry but they're both dead."

Michael hadn't been expecting that. He had known things went wrong, violently wrong. Reasoning with himself, he presumed they had got to his father. *Maybe he could remember the shots.* He thought he could remember his scream, but his mother too. How could that be? That was implausible. He had been protecting her. He strained in the bed.

"Take it easy," said the doctor, but the boy struggled once more. Then he felt a sharp flick of pain in his arm.

When he awoke, he was alone. Two nurses were sitting at a small table at the far end of the room, writing, like they were completing forms or some other bureaucratic activity. They were in the midst of a hushed conversation. Michael set about listening.

"Poor mite," said the first nurse, "some bloke in a suit had to break the news to him. Sad when there is no-one. No-one close to break the roughest news, only some faceless bureaucrat. I'm sure he's glad to be back at home, his day's work done. Not much of a job."

"Well, it's worse for us," said the second nurse, hushing her tones. "We have to live with this all the time. He gets to just pop in, deliver the news and hop out again, back to his pen pushing or whatever it is he does."

Michael nodded off again. It was the next morning when he awoke and the sunlight once again flickered through the edge of the blind. Bernie was sitting on a chair beside the bed. The images, the hallucinations, the noises and dins subsided. Sleep was terrifying. Waking horrific. There was no peace. The facts hit him once again. His parents were dead.

Bernie smiled quickly at him when she saw his eyes were open, then checked her upside down watch and scribbled something on the blue clipboard sitting on her lap. She looked back and forth at the electronic equipment mounted mostly behind him and entered some more information in the notes. A light flashed in his eyes once more. She smiled. "That's fine," she said reassuringly.

She got up and placed the clipboard quietly in the holder at the end of the bed.

"Mum and Dad are both dead," said Michael at last.

Bernie nodded, pulling the seat once more close to the bed and taking his hand in hers. Her grip was firm, warm and soft. It was motherly and he found comfort in her touch, but the tears still welled in his eyes. She held on, making no sound. Michael wanted to hug her, but couldn't easily move. She leant forward and pushed his hair away from his face. Then she kissed him softly on the forehead as a mother would a small child.

Close to him now, Michael could smell her scent. It was clean and clinical, but there was also a mild perfume, a feminine smell perhaps from a soap or shampoo. It reminded him of his mother.

CHAPTER 14

Where Grief Pervades, Hope Glimmers

The body in a wretched state provokes a mental development in the mind, one of expediency, immediacy and pragmatism. In the previous few days, Michael Coglan had had everything he had in the world taken from him. Following such a shock, a mental dilapidation towards oblivion is not uncommon. For many the sheer trauma is sufficient to imbalance the thought processes into a semi-permanent state of denial that can last months or even years causing dysfunctional and unpredictable reactions. But these are only some of the cases. For Michael, who had lived such a melancholy existence for so long, living in a world where tragedy looked always to be etched on his face, in reality he had grieved for years for loved ones not yet lost. He had been conscious of the dangers of his father's job. Mentally, he had not only prepared for such an event but to some degree already existed as if it had happened.

It was the loss of his mother that left him so terribly alone. She represented everything good in the world, his only real stability in the haunted life he lived. Over the days that followed and as his memory of the events pieced together, he punished himself for her loss. *Why did he return home? Why did he confront the assassins? What came over him? Why hadn't the quivering wreck, fearful of his own shadow that had always left him shaking in the corner, deserted him?* Instead, he sought to save and protect. He had confronted his most fearful demons, but to what end? To death, to loss and to misery.

The anger grew in his mind, perpetuated by his own self chastisement as logic gave way to emotion. He could feel a violent rage building in his mind and did nothing to resist it. Roughly, he pulled the catheter from his hand, ripping open the vein into which it fed its nonsense and hurled the stand across the room sending the tubes and wires trailing across the floor, oozing cloudy liquid in their wake. It slammed into the unoccupied bed opposite with a loud crash that echoed in the silence of the night. Tears streamed once more down his cheeks and his hand oozed blood onto the sheets beside him.

He had half expected a major incident to be reported, but a nurse he hadn't seen before turned up not quite immediately and looked him over only briefly before taking care of the mess on the floor. She quietly removed the stand and its contents from the room altogether, before returning to inspect his cut hand. She pulled over one of the little tables on wheels that they rolled about everywhere, with sterile packs of needles and syringes and bandages and the like and set herself down beside him on the bed.

"Do you want me to attend to that?" she asked at last, beckoning towards his bloody hand.

Michael felt indisposed to answer, but he held his arm out all the same, guilty at the mess the blood was making to the sheets and the pyjamas they had given him to wear. She turned and sat with her back to him shielding his view with her body. She wore no bonnet and he found himself watching her narrow neck and the back of her head as she worked. Her fair hair parted sharply on top and he could see the white skin of her scalp between the taut follicles gripped firmly in place by the hair grip on her crown. His hand hurt and he wondered if she was awkwardly having to remove a broken needle or valve from his flesh, but he made no sound. Instead he just watched her work, feeling comfort in her closeness to him, the sharp iodine vapour mingling with the tears that still streamed down his face.

She was young and he wondered if she had parents, or a family or a boyfriend or someone. *Anyone who loved her.* He had expected she would scold him or at least scowl or even worse, try to comfort him, but she didn't. She worked at his little wound, mopping the broken flesh and then finally placed a foam pad over the cut which she asked him to hold while she taped it in position.

When she was done, she turned and looked up at him. He looked at his hand once more. It was clean. The blood was mopped and the stains on the sheets had mostly dried.

"Do you want me to put another one in? I can do it in your other hand."

Michael didn't answer. She got up and looked at the clipboard at the bottom of the bed. Michael had already learned that these sheets on which they scribbled notes and referred to often was now the bible of his life, or at least the case notes that provided continuity throughout his twenty-four hour care. Nothing happened without the clipboard. He watched her diligently as she read.

"There's some pretty important stuff they've been giving you. Really, you should have it. I can put another one in." She looked at him expectantly. "It's no bother. It'll only take a tick."

Michael nodded. She rolled her little table to the other side of the bed and opened another sterile pack. It contained a tiny 'T' shaped tube with a little tap on it. Then she opened another with a needle. This time she faced him and he could see what she was doing. She held his hand firmly, then scrubbed the back with alcohol, before saying; "little prick" at exactly the same time as she slid the needle expertly into the vein on his right hand. It swelled and turned a little purple, then she connected the tap to the body on the end of the needle. Michael watched her work as before, again focusing on her white scalp, but this time he could also see her eyelashes blinking periodically as she worked and her delicate fingernails void of paint or varnish. Within minutes, she was done. "Hold on a minute," she said at last and left the room.

She arrived back a few moments later with a new stand with tubes and poly bags of fluids, just as before and before long had his intravenous drip reconnected. When she was done, she sat briefly on the bed. "They'll change those for you in the morning," she said looking at the blood stains on the sheets. "You gonna be alright?"

Michael nodded and she got up to go. Just as she was collecting the wrappers and swabs together, Michael's eye caught her gaze "What's your name?" he asked.

She smiled, for the first time. "My name is Anna."

CHAPTER 15

Bernie, Would You Write Something Down for Me?

Whatever nurse Anna had put in the drip had a rapid effect, or perhaps his body was just exhausted from the anger that had dominated his mind over the previous few days, but he slept well for the rest of the night. When he awoke in the morning, he felt a tiny flicker of peace in his mind, the first since his admission to hospital. He knew he had to come to terms once more with the loss of his parents, the way he had done every morning, but the mention of the name 'Anna' had jolted his thoughts into a less weary consciousness. The Dutch girl had hardy left his mind since they first met a year and a half ago and almost everything he had thought or done since then, was in her name. However, in the last week, the joint urgencies of injury and grief had dominated his thought processes and the reality of the life he was leading had come to the fore. There had been little room for fantasies of love.

Now she was back in his mind and the thought of her warmed his soul. *She* wasn't dead! She was surely very much alive! His relationship with her was not of the unconditional nature a child enjoys with their parents and he still feared her feelings for him may not be of the same nature or intensity as his for her. However, she was at least a living soul with whom he had some connection. He allowed his mind to drift towards her, visualising her in his mind and enjoying little sparkles of positive energy that began to flicker inside him. At first he felt guilt, like he was smiling at a wake. He felt a painful conflict between the two apparent opposites of grief and love but the short periods when he immersed his mind in thoughts of Anna, lifted his heart and gave him the will to live. Of course, he was no stranger to mental conflict and used to living with such unease. In any case, deep down, he knew his parents would will him well. He knew they would wish love for him and want him to carry on. He comforted himself and thought of his parents, seeing them in his mind's eye, now looking at him as he remembered them. Rightly, he concluded there was no rational conflict between his love for Anna and that of his lost parents.

As the days ticked by, Michael felt his strength recover, and he and Bernie drew closer. She had tended to his every need with a saintly dedication since his arrival at hospital. She worked in the day, and he would watch her go about her business, checking on this and that, but she would also sit with him in the evenings. They would talk a little, with Bernie recounting little tales of hospital life with a rather amusing irreverence Michael rather liked, or relating the occasional more upbeat pieces of news from the world around them. Life went on, even while the ill were ill and the dead lay in their graves. But Michael didn't engage much. This was in no sense off-putting to Bernie who was happy to sit in silence, just being with him, sometimes for long periods after her shift was over.

During these times, she was not primarily a nurse, but rather a friend. At first, Michael had resented the role she played, but she was determined to play it and he had few other visitors. The man from the Northern Ireland office turned up now and again, but usually he had nothing to say. It turned out that as

Michael was still under eighteen, the state had appointed him as his temporary guardian. Michael couldn't remember his name. One or two people from church came, but Michael hadn't been in years and he hardly knew them. The visit was awkward. Some boys and one of the officers from the BB arrived one night, but Michael had been asleep and they were turned away. They never returned.

So Bernie became Michael's friend and confidante as he recovered in hospital in Belfast and the mention of the name 'Anna' put an end to the anger in his grief. As the lonely days ticked by, Michael began more and more to contemplate his future and his thoughts increasingly turned to the Dutch girl. He thought to write to her and set about concocting a poem that might convey his thoughts without causing alarm. It was not an easy task and eventually he set the idea to one side. Then he thought to simply write a letter, chronicling the events of the last two weeks, just to keep her informed. It had been tragic. He'd lost his parents. He was injured, but he was recovering and would be OK. However, he had never been comfortable with the coldness of conventional text and the subject matter was more difficult than he could contemplate. The thought simply depressed him and he allowed his mind to wander to more positive emotions.

Instead, he imagined himself going to Holland. He imagined them meeting again. The cautious pride of new encounter long since gone and now the open smiles of friends who had built a relationship over the months, now reunited once more in physical proximity. That, at least was surely guaranteed, but he knew, as he had always known that his feelings for her were far beyond friendship. He knew this was love. If ever love existed, his love for her was love at its most perfect and he would speak of it. As soon as they were alone, he would tell her immediately. There was no more time for nervous caution, nor the steady pace of engaging minds.

Over the following days, Michael experienced other changes too. Firstly, he felt himself grow stronger. Sleep, dreams and reality fused together less readily than they had done before and facts became much clearer. Little by little he pieced together the events of that fateful night and he began increasingly to come to terms with his loss. But the trauma had other effects too, for his early memory slowly started to return. His dreams had been the first to spark his consciousness, but he could now remember the big house in the suburbs with its wide drive and large, well decorated rooms. In his mind's eye, he could see the conservatory at the back with the peeling white paint and the wind chime with its eccentric tones. He remembered the ivy that grew enthusiastically on the walls, the apple trees laden with fruit and the rose bushes his mother tended so diligently. This had been his dream, but he came to understand that it was not a dream, but a memory, a part of his life that had lain hidden in his sub-conscious for years. A part of his life, now released like a whole new story being narrated in his mind.

He could also remember his old school, set into the hill with its walled grounds and blackened steel gate that led through to the wood behind and the adventures it held. Faces gradually emerged, school friends, neighbours and relatives. There was of course his granny, but there had also been a period when the Coglan household was awash with visitors and Michael could now see their faces. Names were more difficult, but there were faces he remembered.

Then there was Paul. He remembered the little curly haired boy. He remembered them playing football together and climbing in the trees. He remembered Paul's house with its swings and seesaw in the garden. Even Paul's Mum and Dad, he could now see in his mind's eye. His mind flitted back and forward from the beating at the playground that Paul had borne and he felt once more the fear and anguish he had felt then. At first he resisted visiting that particular memory, but after a while he made up his mind that he would have to go there and re-live the experience. And he did. And he sought to reprimand himself no more. He forgave himself and his betrayal in the way his friend must surely have done many years before. Somehow he knew it was necessary if he was to recover his mind and move on with his life.

And move on was something he wanted to do. The grief at his parents' loss was still an open wound, but it was a real wound with pain and suffering and loss and anguish, it was not the false emptiness of the blank mind he had lived with for so long. Now he could see how mentally lost he had been. Now he could see why his mother had fretted so much. Now, he was confronting his demons one by one. From somewhere an inner strength was building in him. He started methodically to separate fear from pain and the past from the present.

And then once more there was Anna. His thoughts began with her and ended with her. At once he realised it was she who was keeping him going through this struggle. She still knew nothing of these recent events and in the end he decided he would keep it like that for now, but his plans were increasingly set. He would go to Holland. He *would* see her again.

However, on that particular day, there was just one small problem that had been lingering in his mind which despite his optimism had forced itself forward and was now gaining his attention. *He really was no longer feeling that well.*

He was still lying in bed, trying to rationally evaluate how he felt, when Bernie came by, as she often did, checking blood pressure, pupil dilation and re-dressing the wound in his neck. She was going about her business, methodically as ever, when Michael suddenly grabbed her by the wrist. "Bernie," he said slowly. "I'm really not feeling that well."

Bernie smiled, that reassuring smile she always offered. "I'll get the doctor," she said and swiftly left the ward.

The doctor checked his chest, listening to his lung function, looked in his ears, closely at his face and his eyes, punctuating his thought process with intermittent 'hmmms.'

"And you say you have been feeling unwell, since when?"

Bernie set about strapping his arm into the familiar sleeve to measure his blood pressure and pumped up the pressure with the rubber ball.

"Well, I can feel myself getting better, but worse at the same time," replied Michael, but his speech was now starting to slur. "It's like I'm getting weaker, not stronger. Breathing is a bit difficult."

"Blood pressure's very low," said Bernie.

The doctor looked alarmed. Bernie unpacked more of the little sterile packages and inserted once more a needle into his arm. Quickly, three phials of Michael's blood had been filled and she walked swiftly from the ward. It was only minutes before a crew descended and he was wheeled once more to the intensive care unit.

Michael knew little of what happened in the following few days for a battle between the medical scientists of the day was wielded with extreme valour against a force that seemed determined that Michael's time on earth was spent. He had contracted septicaemia and his blood swam with bacteria that set about poisoning his body from within causing a severe and destructive reaction from his immune system.

He underwent a series of blood transfusions as well as two further emergency operations. Eventually, his body responded to the antibiotics and they managed to stabilize his situation, but the blood poisoning had already inflicted a heavy toll and several of his key organs had been damaged. The doctors and surgeons who had worked so hard to save his young life became finally resigned to the overwhelming evidence from their tests. Michael would not survive.

When they had done all they could, they brought him round once more. Michael opened his eyes and saw the doctors, surgeons, anaesthetists and nurses gathered around the bed in the same way he had done when he awoke from his initial injury. Although dazed and weak, his body worn out from the war that had waged within him, he was remarkably lucid. He knew immediately all was not well. There was no *welcome back to the land of the living* or the reassuring chuckle of a surgeon pleased with his handiwork. Quickly, he sought out Bernie's dark eyes which now seemed black, all around, like she hadn't slept. She smiled, but it was a despondent smile and when he saw her, he knew for sure he would be joining his Mum and Dad before long.

Gradually the assembled group filtered quietly off. Barely a word was spoken. Once again, he was left with Bernie who by then had taken up her usual position alongside on his left, but the doctor remained with her. He watched momentarily as she and the doctor whispered to each other and caught her discomfited gaze as her eyes fell on him again. "We need to talk to you Michael," she said.

The doctor was still standing and he took up a position behind Bernie, his tall stature stooped over her. He wore the same clinician's coat they all wore and Michael stared at the white image before him, a little slouched, his head bowed. His eyes were sad and empty. When Michael blinked, the white image took a black tone like the negative of a photograph and flashed dark like the cloaked messenger of the grim reaper posing before him. At last he spoke.

"You had septicaemia Michael. We've treated you as best we can and we seem finally to have managed the infection, but it took a while." He paused so long that Bernie turned her head right around to prompt him. "It took *too* long, Michael. Do you understand me?" Michael's eyes widened. If he had had any hope, he could now tell by the tone of the doctor's voice, the direction the message would now take.

"You went into septic shock. The shock has damaged your organs."

Again he paused as if willing someone to help him out.

"Your kidneys are damaged, maybe your heart too. We're not sure, but it is your liver that is the real problem. We've been running tests. There is hardly any liver function. The doctor was hoping Michael's layman's medical knowledge might have been better and he would have known the only outcome of a failed liver, but he just looked imploringly at the doctor, then at Bernie and back to the doctor again his eyes begging for a different message.

"Michael, you can't survive without a liver. There is nothing more we can do. I'm so sorry"

Michael felt Bernie squeeze his hand and he turned towards her, his haunting expression, focusing directly on her, once more begging for a reprieve, begging for hope. Some suggestion of what they would now do, what chance he had, but there was none. A lesser person might have looked away, even briefly, but Bernie held the young man's eyes in hers steadfastly. His haunting expression would be with her forever.

The doctor broke the silence. "Do you want to see a priest?"

"He's not Catholic," interrupted Bernie. Then she went on, taking over the conversation, "someone from church perhaps?

Michael shook his head. "Michael is there anyone you want to see? "Do you want to see Anna?"

Michael's heart fluttered at the sound of her name. *How did she know of Anna?* But Bernie could see the question in his eyes.

"I'm sorry, you mentioned her several times when you were delirious. Michael, do you want me to get her for you. I will find her now. I will bring her here, straightaway." He shook his head once more.

"Can you leave me?"

The doctor looked relieved. Bernie just looked. "I'll be right over here if you need me. Remember, just pull on the handle."

The two went off and Michael lay in silence with his thoughts. It all seemed so surreal. How much sadness was one man's destiny? How could fate strip him of everything he had in the world, then return, unsatisfied for more? What was now wanted? He had nothing left to give.

He thought of Anna. Oh, if only he could see her just one more time, just one more time. Bernie had said she would call her. She would find her for him. A dying man's wish, she would surely come. She would come for him. But was there even time? And to what end? Inflict on her the contagion of Ireland's hatred for itself? No, this was something she shouldn't see. His life was over, but hers would be perfect. Left alone, she would find a husband, and she would make him as happy as she might have made him. And children? Oh yes, she would have children. Left alone, Anna would still have a wonderful family and bring up her children with the unique love he knew she possessed.

The thought shed a glimmer of light on his fading mind, but it didn't last long.

He thought of the Trumpet Major. *Watch what you wish for.* Oh the irony! He had just assumed the soldier would end up with the beautiful girl, but now he had finished the novel. The love that had seemed on the verge of blossoming for most of the book had never materialised and the Trumpet Major lay slain on a Spanish battlefield. His love, like Michael's, unrequited.

His thoughts tailed off. She would forget him. She *should* forget him. That was right, but the loneliness of death was bleaker than he had ever imagined. There was nothing ahead, just nothing. Beneath the blankets, he clasped his hands firmly together as he had done as a child at church. He could hardly feel them and wasn't that sure his hands were even connected, but he squeezed. He didn't know what to pray for. He knew he wouldn't be saved, not for this life anyway, so he prayed for salvation. He prayed for a smooth transition as life and death connect for that short moment when all uncertainty is certain and all questions are answered.

Over the hours that followed, Michael lay in thought, his eyes closed. Bernie came by several times and took his pulse. He felt her presence, but he didn't react. He just lay there, the last of his mental powers focused on a final errand his mind sought to complete before he finally succumbed to the inevitable. At last Bernie's shift ended and she came and sat by him the way she had done so often over the past few weeks.

After thirty years of nursing experience she had seen numerous successes where unlikely lost cases would suddenly revive and achieve a full recovery. She would smile openly as they thanked her and watch them stroll from the ward, once again set to enjoy the virtues of the world and endure its challenges. That's why she got into nursing. But she had also seen a few like Michael's where comparatively minor injuries had been plagued by a succession of complications that all led to a sorrowful ending. They were never easy, but for most they had been surrounded by family and friends and Bernie would be only a witness to the departure, comforting the bereaved, not the dying.

Michael was different. There were no family and friends. There was no one to comfort him. No relatives who would leave the ward, their eyes red with grief. She had grown close to the boy no one seemed to know. They had talked a little in the evenings, but mostly she had just sat with him and watched, firstly as his recovery began, then as he came to terms with the death of his parents, then in horror as his final sentence was delivered.

She knew him to be a deep individual who possessed inner qualities as yet unclear to her. She knew her purpose in nursing and in caring for this particular patient would never be surpassed. She knew no case would ever touch her as profoundly as this one. She knew she would never forget Michael Coglan, but the poignancy of what would now happen in the final hours of that young man's life would stay with her forever.

The tears were still in his eyes, when she sat down beside him. Crying for himself for no one else would. Crying for what might have been and that that never would. She held him by the hand once more, firmly, softly the same way as she had done over three weeks ago when he had awoken. Michael looked at her. She smiled once more, the same smile she had smiled that first day. It seemed like it had been a long time ago, yet only a blink of the eye. Never and forever, all rolled into one.

At last Michael spoke. "Bernie, would you write something down for me."

"Of course," she replied. "Look, hold on. I'll go and get some paper." She walked off, quickly as usual. She always walked at the same speed and in the same determined way, whatever the situation. It was part of her professional composure. *Never let the patient see you're in a flap*, her first Matron had told her. In minutes, she arrived back with paper in hand and a pen. She lifted the clipboard from the end of his bed with the patient notes and their damning message still in place and clipped a fresh new sheet on top.

"OK," she said. "I'm ready."

"Just as I say it Bernie. Please. Please write down just what I say."

His voice was soft and his breath short, but in the silence of the night Bernie could hear his words with remarkable clarity. She nodded.

So Michael began to dictate. His words. His final words. She had wondered what it would be. A confession? A last will and testament? She had written several lines before she realised it was a poem and she could see the little rhymes emerge. As she wrote, the words engulfed her senses and her hands shook, the one shaking the clipboard and the other shaking the pen in her hand. In the moments that followed, Bernie deserted her professional composure, not simply from the grief of the moment, but from the power of the words he spoke. Here was a young man in certain demise who still seemed able to cast the most profound message of forgiveness in this, the most challenging of theatres. Here was a young man, a life yet hardly begun whose selfless love bestowed all that is good on those who remain. Here was a young man whose voice now faded to a whisper, yet whose words still cried aloud with passion and love. And as Bernie wrote, she let the emotion take over her mind as a lover succumbs to lust and the tears dripped from her face as her quivering handwriting recorded his words.

She didn't understand everything and some words had to be repeated and others spelled for her, but she did her best, stroking through mistakes and re-writing where necessary. It was about thirty minutes before the work was finished. Bernie thought to ask if he would like her to read the poem back to him in its entirety, but she lost her composure and realised that that would be impossible.

At last Michael asked her to leave. He had never done so before and took great comfort in her presence, but he knew the end was nigh and there was something he wanted to do. Bernie held his hand tightly, hoping that if she didn't let go, things might be alright, her emotional wishes overwhelming her professional knowledge.

"I don't want you to be alone" she said at last.

"I won't be alone," whispered Michael.

Still holding his hand, Bernie cried, for she had become close to the boy over the few weeks just gone. Indeed, they had passed far too quickly for her, because despite their sadness, she knew her own personal worth was enhanced in his presence. This was not just by the sympathetic and comforting actions she took, but by the force of the young man's presence.

Here was someone whose life seemed hardly to have touched anyone at all. He had had few visitors and of those who came, no one seemed really close to him. Yet, Bernie could now see the true depth of his complex thought processes, his talent for expression and his almost godlike capacity for forgiveness. The more she understood him, the more tormented she was by his imminent departure.

At last she left and Michael settled down to the inevitable, but he retained a sort of determination to die on his own terms. Of course he couldn't influence the outcome, but he knew where he wanted his mind to be when it happened. He sensed a sleepiness come over him and he knew the clock was ticking fast. He felt his organs shutting down. He could hardly move and barely see. His existence, he found already in some form of semi state and he imagined that he would not see the night through, but his thoughts continued.

At last he closed his mind and fixed the image of Anna he kept in his mental vision, the one he could remember so well from that first and only time they were together. She would look at him, her blue eyes seeing him in a way he had not been seen before. Then she would look away, biting her lip as she processed her thoughts, before once more looking him in the eyes. It was almost like she was about to speak, but instead the movie in his mind repeated several times.

As he lay in bed, during those last few moments, his hand twitched unexpectedly as he felt once more the same transcendent touch that he had felt before when she had touched him. The picture slowed and he felt her presence near to him as she looked into his eyes for the very last time, her soft features caressing his soul as it prepared for flight. "You have to go" she said.

CHAPTER 16

Anna's New Love

Anna's elation was not to last. Michael had always replied so promptly, but the post came and went on the Tuesday, then on the Wednesday and there was no reply. Nothing came that week at all and by Saturday, she couldn't shake off the clouds of doubt that followed her around. She pondered her invitation; so warm, so open with barely the scantest protection of her feelings. It began to prey on her mind. Had she been too bold in her text, too audacious? Were her words, so carefully chosen to *convey* her affection, which was after all the message she wanted to send, simply too blunt; too obvious?

As her thoughts developed, she tried to rationalise. Michael's poems were not *love* poems. NOT messages of love. She scolded herself. They were beautiful, wonderful and exquisite. She danced in her mind at the thought of them, but they were about nature and art, about humour and life. They were not messages to *her*, she decided. She was simply his outlet, perhaps his only outlet for his bounty of creative expression. Perhaps her remoteness, the very fact that he didn't see her every day, that she was just a name on an envelope, was what made it all possible. If they were to meet again, become familiar as she had hoped and imagined they would, perhaps his talent would seal itself away. Perhaps he thought or even knew this. Perhaps she was his liberator, not his chalice. Perhaps he had already moved on to the love poems, but they were aimed elsewhere. Perhaps he had already been reciting them to another on a picnic rug beneath soaring trees in the Irish meadows. Perhaps there was already a sweet *Colleen* engaged in his soft charm, transfixed by the words that had opened her world and lit her fire. *Oh woe, oh woe* she thought.

She reflected back, trying to remember exactly what she had written; checking word after word, first against the Dutch translation, but also in her English language dictionary to catch the subtleties of meaning. In truth, she found little to reprimand herself for, but the gradual ebbing away of her confidence, the disappointment of day after day, her hope rising with every visit of the postman, then quickly falling back, left her steeped in sorrow.

"He's found someone else" said her mother.

She had embraced her. Her mother had struggled to find words, other words that might not have hurt so very much, but she could find none. Her daughter, so joyous, so certain of her future path only weeks earlier became sad and despondent as her confidence and zest for life evaporated. Yet, still, now even against her will, the endless tide of hope rose and fell with the postman's daily visits, pestering her like a chronic ache.

At last she knew that only acceptance would free her from the endless sense of loss, but before she could do that, she knew she would have to confront another possibility. Something worse. Something far, far worse than this sudden apparent abandonment. Lingering in the back of her mind, waiting to prey on her weakness, a fear arose in her. Acceptance opened a new door, a thought, not so dependent on her fragile sense of self-worth for validity, but a practical notion that chilled her emotions. Perhaps Michael did love her? Perhaps everything she felt, he too had felt. Perhaps everything she wanted, he wanted too. Perhaps the laced messages in his texts that spoke to her were as true and honest as she had always thought them to be. Perhaps he was injured! Maybe he was dead!

There is a process by which a thought emerges, first from the subconscious, then to the semi-conscious. In truth this thought had sat in her mind for some time, but engulfed in her own loss of self-esteem it had failed to fully materialise. Now her recovery of mind and acceptance of her loss had opened her eyes to another possibility; the *nature* of that loss.

She did know of the political upheaval in Northern Ireland. She knew there was danger there, terror and misery, but of course Michael had never spoken of it. The so called, *Troubles* had been reported in the Dutch news, but as the 70s had ensued, the incidents had failed to attract much on going attention among the Dutch people. Recently, the subject had fallen some way down the priority list and even off the radar of the main Dutch television news programmes.

She had also never concerned herself with it. She bore no political view and knew of none that Michael held either. There was nothing of that she wanted to know. She had closed her mind to it, left it in the background from where she thought both she and Michael were safe. Neither of them wrote about it. It wasn't an issue. It wasn't there. Now suddenly, it hit her like a boulder from above, crushing her recovery and distorting her acceptance of reality. Could he really be dead? Had he been caught up in some random act of violence, shopping or at school or… Really she had no idea and the thoughts were so unpalatable she could hardly comprehend the notion. She shivered with worried dread at the thought.

But, if he was dead or injured, then why had no one

contacted her? Surely his parents would have known of their relationship. The letters had been going back and forward for 18 months, *someone* must have noticed. She knew he was different, insular, quiet and intense. She knew he was shy of his emotions, secretive perhaps, a loner. She liked him, but she knew he didn't have many friends. But surely, if he had been hurt, *someone* must have known of the ardent correspondence that had occupied so much of his time.

So she reverted back to her first thought. In the end, this was more palatable, preferred and she concluded, also more likely. He didn't want her anymore. He had found someone else and despicable as it was, he had shied from his responsibilities and failed to tell her properly. And they had never been lovers. In reality, he had no obligation to her at all. She was charmed by his words, the poignancy, the sensitivity and the wit, but wouldn't *anyone* have been? He was a pen pal, just like any other pen pal might be. Just like the Swedish girl she had exchanged letters with a year or two back. The letters had just stopped. She couldn't remember if it had been herself who had stopped writing or if it was Ingrid or Inge; she couldn't quite remember. Nothing sinister, hardly even impolite, not really, just the way things are. Just the way it goes.

She scolded herself once more at last. She shouldn't have allowed herself to become so involved, so emotional, so connected. Not with someone who she had met only once for a few hours. He was fine. She was sure he was fine. He had found someone else. A girlfriend. A *real* girlfriend. Rather surprising herself, she smiled. She could now see him hand in hand with another. An Irish girl of course, from his own land. One of his own people. That was the way it would be, she reassured herself. He was well, happy too of course. *Oh the perils of teenage angst.*

And so the gradual recovery of the young Anna began. Who has not loved and lost at the age of 16? Who does not know this pain; this arbitrary emotion? Most do live to tell the story! And so, she put her thoughts of Michael behind her. There was school, her family, her friends. Perhaps she had been neglecting them a little. Maybe she should pay those around her, those who lived in the real world, her world, more attention. Michael would always be a part of her life. She was glad she had met him and remembered him fondly, but he was part of the past, no longer the present. She put his poems in a drawer.

And so as time went on, Michael became a memory, mostly warm, sometimes confused, a little vexing, but a memory all the same. The emotions she had for him remained rather exclusive to him, not by design or intent, just by chance. As her teenage years progressed, she sought little of love and did not court its feeling. Although, she had no shortage of offers, she disallowed herself progression once more into this vulnerable state, where her emotions dominated her thoughts.

Instead she became adept at polite refusal. She could spurn advances with a shy flutter of her eyes and a soft, warm rejection that protected the humility of her suitors but did nothing to dampen the disappointment. As time went on, she gained a reputation for being a little distant, not cold exactly, but rather inaccessible. Some of the more confident young men saw her as a challenge, a test of their charm, but the flattering chat of the well-practised lothario appealed little to her. In some respects, she was a coveted prize, but as time went on, increasingly she found herself a little side-lined as the other girls found boyfriends and lovers.

Anna had always been studious, but since the disappearance of Michael, she had rather intensified her effort. It kept her mind busy and fulfilled an emotional need she could not find elsewhere. She graduated high school with very excellent results before winning a place at the University of Utrecht, about 40km from her family home.

There she studied English literature as her major subject. It had always been her passion, even from before she met Michael, though it was he who gave it the greatest boost. She quickly developed an advanced understanding, not just of the language but of Anglo-Saxon culture in general and how it manifested itself in literary styles and genres. The spoken word was also interesting to her and she studied accents and dialects. Quickly she became proficient at separating American Southerners like those characterised in Mark Twain's books from Northern professionals from Boston. She could also easily identify the colourful English accents of Liverpool or Newcastle, the Cockneys with their slang and soft consonants and the Scots with the rolling *R*s familiar in her own language. But for her own speech, she continued to cultivate the vowel sounds of the BBC at the time until her own accent was hardly discernible from that of an affluent inhabitant of Surrey or Hampshire whose speech had developed in private schools and exclusive social spheres.

She read extensively, engrossing herself in texts from Chaucer to Shakespeare but it was the Irish writers like Joyce, Shaw and Wilde who really inspired her. She developed a diversity of intellectual comprehension, supplemented by a sound understanding of German and French structure and vocabulary as well as that of her mother tongue. As university life progressed, she quickly developed her personality and interests and at the same time grew into a very fine looking young woman.

Her straw blond hair faded and darkened with the seasons and curled naturally. She might have looked a little dishevelled in the tent when Michael met her but the quickest stroke of a brush turned her hair instantly into a mop of sparkling locks that men admired and women envied. She wore little makeup and her pale skin dotted with blond freckles kept her face fresh and youthful. The pale blue eyes that had transfixed Michael contrasted with the blackness of her pupils which would dilate and contract betraying at once her feelings to those adept enough to observe. Her particular look cast an emotion in men, not only of physical attraction, but of endearment, charm, a fantasy of times gone by. Anna was not immediately someone men wanted to sleep with, she was someone they wanted to marry and to settle down with. It was easy to imagine Anna baking the apple pie and calling to the happy children playing in the garden sunshine to come in for supper. Indeed that was not just an image others saw in her but one she could easily see in herself and a role she sought to play. Her personality emitted a warm dependability, a permanence, an air of dignity and of quiet solitude that both comforted and charmed those around her.

So, despite her academic aptitude, as her university days drew to a close, Anna found little inspiration in the prospect of work. Instead it was in the much more traditional role of wife to a good man and mother to a hoard of lively children that she saw her future. Her experience with Michael was now many years behind and for some time she had been open to the prospect that one day someone would come along and light her fire once more. However, she was also troubled that no one had. She had been on the occasional date, but charming as some of her suitors were, there were no flutters of excitement on her part. Not since Michael had she had any idea of love as an all-encompassing passion that gripped the senses. In the end she came to dismiss this particular feeling as the stuff of fairy tales, of adolescent innocence. Instead she came to see love more pragmatically, more in terms of comfort and security than passion and desire.

It was in her last year at university that she met Cees Bouwmeester. He was several years older than her and although he worked at the university, was externally employed by a large research organisation while he completed his PhD. He was a good looking young man who certainly had options as far as the selection of a partner was concerned, but he was also wedded to his academic development, his science and the expectation of an interesting and exciting career. That was something he would surely have, for he was talented intellectually, but also possessed an innovative flair and pragmatic reasoning that made him a valued player in any research team.

Although he was inspired by science, he was also meticulously organised and had every aspect of his life carefully planned. A wife and family were very much part of this agenda, so he reserved some time for girlfriends and enjoyed a modest social life. He would accept the occasional invite to meet a friend of a friend or attend a dinner party as he kept an eye open for suitable contenders for the title of *Mrs Cees Bouwmeester.*

It was at one such matchmaking event that he met Anna. She offered the homely charm he sought while he offered a very pleasant combination of attention and indifference, that whet her appetite in a way that previous over-enthusiastic suitors had failed to. He cared for her of course, but she enjoyed not being completely the centre of his world and he was adept at compartmentalising his life, such that he reserved time for Anna and showed genuine interest in her. It gradually became apparent that their wants and needs in life were really quite well aligned.

Anna might have been comfortable for the relationship to develop at a rather sedate pace, but Cees, saw it as an action to be ticked off in the organisation of his life. One evening in a small Italian restaurant, just after Anna had graduated, Cees proposed marriage. She had thought quickly as he looked at her over his wine glass, smiling openly with only the faintest betrayal of his apprehension displayed in the lines in his face. It was the most vulnerable she had seen him and she had not expected the proposal, but she knew her answer straight away.

The couple were married in the summer of 1987 and bought a house by the canal, in the town of Veenendaal, not far from her parents' home in Pijpersboss. By 1989, she had become pregnant with her first child, a boy, whom they named Marcus. Anna quickly gave up her job as a receptionist at a doctor's surgery and became a full-time Mum. Marcus was quickly followed by another boy, Johan in 1991, then the family was finally completed with a girl, Esther in 1994.

The marriage was a happy one. Anna proved to be a loving wife and expert homemaker and Cees provided well for the family in every respect. He built a very successful career, but he was also adept at sharing his time between his work, always his first love, but not his only love, and Anna and the children.

Anna never told Cees about Michael. This was not for any reason other than a lack of relevance. In any case, who would want to hear stories of their spouse's past loves especially ones that never actually materialised. As the children grew up the name of Michael Coglan hardly entered her mind save for occasionally when she heard a word or phrase she had learned from him at the time or when a glint of sunshine reflecting on the water, reminded her of a line or two of his poetry. She would smile briefly, and think back to the shy young man she met only once, wondering where he was and if he was happy but she never allowed the thought to linger long. Then she would get on with family life, picking the children up from school or cooking dinner. She was happy and content and Michael's letters and poems rested silently in the bottom drawer of her dresser.

CHAPTER 17

An Outspoken Judge

The two culprits were quickly apprehended. The gun, lodged in the hawthorn bush, had been swiftly traced and the security services already had intelligence linking the two men together and their positions within the terror group.

The older of the two, Patrick Flannigan was already well known to the police and he had previous convictions for more minor sectarian activities. Even those who knew him would have described him as cold. The younger man, Sean Bradley, had cracked easily under police interrogation. Actually, he had really cracked some seconds before the gun went off. He had confessed everything, his position in the active 'unit', his relationship with Flannigan, though had been wise enough to stop short of providing any further information outside of his own personal involvement. In truth he knew little.

The two men were sent for trial. The proceedings were presided over by Justice Oliver Bailey. The barristers, clerks, police, prison guards, the accused and the convicted, even politicians all called him the 'Ole Bailey'. He had been born and raised in England but of Irish stock. His great grandfather, Thomas Bailey, had grown up in poverty in Ireland and together with his young wife and baby son, moved to London in the 1870s. He quickly found his feet and became an astute investor in the booming city of the day and developed considerable personal wealth. The couple had many more children and the family prospered, but always retained their Irish roots. There are now over ninety direct descendants of Thomas Bailey littered around the world. Justice Oliver Bailey was one of these.

He had studied law at Cambridge but his minor subject was Irish history and later he participated enthusiastically in the small Irish community in Norfolk, where his family had lived for years. It was here that he met Maria, a young woman from County Down and took the opportunity to move to what he always considered his true homeland. This was in the comparative calm of the early 1950s and while his legal career developed most satisfactorily, so did the tensions and conflicts in the communities where he had now made his home.

Justice Bailey was never known for understatement. Candid and outspoken, sometimes offensive, often controversial, he was a well-known and respected senior member of the legal system in Northern Ireland. Some thought him harsh, others rather too lenient, but none doubted his commitment to the welfare of the people of Ireland. Somehow his early years in England had made him able to see the Irish people in a way they seemed so completely unable to see themselves.

Both men were given life sentences. In summing up Justice Bailey first rounded on the young Bradley who stood in the dock, red faced, his head slightly bowed, shaking.

"You have shown remorse", he said, "no one doubts that. You claim the gun went off by accident. Some will believe you, others won't, but the fact is that you went to that house that night with very clear pre-meditated intentions. You went to kill. To kill in cold blood. To kill a man you had never met and who had done you no wrong. You went to kill because you were told to by those more powerful than you. This court accepts that, but in its acceptance it cannot absolve you from responsibility for your actions. You *are* responsible for your actions."

He stopped suddenly then exclaimed;

"Good God man, what were you thinking of? It was a Friday night. Why weren't you out chasing women or drinking beer or listening to music? Why weren't you playing football or hurling or whatever might take your fancy? Can these things only be done in the new different, better Ireland you claim to desire? Instead you and your accomplice went on a mission to murder. And murder you did. In cold blood. Your bullet killed both Susan Coglan and her son. Simple, ordinary people trying to get through difficult lives as best they could. Michael Coglan was but a year younger than you. I know your politics. Jesus Christ, we all know your damned politics, but where was the compassion, the humanity"?

Bradley stood stunned, tears now streaming down his face. Judge Bailey now in full flow paused slightly, his tone lowering a little.

"The truth is, in another world, on another planet, in another universe where sensibility and sanity might triumph over hatred and skewed logic, Michael Coglan might even have been your friend. Who knows how it might have been without the wretched Irish curse. I would have avoided such a notion if anyone from his family had even survived to be appalled by such a thought, but there is no one. They are all gone. You killed his parents. You killed him, his future and his blood line. You killed his family before and after. I am sure there are some who will celebrate such a fact. The man standing next to you is certainly one."

With that he turned to Gallagher.

"You on the other hand have shown no remorse whatsoever. I have sat before many like you. You were lost many years ago. There is no salvation. You claim your objectives are political. Well, maybe they are. If they are, they are bad politics. The history of the world, not just of Ireland, is full of individuals who claim their ends justify their means. They never do. Murder is murder. There are no politics in shooting an unarmed man, his wife and only child in his own home. But still you do it. You feign enlightenment but deep down, we all know there will always be hatred in your heart and murder on your mind."

He stopped once more, his own hands shaking with anger as he shuffled the papers on his bench. He sighed.

"Maybe it is not *all* your fault, for the speciality of Ireland is the efficiency with which such hatred is handed down from generation to generation. It's like a cause celebre. All too often, hatred is worn like a mantle by parents and gifted to children in the greatest sadness on earth. Let none forget. This is the cancer in our society. It is not about the one event, the tragedy or the fault, it is about the perpetuity and no generation seems quite capable of escaping it."

"We exist here in this part of Ireland, but also in the South and where Irish people live throughout the world, as a divided people. We share so much, yet nothing. We just live in our cliques and groups, bitching at each other. Criticising and complaining. Few friendships cross the divide and some that do are disrupted by the judgement of others. The voices of dissent are few. There are some, but they are few. Religion and national identity dominate the psyche."

"We meet new people, perhaps a new colleague or just the guy who fixes the heating or the local doctor, but we can hardly relate to them till we know what they *are*. We hear of a tragedy, a death, maybe even a murder, but we don't quite know what to feel, not till we know what the victim *is* or in some cases *was*. Yes, we are always appalled, our condemnation sincere, but somehow as if by subtle instinct our feelings are amended and qualified according to what we now know. In which camp did he sit? Our very humanity is tarnished by our culture. Who in this courtroom can say it is not so? *WHO IN THIS COURT ROOM HAS NOT CONTRIBUTED TO THIS MESS?"*

Besides the dinning voice of the angry man, you could have heard a pin drop. Even the journalists had stopped scribbling. Bradley's demeanour had turned to a shaking figure in the dock. Even Flannigan now fidgeted as he stood, though his cold stare remained unchanged.

"We, in this city, and on this Island possess a subtlety of humour unmatched throughout the world and a culture others can so easily warm to. Instead we live in tragedy and pedal hate. Branny Coglan, his wife and child lie dead. These two will serve their time in jail. That is just. It will be so. But, perhaps it is also time we all took a long hard look in the mirror. Are the rest of us all quite so innocent?"

The judge was now tired. A large lock of his hair had escaped from underneath his wig and fallen over his face making him look scruffy in appearance. He slammed his gavel hard several times on the bench.

"This court is adjourned."

Patrick Flannigan was an awkward and aggressive prisoner, prone to violent reaction and participating at some level in the various protests that would become part of his incarcerated life. He was released in 2000 as part of the prisoner release programme resulting from the Good Friday agreement.

Sean Bradley served almost 10 years of his sentence. He was released in the Spring of 1989 on a date that is unrecorded in the public records. On that day, an unmarked prison vehicle took him to the airport where he boarded a plane to London. There he was met by a rather podgy, grey haired man wearing a tweed sports jacket and polished brown shoes. He shook his hand warmly and handed him a brown envelope. Inside was a brand new British passport in a name that had not existed until a few weeks earlier, together with a birth certificate and some other notes and documents.

"Where's your luggage" said the man.

"Sure, I haven't got any. There's nothing I want to take from here"

"Ah." He paused thoughtfully. "OK. Just don't want to arouse suspicions old boy. Airlines can get a bit funny if you have no bags. We can fix it of course, but no point in inviting trouble."

He shrugged. "Still, not to worry."

The British government has reciprocal arrangements with several countries around the world to enable resettlement of individuals whose lives have become untenable in their homeland. It is sometimes used for the rehabilitation of offenders but more often for the protection of witnesses in major and controversial trials where there is thought to be a serious danger of intimidation or extermination.

Sean Bradley didn't exactly fit into this category, but he had asked to go. In recent times, various prisoners, perhaps prompted by Flannigan himself (there was no love lost between the two men) had mooted comments that Bradley had been a little too cooperative with the authorities.

At Heathrow, he boarded a plane to Toronto Canada. Within

a few months he had adopted a Canadian accent. About five years later in accordance with Canadian law, Sean Bradley applied for Canadian citizenship and in a small ceremony in Ottawa in September 1994 he, rather ironically, pledged allegiance to Her Majesty Queen Elizabeth II and of course to Canada, his new country.

He has never had any contact with his old life, except for one day early in the new millennium when a small package arrived at his home. It was post marked London W1. Inside was a hard backed book entitled; *The Troubles in Poems and Prose*.

With it was a short handwritten note, neither signed nor addressed:

I thought this might provide some interest and perhaps comfort to you. I know you will treat it with any discretion required.

Sean Bradley has never married and always lived alone. The book is his only treasured possession. He keeps it in a locked drawer beside his bed. He reads it often.

CHAPTER 18

All Traces Removed

A nd so ended Michael's life and the life too of the little family. Like so many before and so many who would follow, they became statistics in the history of Ireland and its relationship with its own people. The house remained cordoned off as a crime scene for several weeks after the murder. No one lived in the property again. The area itself, the surrounding streets and community continued to suffer the havoc and deterioration that follows war and political strife wherever they occur around the world. Eventually the house was boarded up to prevent vandalism and when others in the street were vacated, they were not re-let but boarded too.

In the mid nineteen eighties when plans were drawn up for the new motorway extension to the North of the city, the last residents were moved out, re-housed elsewhere and the demolition process began.

The men arrived with lorries, plant and heavy equipment. They worked diligently along the street, firstly removing lead and slates from the roofs, then rafters and beams before moving inside to remove floor boards and joists. The houses were systematically stripped of their copper pipes, their wiring and anything else of value that could be re-sold or re-cycled, like carrion feeders at a corpse. And corpses they were, as a house, like a life, has a beginning and an end. When the people move out the life is gone and the shell remains standing exhausted and useless, awaiting the inevitable process whereby all life returns at last to its beginning; ashes to ashes and dust to dust.

Finally, when the heavy equipment had moved out, the street lay silent once more, like it had done more than a hundred years earlier when Belfast was expanding with hope and expectation as industries developed and new people moved in. The bricks, mortar, stones and dust that had seen so much lay piled in heaps of surprising uniformity, awaiting onward transportation to their final resting places as hard core for the foundations of new developments.

When they had finished, they had removed every last trace of the life of Michael Coglan. It was as if he had never existed. As the dust settled, the demolition workers stood around for a moment as they often did at the end of a job, in a kind of silent reverence to the lives that had now moved on. Had any of them thought or cared to look, just by where Michael's house had once stood, Anna's letter lay still unopened in the dust.

Part II

Anna

CHAPTER 19

Veenendaal, The Netherlands, 2007

The two women hadn't seen each other for many years. After school they had attended different universities, but had maintained a healthy contact by exchanging letters and occasionally meeting up with each other when they were both visiting home during the holidays. However Grietje had met a young man and gone off to live with him in Amsterdam. Over the years that followed correspondence became less and less and finally dwindled out the way it sometimes does even with the best of friendships as lives move on in different directions.

Grietje had recently split from her partner, as she called him, they had never married. He had informed her in a shock message that he had found someone else and after over twenty years together, was off to build a new life. Apparently he hadn't been happy for some time. They had no children, just some property to sell and the proceeds to share but otherwise the 'divorce' had been quick, cold and eventless.

They smiled at once as they recognized each other, hugging warmly. They had been good friends, protecting each other through those delicate formative years and the sense of belonging, of closeness and of friendship was still present in the two women though now both in their early forties.

After the initial smiles and mutually admiring comments of how good they both still looked, they went for lunch at a fish restaurant in the centre of town where Grietje had made a reservation. The waiter showed them to a table outside on the raised terrace that overlooked the courtyard and the little 16th century church that still defined the centre of town. It was a rather grander establishment than Anna was used to with tables covered in starched white linen laid with two sets of cutlery and glasses at each setting, the restaurant rather optimistically having prepared with the most profligate of customer in mind. Occasional light wafts of garlic and herbs swirled around mixing with clinks of glasses and happy chatter. It was June, but the sun canopies were not yet raised and the sun shone brightly casting moving shadows over the pair as the trees waved in the light wind.

The waiter smiled approvingly at the two smartly dressed women, responding positively to Grietje's mild flirtations as he took their order causing the two to giggle playfully as they sipped the chilled Prosecco they had ordered as an aperitif.

"So, it's been how long? At least 15 years," Grietje answered herself.

"Yes, I think the last time was before Esther was born and she's fourteen now," added Anna.

"My, how time flies. And Cees, is he well?"

"Oh yes quite well" replied Anna enthusiastically. "You know him, he's happy as long as he's making some great contribution to mankind. He's been working on some drug, a designer drug he calls it that will no doubt make us all live longer and happier lives!"

She paused a little while pondering her next remark. "So things didn't work out with Rik?"

Grietje sighed out loud. "No. After 20 years he decided he didn't want me. Ran off with some bimbo half his age with tight skin and firm breasts. *Bitch!*" The two friends sniggered briefly, for want of a better reaction to Grietje's obvious discomfort. "Actually, she's lovely. I met her a few times. Well that was before I knew what they were up to. At least, I can see the attraction, apart from being a marriage wrecker that is."

Anna smiled sympathetically. Grietje had always been the more adventurous of the pair and had been popular at school. Anna had even been a little jealous of her easy manner and convivial personality. She had a lovely knack of being able to make people, especially the boys, feel good about themselves.

Grietje lifted her glass. "Mothers batten down the hatches, get your sons inside, Miss Chaos is back in town! Actually," she paused a moment, blushing a little. "Do you remember Karel van der Klaas from school?"

Anna smiled, nodding expectantly.

"Well, we've been sort of liaising on the internet recently. We got together through one of those *school reunion* type websites. It seems he was married to another of the world's ample supply of emotional train wrecks. Anyway, she took off. Went to live in Africa somewhere with this bloke she met on the internet. Crazy! Anyway, he thought he would give it a try himself, the internet that is, not running off to Africa," she smiled once again, "and hey presto, he found me!"

"Together?"

Anna noticed her friend reddened a little easier than she remembered.

"Well, yes. I hadn't really thought to define it that way, but yes, *together*. We met up in Amsterdam a few months back and it seemed to go well and we've seen each other several times since. Then we went on a short holiday together to Venice, not that the location mattered much."

She leaned across the table beckoning her friend closer and whispered, "more of a major bonking session really. We hardly left the hotel room!"

Anna's gasp quickly turned to a shy titter as her friend, whose language always seemed a little devoid of euphemism, smiled coyly back.

"He still lives out this way and I am a bit fed up with Amsterdam now, so I thought, well, why not. I'm single, he's single. After all, we did go out a bit at school. It didn't last of course. Well we were young. Anyway, I thought, life's not much fun on your own is it? "

Grietje looked a little sullen, then collected herself once more.

"So, what have you been up to?"

"Well, not much actually. Cees is fine, the children are fine. Marcus is at University, Johan and Esther are still at school."

"Don't you have a job?"

"A job? I haven't worked since Marcus was born."

"Ah, so, you're a homemaker, then?"

Anna paused, figuring this was a new term for *housewife*.

"Well, yes, but I am getting a bit tired of that. The children are older now, they don't really need me. I feel a bit lost, redundant even. Can you understand that?" Grietje nodded, but Anna didn't really wait for an answer and pondered a little more as she gazed across the cobble-stoned square, her thoughts developing as she spoke. "It's about Cees too. I wonder if he might be getting just a little bored with me. When the children were younger, I could always tell him about my day and the things we had got up to and he could tell me about his. Now I just don't have anything to report any more. Also, intellectually, I think I am now suffering, missing out a little. It's like my mind has stagnated and I don't know how to jolt it into action again. Also, it's been so long since I worked, I really don't even know how to go about it. I don't know about computers and all that sort of thing, I just don't think anybody would employ me."

Grietje raised her eyebrows and held her gaze in a sort of mock incredulous look.

"Well, that *was* quite a speech! For God's sake Anna, anyone would employ you. You have a first class degree in English literature. You can learn to use computers in about a week, then join the rest of us who perpetually still don't know what we're doing! You must be able to use the internet?"

"Well, yes, OK, I can look up the weather and so on and do emails, but it's just everyone seems to use jargon today that I don't understand."

Grietje chuckled. "Still the same old Anna. Really, you always spent so much time fretting that you couldn't do things, then you would get much better marks than anyone else at school."

Anna smiled a polite acknowledgement of her friend's flattery while the discussion continued in her mind. "Cees isn't that keen. I guess he just likes being looked after and frets that I won't be home to make his dinner."

"Well bollocks to that! Let him make his own dinner for once. Who's he to tell you if you can have a job or not?"

Anna smiled once again. "I know, but he does provide for me and the children really very well and I like being there for him, really I do. Also, we have a good relationship and I don't want to compromise that."

"No but still, it's good to have a bit of independence though."

Anna nodded.

"So, tell me. What ever happened to that boy you used to write to all the time back at school. You know, the English guy. You were quite sweet on him as I remember." Grietje smiled knowingly, looking closely at her friend. Then she set her glass down with a firm thud. "Poems! He wrote you poems! I remember now. Oh dear, Anna, I do recall you were just a little bit in love with him!"

Now it was Anna's turn to blush. Her friend always spoke more openly, more freely that Anna might herself and it was the term love, her love, Anna's love for anyone other than her husband that had caused her a little discomfort.

"Oh it just petered out. You know how these things go." Momentarily her face took on a pensive mood and she paused briefly slowly pulling her soft lower lip through the measured grip of her teeth. "He was Irish actually, not English," she emphasised, as if it made any difference. Her thoughtfulness didn't last and she went on, looking up once more at her friend.

"Are you staying with your parents? How are they? My mum says she sees your Dad around now and again, doing the shopping."

"Oh they're fine. Getting older of course. Mum has arthritis and can't get around much, hence Dad is out doing the shopping. It does make me laugh a little. I don't think he had ever even been in a supermarket until a few years back, now he is an expert on the selection of produce and the available bargains which he insists on recounting at home, seemingly oblivious to how completely boring he is being! They manage OK. Funny seeing old people together, they know each other so well."

Grietje stopped talking and sat thinking for a moment. Anna watched her closely. She could see the little grin she knew so well develop in her friend's features. While Anna would pause to ensure the words she planned were correct and appropriate, a similar pause from Grietje tended to indicate impending gossip or mischief. "So did you stop writing to him or did he stop writing to you?"

"Who?"

Grietje smiled openly, teasing her friend, but didn't answer. "The Irish boy?"

Suddenly, Michael came to her mind once more. Today was the first she had thought of him in many years and she smiled inwardly to herself.

"Did you ever hear from him again?"

"No, Never."

"You don't know what happened to him then?"

"No. He just stopped writing. I don't know why." Anna paused once more, hoping Grietje would pitch in and move the conversation on quickly, but there was silence. "Well maybe I do. The last letter I wrote to him…" Anna's voice tailed off as she remembered back, long ago, so very, very long ago. She swallowed. "Well I more or less said I loved him."

Anna's unusual candour surprised her and she blushed. It was a warm, soft vulnerable blush that was so part of her personality. Her friend looked back at her searchingly, now sympathetic.

"Ah, and you think he took flight. Maybe the ball fell out of his pen! Or more accurately he caught a major dose of commitment phobia and couldn't actually manage the gigantic task of letting you know. Bloody typical. Men!"

Anna opened her mouth to reply, but Grietje went on, "I do remember. You were upset at the time. Actually you changed just then, back then. Maybe you didn't notice it but I did. I was your friend and I could see it. The harsh reality of love." She pouted sympathetically.

"I just grew up. That's all," replied Anna matter of factly. "Maybe it takes a little blow now and again to let us understand the world. Understand reality. What do you mean, *changed*?"

Grietje, sat back a little in her seat and left an uncharacteristic pause as she quickly digested the mild agitation in her friend's response. "Well, you never dated anyone at school for a start. There wasn't a boy in class who wouldn't have been delighted to walk out with you but you brushed them off. You brushed them all off."

"Well, there wasn't anyone there I fancied."

"The *Ice Princess* they called you."

"*What*, exclaimed Anna," now irritated by the way the conversation was going.

"The ice princess. That's what the boys at school called you. They said you were cold. And you were cold. I remember it well. Come on Anna, you were a little elusive. You must admit that."

Anna just stared. Maybe she wanted the conversation to end there, but it didn't.

"I think some of them liked that a little. After all, not everyone is after the party girl, but nobody really got through. In the end, they just gave up. Don't you wonder what happened to him?"

Who?

"You know who. The Irish boy. What was he called again?"

"Michael," said Anna quietly.

"Yes, Michael. I remember now. Of course we met him on that trip to England with Geert and his friends. He was with those weird religious kids with the funny uniforms that camped up the hill from us. I remember now. Have you googled him?"

"What? Googled? No of course not. Why would I do that?"

"You can find most people on the Internet nowadays. Usually quite quickly. That's how I found Karl. He sends his love by the way," she interjected casually. "If you know what school he went to he's probably there on some sort of alumni site or whatever."

Anna bit her lip in the way she often did when she was thoughtful or pondering her answer to a difficult question.

"It was a long time ago," she said at last. "He's probably married with kids and so on just like me. What's to be gained? Nothing."

She sighed concluding her thoughts on the subject, but a seed had been planted and it planned to grow.

CHAPTER 20

The Power of the Internet

On the way home, Michael came to her mind once more. Maybe it would be nice to find him, to send him an email. To send her greetings at least. Maybe even find out what happened. It had been an abrupt end to the correspondence that had at first been so plentiful. *Grietje was right*, she admitted to herself, she *had* been upset at the time. Did it change her? Well, yes, if she was objective and dropped her natural defences, it had changed her a little.

She wondered how he had turned out. How he was getting on with life. She didn't love him now, it had just been one of those adolescent romantic ideas when *passion whisks you up in a breath of warm air and leaves you shaking with excitement*, but it wasn't real. She had always described it like that. Love was just an illusion, a fantasy that children have, not a real emotion. She loved. Yes of course she loved. She loved Cees, she loved her children, but pure romantic love, the sort of love that sweeps you off your feet and has you swooning in ardent delight, that was a fantasy that belonged in fairy tales and novellas, not a practical aspect of the modern world.

Still her thoughts toyed with her mind. *Maybe there was no harm in having a look.* Unexpectedly, she felt a little flutter of excitement but it wasn't to last. He hadn't come looking for her, she suddenly noted, rather startled at her inclination to reserve her emotions, as if they were teenagers once again, hiding their feelings to protect their own vulnerability. She pondered a little further and the question vexed her mind a little more. *Why hadn't Michael dropped her a line? Why hadn't he sent a little message to say hi?* He would surely be more Internet savvy than her. *Everyone* was more Internet savvy than her. Why hadn't he come looking for her?

She felt a shudder run through her. It was a bad feeling, a sick feeling and it wasn't the first time she had felt it. Twenty-seven years ago, she had felt the same. No letter arrived. Michael lived in a troubled place. Bad things did happen. Bad things did happen to real people. Real people with real loved ones.

She felt unsettled once more. *Damn Grietje* she thought. Trust her to dig things up again. Maybe her life was chaotic, with her failed relationship and her new love, but Anna's wasn't. She was settled. She was happy. Why go trawling through the past again? Michael Coglan was history, ancient history and he should stay there.

Grietje was right in the practical sense though. He could probably be found quite easily. Just type his name into Google and see what comes up. Perhaps there was no real reason not to. After all she was not some love struck teenager, she was a happily married mother of three healthy children with a wonderful husband whom she loved dearly. She looked at the laptop sitting on the small desk in the lounge that Cees used, typing reports and sending emails while talking to her and watching the television all at the same time. It always sat there. She used it occasionally herself to find recipes or send an email now and then, although the latter always appeared in his name, his email address and often people weren't sure if it was him or her they were corresponding with. She really should get a job, she thought once more.

She opened the lid and hit the *on* button. The machine

powered quickly to life, the whirr of the fans suddenly breaking the silence of the room that must have always been present, but she hadn't really noticed before. The sound was eerie. She looked around and behind herself, nervously as if she was set to commit some sort of crime or betrayal. The feeling unsettled her. She pressed the keys; Control, alt, delete. She was in. The system quickly defaulted to the Google homepage with its familiar logo and empty text box awaiting its latest command. Hesitating a little she typed in his name, *Michael Coglan*. It was easily done. Suddenly she realised she might now find the answer to a question that had troubled her for so long, and she might find out fast. It was simple. It was *too* simple.

She hesitated once more. All she had to do was press the return key. She was face to face with the power of computers, the power of the internet and the endless knowledge it provided, only a keystroke away. She hadn't really thought about it before, but suddenly it seemed overwhelming. Yet, the motivation to look was intense. Already she knew she would do it. Already she knew that the urge to know the truth would overpower any reservations she had about the nature of that truth, but she needed time.

She closed the lid, went upstairs to the bedroom and sat at the dresser. It was the only piece of furniture in the house that was exclusively hers, everything else they shared. Her toiletries were carefully lined up on the little shelf as was her way. Perfumes with perfumes, moisturisers with moisturisers and talcs with talcs. As she sat, she caught the sight of her own image in the mirror. She stared at it for a minute. She looked older today. She thought back to the young girl she was when she had been exchanging letters with Michael. It all seemed long ago and far away, in another time and place, not real, a surreal experience.

She picked up the brush from her dresser and slowly pulled it through her hair untangling it as she did and causing a few errant strands to lift and hover jolted into independence with the little static current the movement created.

She opened the third drawer of the unit. It contained mostly her underwear as well as a few personal odds and ends, like some cufflinks from her father and a few loose photographs of herself and her family from when she was growing up. She set these aside. Underneath was a well packed A4 manila envelope, old but in good condition. Inside were Michael's letters. She hadn't looked at them in well over twenty years.

Cees didn't know about Michael. She had never mentioned him. Not that there was much that was private between them, indeed he could easily have looked in the drawer himself, there was nothing stopping him. There was no lock and no key. He could even have read the letters for the envelope was not sealed and it would have been easy to read them and replace them without leaving any evidence behind, but that would not have been like Cees. He was always respectful of her and was in no sense the jealous type. Actually he wasn't that emotional at all really and this had been one of his principal attractions when he came onto the scene.

The letters had been stored carefully in chronological order. She had sorted them this way when she concluded her memory of Michael many years ago. That had been part of the closing process for her. Things had to be archived properly. On top was the still crumpled little poem with the wit and craic. She lifted it gazing at the scribbled text and smiled as she remembered the day when Grietje suddenly pulled it from her bag. Unexpectedly, a warm glow lit inside her and she affectionately stroked the crumpled paper imagining him diligently setting his words to the page.

There was the strange poem seeking cadmium yellow. She had never heard of cadmium as being particularly a type or shade of yellow but she started to read it once more:

In Search of Cadmium Yellow

In autumn mist of davys grey I set upon my task
To find the shades of artist's flair both modern and time past
Where distant hills of violet blue do blend to shady meadow
Of Phthalo green, Sienna sap and Naples hue of yellow

All through the wood the trees were decked in umber burnt and raw
Where alizarin crimson leaves with yellow ochre tails
Did fall like golden snowflakes upon the forest floor
To rot in piles of madder brown when summer is no more

Then climbed I out on cobalt rock and gazed into the sea
Of Prussian blue with zinc'n waves that washed on rippled sands
As giant clouds of titans white far off with wind they blew
And sun shone from a perfect sky, pure cerulean blue

But though I searched I couldn't find a cadm'um yellow hue
And dandies bloom or buttercup would never really do
For tis not flower but plant I seek, man-made upon the earth
Alas poor yellow cad may be unfound in this wee verse

Then off toward home and o'er a ridge I craned my neck to see
A sight so grand in all the land was there before the sea
In chuckled mirth, in city fare, in dual, yellow triumph
In primary shade of form and tone, stood Samson and Goliath!

As she finished, she chuckled to herself. She never did find out what Samson and Goliath meant! She set it to one side and filtered through the other pages. There was the heart wrenching little story of the starling chicks. It all came flooding back only now a mother herself she felt the final anguish of the distraught bird all the more.

She read his last letter once more. She had read it many times before, looking for evidence, a reason, any reason for his sudden stopping writing, but she found no more this time than she had done before. At last she left them sitting in a pile on the bed and returned to the lounge.

She touched the space key. The fans whirred once more and immediately the computer sprung to life. *Michael Coglan* was still printed in the search box. This time, she pressed enter. Google reported that it had found 26,000 results in less than a third of a second. She scrolled through, quickly scanning the entries, speed reading little snippets for hints that might point her in the right direction. There was something about a legal practice in New York, a chiropractor, a few articles and references. She went back to the search bar once more and typed in *Michael Coglan, Belfast*. She started reading from the top of the page. Quickly her eyes widened and her heart skipped a beat. It was an archived newspaper story:

> *The funeral was held today of Michael Coglan, a seventeen year old school boy who lost his fight against injuries he received in the shooting four weeks ago in which both his parents died. Not having any living family, the funeral was a small and quiet affair attended by some members of the church, a few pupils and teachers from his school as well as one or two medical staff from the Royal Victoria Hospital where he spent his final days. The*

funeral was also attended by Mr Peter Gilbert, reported to be the young man's guardian along with politicians from both sides of the political spectrum who issued a joint message of condemnation of what they described as a heartless and needless crime. It is understood that his assailants are already in custody and a trial will be held in due course.

It was dated Wednesday 13th February *1980.*

Anna's eyes froze on the screen and her limbs shook as she struggled to absorb the information. Her mind went into overdrive as it fought to rewind the years as if showing her whole life in an instant like the momentary vision in a near death experience. Everything she had thought about the young man suddenly needed to be re-written like a book whose plot derails the author's work by taking an unexpected twist just at the end, requiring a complete rewrite from the start.

That newspaper article, a brief report from long ago now explained everything about Michael. He had not deserted her. He had not found another love, another muse for his talent, another partner to his hopes. Instead he had been lying struggling for his life in a hospital, surrounded by people he didn't know, an orphan, his parents slain. The thought was too awful to comprehend; the only fact that could make the story any worse was her part in it.

She had denied him at the first challenge. Like St Peter before the crowing cock, she had thought herself to love the man, but deserted him in an instant at the first hurdle. She was caught between her own reproach and her torment of his sad, lonely death. *God in heaven!* She pleaded to above, searching for some merciful solace in her troubled mind. *He had died alone, all alone. That poor, poor boy.* Her reproach turned to self-denigration, then worse, a kind of self-hate as she looked inside herself. How could she have thought him so shallow, to have just gone off, and forgotten her? Of course, that wasn't so, that couldn't have been, that could *never* have been.

She should have been there, holding his hand, willing him to survive. Instead he met a solitary end, alone in a hospital. The tears welled in her eyes and fell like raindrops from the clouds of desolation that now occupied her heart. She was beside herself with remorse. Perhaps it was to suit her convenience. Who would want to become involved in that? In trouble, politics, murder. These were someone else's problems, not hers. Perhaps subconsciously she knew Michael's silence was enforced by tragedy, but her passive self-protection had soothed her mind into more palatable thoughts, protecting her from reality. Perhaps she had known all along.

No, that was too far. She did deserve reproach, but not at that level. Her failing was not in her faith in him, not in her own trust. She had done her best. If she was at fault, it was her own self confidence that had let her down. It was her own willingness to believe her self-worth was such that she deserved no explanation that had been her failing. She had been wrong, badly wrong and she knew it, but she had done her best. Had she known, she would have surely gone there. She would have sat by his side. She would have nursed him herself. She would have loved him back to health.

But why had nobody told her. He must have had her letters at home. Didn't anybody think she might have *wanted* to know. But then, his parents were dead. Who would take on these duties when no one is left? Some government official she wondered. Twenty-seven years she had doubted him. Twenty-seven years she had doubted his love for her. Oh, it was too awful for words, too awful to contemplate. Oh, the folly. *Trust your heart, not your head.* Her heart had been right all along, it was her head that was lacking.

She sat, weeping, there on the settee, the sun shining outside. It was the same sun that had lit the world every day for the past twenty-seven years as it revolved in its timelessness. It was the same sun that flickered through the thick summer foliage of the trees in the garden, or rose slowly over the polders in the winter chill. Outside, the birds sang in the trees and all along, Michael's body had lain cold in the ground following a funeral attended by officials and a few politicians trying to make gains from it however virtuous their intentions. She was stunned and in disarray. He had surely loved her though. If she could find any sliver of light in her misery, it was that.

CHAPTER 21

A Supportive Husband

A nna was still sitting motionless on the settee in a daze of lost thoughts, her eyes reddened with tears, commanded by an anguished heart, when she heard the tyres of Cees' car grating on the gravel drive outside. Her senses suddenly restored, she jumped up urgently, patting her swollen face and trying to regain something of her usual composure. This was not in order to conceal anything from her husband, but so that she could quickly reassure him that there was not *actually* anything wrong. The children were all fine, that would be his first concern. She too was fine in herself. She would be able to explain to him the reason for her condition, but she would need sufficient equanimity to do so, otherwise he would be frantic with fear if she could hardly speak through tearful distress.

She met Cees at the door, quickly mollifying him with assurances, hugging him and holding him close while whispering in his ear;

"It's alright. Everything is fine. Every*one* is fine, she emphasised. I just got some bad news from long ago and it is upsetting, but it's nothing more than that."

Cees pushed her gently away as soon as he felt able, clutching her firmly on the upper arms and focusing his eyes on hers. Anna felt reassurance in this. He was her friend as well as her husband and lover and she trusted him to be there for her. She would tell him everything now. Michael had never been a secret, he just hadn't been relevant to their lives together, but now he was, at least a little.

She led him to the lounge where she had been sitting for some time. Cees sat beside her, placing the laptop on the coffee table, seemingly unaware of the message it held. Anna recounted her story. She started from the beginning; the meeting in Morecambe, the letters and poems, her invitation to visit and finally her assumption that when the letters stopped he had just got bored or found someone else. Now she had discovered why.

"You know how fickle things are when you're that age," she reminded Cees, "I just presumed he lost interest and it was time to move on."

Perhaps Cees may have felt a little pang of jealousy. Perhaps he may have considered that if Michael had lived, he may never have met Anna. Perhaps they may never have married and the wonderful life they enjoyed, may never have been. If he did feel any of this, he didn't show it.

"I did love him though," she ventured. She paused to gauge her husband's reaction, but he just looked intently at her. She had considered not saying it, certainly not using those exact words, but she had denied Michael all those years ago and was not in any mood to do so again. If it caused a few waves, then so be it. She could reassure Cees later. She couldn't do anything about Michael.

Cees smiled encouragingly and Anna bit her lip once more, pouting a feigned smile in return.

"Well is there anything more on the internet about this young man?" he said at last, the rational scientist in him coming to the fore.

He lifted the laptop from the table and awoke it from its

sleep. Once again the cooling fans whirred to life as he scrolled through the results, running through page after page. "You would think there would be some report of the incident itself," he commented as he speed read quickly through, "but I can't find anything. Still, these events really pre-date the internet, so they probably only put snippets of information on line." Then he scrolled back once again to the beginning to check further the most relevant results.

"There are a few Michael Coglans around," he commented at last, "one or two in the States with some sort of Irish connection, nothing much more relating to Belfast though. He paused a little. "Here's one though," he said opening up the page, "something about schools in Ireland." He read through a little, muttering the occasional phrase; *agreement reached that English literature curriculum...* His voice trailed off. ... *now to include modern Irish historical content.* "Ah no," he tutted, "that's from 2002. Too recent."

Cees scrolled further. "OK, here's another. Some political thing, not sure. Something about the *Good Friday Agreement.* I think that is the peace initiative they agreed, but that is also too recent, just a few years back. What did he do for a living?"

"He was a *school boy,*" retorted Anna, showing the first emotion that wasn't conciliatory since Cees had arrived home.

"I'm sorry Anna. I'm just trying to help."

"Oh, I don't know, what's the point," said Anna softly. "I know now, that's all. I'm glad I know and it is upsetting, it is painful, but maybe it would be better left alone."

"Well it's up to you, but Anna," he paused a little, gripping her once more on the arms and smiling softly as he looked deeply into her reddened eyes, "though you've been crying half the afternoon by the looks of it. Your blouse is soaked through."

He indicated at her clothing, damp and sticking to her body in places. She looked down at her herself and smiled back at him, taking on the role of the child in the relationship. He was right. The tears had cooled and her clothing now stuck uncomfortably to her body. *Oh goodness, what must I look like*, she thought suddenly, patting her reddened face and pushing the hair that had fallen forward, backwards so she could see him properly. She mustered another smile.

"It does sound like you have some unfinished business though. Maybe you should try and find out a little more, contact his relatives or something."

"His relatives are all dead," snapped Anna, "didn't you read; his Mother and Father were both killed at the same time."

Cees paused, taken aback a little but not accustomed to backing down from any situation at the first sign of difficulty. "Well, there must be somebody." He hesitated, only briefly, collecting his thoughts and mentally evaluating what he was about to say. He quickly read the article again himself. "If you do want to find out some more, I guess we could contact the newspaper that this article is from; *The Belfast Telegraph*. Journalists hoard information like autumn squirrels hoard nuts only, especially with historic stuff like this, they're usually delighted to share what they have. If you want, I can send out an email to this newspaper tomorrow. If anyone has any further details, I guess it would probably be them."

He paused looking lovingly at her. The institution of marriage is successful for many reasons. One of these is the ability of the partners to provide an infrastructure of support in crises that their spouse would never be able to muster themselves.

"Ok?"

"Ok," she replied

CHAPTER 22

Sarah Thompson (Miss)

It was late the following afternoon when Cees remembered his undertaking. The Belfast Telegraph was easy enough to find, the availability of contact being among the most important requirements for the operation of a successful newspaper anywhere in the world. Cees sent a simple email, without much in the way of facts, just referencing the article he and Anna had read the previous day and asking if, despite the passage of time, they had perhaps any further information about Michael Coglan.

The following morning there was an email in his in box:

Dear Mr Bouwmeester,

Many thanks for getting in touch with us regarding the late Michael Coglan.

Obviously outside of what you know already, there is really very little more to say. His parents are of course both dead, but we also have no record of any living relative. Furthermore, he was known to be a solitary and introverted sort of individual with very little in the way of friends or an established social circle, people we would certainly have interviewed ourselves, given the circumstances.

The only person I know of who might be able to fill in a few details for you would, of course, be the nurse who tended to him at hospital just before he died. As you might know already, her name is Bernadette O'Callaghan (Bernie). She has been retired many years now, but I believe she still lives in Belfast. If you give me a day or two, I will try to get in touch and see what I can find out.

Best Regards,

Sarah Thompson (Miss) – Assistant Editor

After lunch that day, Cees was just about to go down to the laboratory to check progress on a short experiment he and some others had been carrying out over the last few days when the phone rang. It was Sarah Thompson. She had a strong Belfast accent and talked quickly interspersing her speech with apologies and comments on what she had just said or what she thought Cees might be about to say.

"Oh, Mr…eh, yes, Bowmeester. Thanks so much… thanks so much for getting in touch. Now, I am sure you're busy, well of course you're busy, everybody's busy these days, but I thought I would call and see, well, it's like this you see. The nurse, that's this Bernie O'Callaghan. Well, you know that; *of course* you know that. Well, I can say that she is still very much alive and well and living in Belfast. So, yes, yes that is the good news. That *is indeed* good news."

There was a short pause and Cees could see her in his mind's eye shuffling papers in the sort of confusion her speech conveyed.

"Well, the thing is this,…er, Mr…Bowmeester. Look, yes, we have tried to talk to her before about Michael Coglan. Well, you see, that is not easy. This lady, well she is retired many years now. No, no, no of course not, yes, she is still, well, how should I say it, well, yes compos mentis as they say, well you know what I mean. Yes, she's fine, but she is quite reclusive. Not on the telephone, well at least we don't have a phone number for her, maybe she has a phone, indeed she may well have a phone, but we can't find a number for her. Maybe she has a mobile. Well, I'm really not sure…"

She sighed, perhaps aware of her digression and took a long inward breath ready for her next prolonged sentence while Cees quickly summarised in his mind what he could understand.

"Well, the point is this. A few years back when this story broke, we did try to interview Miss O'Callaghan, but she really wouldn't say much. Well, that is our job, to find out the facts and she seemed to be the only person who really knew the boy at all well, only she always declined to say anything much other than that she had spent some time talking to him in hospital before he died."

Cees rather considered that twenty-seven years was more than a few years back but kept listening.

"The point is this, Mr Bowmeester. Well, look here's the point. After I sent you the email earlier, well, I just got in my car and went up there and knocked on her door. She lives quite near the hospital, not far really. I had never met her before, you see, I am quite new to the paper, but well look, she won't talk to us journalists, but well, I mentioned you and your wife and it seems she *would* be quite willing to meet you.

There was a long pause. "Mr Bowmeester, are you still there?"

"Yes, yes," replied Cees. "Meet us? What in Belfast?" asked Cees, incredulously.

"Well, yes," replied Sarah. "I don't suppose you would be willing to come over here and talk to her. Would you?"

Cees was a little taken aback. A visit to Ireland was not

something he had been considering any time soon.

"Well, we just wanted to know a little more about him. I'm not sure it's really that important." He paused. "OK, look, I'll think about it. Let me talk to my wife."

CHAPTER 23

An Unexpected Trip

Anna was in the kitchen when Cees arrived home that evening. She had been amusing herself cooking rhubarb into a rich paste and had already rolled the pastry out to make a delicious tart with a sour tang that she always claimed was an antidote to summer colds. She heard Cees arrive, but with her hands covered in wet pastry and flour, was rather indisposed to give him his usual welcoming kiss. Cees leant against the jamb of the kitchen door, watching her casually for a moment. He marvelled at how beautiful she looked with her sleeves rolled up, stirring the pot, which emitted a sharp acidic odour into the air, with one hand while cutting the pastry to shape with the other.

Even in her melancholy state she retained a classic beauty and stirred a feeling of love and cherishment in his heart that was as alive today as it had been on their wedding day. *Poor Michael really missed out*, he thought to himself rather irreverently. Still she seemed in better form now. Sure, her news had been a shock, but she had already cheered up quite a bit the previous evening. Although he could see she was thoughtful, she smiled broadly when she saw him as the early evening light shone through the thin mist of flour in the kitchen air.

"Well, this Michael guy. You know, I do think I have something to report," he began.

Anna looked up earnestly.

"Well, I had written an email to the newspaper as promised and this morning I got a reply from a journalist there. Actually, her email said she was the assistant editor. Apparently Michael became very close to a nurse at the hospital during his last days and reading between the lines a little, she thinks maybe he confided in her in some way. The funny thing is, she is retired and pretty reclusive and won't usually talk to anyone, but she says, she *will* talk to you."

"Great," said Anna, "did you get a number? Maybe we can we give her a call."

Cees smiled. It was a smug smile she knew well. It was a smile that said he knew something that she didn't. Anna looked at him intently unsure whether to join his grin or exercise caution towards the plan she figured was coming. "Well, that's just the point," he said, "she's not on the phone. Sarah, that's the journalist's name, suggested we go there and meet with her face to face!"

"What!" exclaimed Anna, "In Ireland?"

"Well yes, in Ireland."

"No way. We can't just go and jump on a plane to Belfast."

"Well, that's exactly the point, we *can*." replied Cees. "It's really quite simple. There are direct flights with Easyjet. You just buy a ticket, book a hotel and go. Such is the modern world my darling." He smiled openly.

"No! What about Esther? When would we go?"

"Esther can stay with your Mum for a few days. If we went on Friday, we could easily be back by Sunday. They can do without me at work for one day."

"No. I don't want to go raking it all up again. It was a shock, I was upset, grieving I suppose, but really I'm fine now. I don't see what's to be gained."

Cees looked intently at his wife. "Look, it's up to you of course, but I think you should go. You were obviously very close to this guy. Maybe you just need to go and have a look, see where he lived or whatever. Maybe talk to this woman. Sure, why not. Maybe he mentioned you before he died. I don't know, but you won't rest, not really until you have all this sorted in your head."

Anna bit her lip in thought once more.

"Besides, we could do with a few days away, just the two of us. And, Ireland, well, I've never been, nor have you, unless you have some more secrets you're not sharing." Anna smiled. "This'll be good for you. It'll be good for us. You'll see. You see Anna, I'm your husband and I love you very much, even if I was second choice!" He smiled broadly once more as she threw a flour covered tea towel that emitted a white puff when it hit him. They both laughed. He took her in his arms and held her close and as he did, a little tear escaped from her eye and ran down her cheek making a bright narrow track in the film of flour on her skin. "Won't we have to pay top prices on *Easyjet* if we book this late?" she said.

So arrangements were made. The next day, Cees got in touch with Sarah Thompson once more, who seemed delighted with the news. She said she would call with Miss O'Callaghan again and try to agree an exact time for their visit.

CHAPTER 24

A Cosmopolitan City

They arrived at Belfast International airport early on
the Friday evening. Although it was late June, the sky
was overcast and a cool wind was blowing. A light
drizzle filled the air. They took a taxi for the city centre and sat
relaxing in the back seat as the driver sped through the Irish
countryside, the car lifting and falling joyously on the little
undulations on the road. After a while they stopped at a
junction. There was a small house situated on the corner, a
simple bungalow with a little window in the roof. Beside it was
a makeshift sign at the side of the road. It read; *If you lived here,
you'd be home by now.*

Cees read it with a little confusion as he peered through
the spot he had cleaned on the steamed up window. "Here
Anna," he said at last pointing. "Your English is better than
mine. What does that sign mean?" She leaned over and looked
out, reading it quickly before settling back in her seat. She
glimmered a smile. Cees looked on expectantly. "It means if you
lived here, you'd be home by now," she said nonchalantly in
Dutch.

Cees looked perplexed, opened his mouth to speak but
reconsidered and went back to his own thoughts.

After a while the roads became larger and the landscape
more urban with houses and larger buildings dominating the
skyline as the green of the countryside first engaged, then gave

way to city streets. Belfast wasn't quite what they had been expecting. The only images either of the two foreigners had already imprinted on their minds were from the 1970s and 80s when political strife tore through the city and pictures of the results were broadcast around the world. Now, the place seemed rather well developed, affluent even. German cars sped past on the wide roads and as they approached the centre, they could see large developments of apartment blocks and entertainment complexes befitting of any modern West European city.

The streets were busy and the traffic slowed as the pavements filled with throngs of citizens as those late in leaving work mixed with others heading out for a Friday evening on the town. Anna observed them carefully, contemplating which ones might be Catholic and which ones Protestant and wondering how one could ever tell the difference. She pondered how whatever differences there were could ever have descended into the violence that had claimed so many lives, including the life of her first love.

Eventually they arrived at the hotel. It was a large, modern and rather luxurious establishment which towered some twelve floors into the sky. Outside there were a good number of prestigious cars picking up and dropping people off at the hotel as well as the theatre next door.

They checked in and were shown to a large, well decorated room on the sixth floor.

"Bit flash isn't it" remarked Anna as she laid her suitcase on the stand that sat below the window at one end of the room.

"Well, yes. I think this is one of the best hotels in the city," replied Cees, smiling broadly. "I thought why not make a thing of it. We get away, just the two of us, nowhere near often enough."

"City seems nice," added Anna. "Not sure what I was expecting, but I suppose I thought it would be, well certainly less busy. Maybe a little run down still, but it really is quite vibrant. I guess this is the peace dividend."

"Yes, that and the Celtic Tiger."

"Celtic what?"

"The Irish economy is the fastest growing economy in Europe at the minute. They call it the Celtic Tiger."

"Yes, but that's surely the South. This is the North."

"Yes, but it looks like the effect has spilled over to the North too." Cees chuckled. "Maybe they have discovered making money and decided to put their efforts into getting rich instead of killing each other."

Anna scowled, disapproving of his casual reference.

"Sorry," said Cees, noting his impropriety. "The place does look affluent though."

They had eaten at Schiphol Airport before they left and weren't that hungry, so after they had settled in, Cees suggested they go out for a drink to sample the local nightlife. Outside the sky was overcast and a cool wind was blowing. A light drizzle filled the air. Across the road was a pub and the welcoming atmosphere of the townsfolk drinking, talking and socialising spilled invitingly out onto the street in a noisy hubbub of activity.

They looked approvingly at each other and entered. It was an ornate, Victorian establishment with etched glass mirrors and dark, hardwood panels. The room was much larger than they would have been used to in Holland and the serving bar stretched the full length along one side with a marble top, smoothed to imperfection by the years of casual leanings of the townsfolk awaiting service. It smelled of beer, wine and whiskey, but it also smelled of history and nostalgia as if both were a permanent presence in the building. Animated couples and groups stood chatting enthusiastically with mannerisms buoyed by the satisfaction of a week's work now done and the prospect of a relaxing unwind with friends, colleagues and family. Some were dressed in smart business wear, while others were more casually attired. A few even wore rough work clothes, soiled with the marks of their respective trades.

The remainder of the room was taken up with cubicles or private snugs elaborately carved from mahogany panels that looked to have witnessed many a negotiation, plan, scheme, argument, triumph or other human experience since time immemorial. Boisterous laughter could be heard from some, while in others, groups talked in hushed tones of issues more private or personal in nature.

The two foreigners went up to the bar. "Better try the local brew then, Anna," said Cees.

"That'll be the Guinness, I expect."

Cees paused a moment and looked at her. "Is it one Guinness, but two Guinnesses, or is it one of those words where the singular is the same as the plural, you know like sheep?"

Before she had time to reply, a voice interjected. "It could be either," he said, "but of course it could also be one Guinness, two Guinni or two Guinnessi, like from the Latin!" Anna laughed and gazed at the mirror above the bar. *Guinness is good for you*, it said.

The man appeared to be in his late seventies with thin back combed grey hair that yellowed at its tips and an unkempt, bushy moustache that looked like it had been dipped in rather too many pints of Guinness over the years. Anna recognised his accent as quintessentially English in nature, the tone of which defined his social class, as rather well to do, much more so than his regional origin.

"Well," he went on, "there is a lot of Latin in the English language. Indirectly, of course, mostly from the French, following the Norman invasion, you know, 1066 and all that."

"1690. What's that? 1690?" interjected his drinking partner, a tall, elderly man who spoke with the sharp musical tones of the authentic Belfast accent. He was waiflike thin and his body seemed to buckle under its own weight as he stood.

"Not 1690 Tom, 1066. The Norman invasion. You know, William the Conqueror."

"William of Orange?"

"*No* Tom, not William of *Orange*, William the *Conqueror*. The battle of Hastings. 1066. He had everyone speaking French for years. For God's sake put your hearing aid in."

In the meantime, the barman had arrived and Cees ordered two pints of the establishment's *best* Guinness, he emphasised, cleverly pluralising the word pint, thus making the plural ending of Guinness unnecessary.

"It's all standard," said the barman dryly. "We don't have different grades of Guinness, but you can have extra cold if you like."

Cees, looked at his new friend who shrugged, "I always stick with the original, sort of warmer one. The cold one hurts my teeth, the few I have left!"

"Just normal then," said Cees.

"It's not that standard at all."

Cees looked up.

"The Guinness in England is nowhere near as good as here. Something about the water they say. Irish Guinness is brewed from water from the river Liffey, which apparently gives it an extra quality unavailable anywhere else in the world. You can definitely tell the difference."

The voice came from another man who had joined them at the bar, money in hand, trying to catch the tender's eye. He was young and casually dressed with short hair and glasses and spoke in a younger version of the Belfast accent, dodging his head from side to side in a rhythmical motion as he spoke.

"Also, it all depends on volume. You can't leave it in the keg too long. It doesn't keep. Sometimes in England it's been sitting around for a while. I never drink it unless others are." He smiled at Anna, who was still pondering the Guinness advertising mirror.

"Of course, that couldn't really be," she said casually. The Englishman raised his eyebrows. "Well," Anna went on, "Latin plurals are really only found where the word ends in –us, like radius; radii or alumnus; alumni etc. Guinness ends in –ess, not –us, so whatever its origins, it wouldn't really take this type of ending"

"Ah, you're clearly a well-educated young woman," replied the Englishman, a mild flattery in his voice.

"Well, yes." Anna nodded shyly, "I studied English literature at university and the origins of the language particularly interest me. As well as being arguably the most widely spoken language in the world, English has openly welcomed new words into the vocabulary. This gives it a rich diversity which makes its literature so particularly fascinating. While its core origins are Germanic, as you mentioned, most words in the French language can also be found in some form in English. Usually the meanings are derived, but they are there all the same."

The man watched her intently, shuffling his weight from one side of his body to the other before responding. "Do you mind if I ask where you studied?"

Anna chuckled openly. "Ah, well, I studied in Holland, at Utrecht actually." She pronounced the city's name locally with a soft Oo-trecht, rather than Uu-trecht as it might be pronounced by an English speaker, providing the first indication that she may not hail from England's home counties. "We had a long established English department there," she went on "and liaised with all the premier universities in the English speaking world."

"Ah, so hence the knowledge of the vagaries of Latin." The Englishman nodded approvingly as he nonchalantly tapped his walking sick on the tiled floor.

Finally the two pints of stout arrived on the counter, already settled with the dense black liquid topped with the familiar creamy lather. Anna's eyes widened, "I'm never going to drink all that," she said looking at the large pint glass and taking a sip leaving a comical creamy moustache remaining on her upper lip, a fact noted by the company but not commented on.

The younger Irishman ordered a pint and stood waiting for its delivery. "You are English though?" he asked expectantly.

"Oh no, we're both Dutch. I've only ever been to England once for a short holiday." Anna's face took on a pensive expression as her mind wandered briefly to the reason for their visit, "but the language has always been my passion."

"Of course you will know," chimed in the Englishman who had now rather deserted his hard of hearing friend, "the Irish have made amazing contributions to English literature. There's George Bernard Shaw. Yes and Oscar Wilde…"

"Gay!" said a voice. It was the Irish guy who had now turned to face the accumulating group.

"What does it matter if he was gay?" asked Cees, suddenly becoming defensive on behalf of Dutch liberal opinion.

"Well, it doesn't matter, it doesn't *matter*, I'm just saying he was gay, that's all."

Cees thought better of pursuing the subject and the conversation skipped cheerfully on.

"Then there's James Joyce," said the Englishman, clearly happy with the subject of the discussion. He paused thoughtfully. "Ah yes, Ulysses. The most famous book, nobody has ever read."

"And the longest!" interjected the young Irishman who now had his pint in hand and had joined Anna in a creamy moustache though he seemed indisposed to lick it off, rather leaving it to dribble slowly into his mouth as he talked, periodically catching the drips with his tongue.

"Then there's C S Lewis. He was actually born in Belfast, you know. Also what do you call that kid the children are studying in school?"

The Englishman tapped his stick repeatedly on the floor as his mind sought out the answer on the tip of his tongue, more recent events having become rather more difficult to retrieve in his later years. However, before he spoke, Anna once again found herself contributing to the dialogue. "I've read it." She paused briefly, then repeated for clarity, "Ulysses, I've read it."

Once again, the company turned to face Anna's modest features. Happy with her audience, she went on. "It has been voted, admittedly in literary circles, as one of the best novels ever written in the English language. It's full of riddles and puns, so much so that even the most sophisticated scholar can only hope to decipher a minority of them. I thought I should read it."

"And..." asked the Irish guy.

She smiled. "Actually, it's not that bad. You need to be

content to not understand it all or even most of it and also to know that there is still more you don't know you don't understand, but it's irreverent, sort of fun too in places. It's made up of a series of short stories, linked, but also self-standing in their own right. You could do worse than read just one or two of the episodes and see what you think."

The conversation was interrupted as the door of the bar swung enthusiastically open and about a dozen people marched in. They were mostly in their twenties or thirties and casually dressed, but smartly so in blue jeans and designer pullovers, some with satchels across their shoulders. They milled around, looking above and to each side surveying the establishment as they pushed through the regular Friday night drinkers.

Eventually, two men approached the bar. The young Irishman who turned out to be called Sean, quickly engaged them in conversation and suggested they should ask the barman for his *best* Guinness, carefully explaining that sometimes they don't supply their best grade to foreigners as they don't think it will be appreciated. This they did receiving the same dry response that Cees had received an hour or so earlier, much to the amusement of the little group. The newcomers spoke in slow English punctuated with pauses and stutters and fiddled about in their purses for money to pay for their drinks.

Sean watched carefully before once again catching the eye of one of them. "You folk aren't from around here then are you?"

"No, no, we are from Croatia," came the reply.

"Croatia!"

"Yes, there is many coach load of us, but most of the older peoples are staying in the hotel. We are thinking we would come out and visit real Irish bar."

216

"Bloody hell! Now we have coach trips from Croatia visiting the city," remarked Sean, swaying joyfully as he spoke, the effects of the alcohol now becoming evident as he had already been present in the establishment for some time before Cees and Anna arrived.

"The thinking man's holiday destination," added the Croatian visitor. "Look here." He pulled a brochure from his bag, printed in a Balkan language of some sort, but with the slogan, *Belfast, the thinking man's holiday destination*, printed in English on the front cover. He handed it to the Englishman who was now gazing attentively.

"Well, I've lived in this city for over fifty years and I never thought I'd see this day!" He chuckled as he leafed through the pages full of illegible print but with familiar photographs of the city and surrounding countryside he knew so well. "Here we are, me an Englishman, two Irish, a Dutchman and his wife, two Croatian tourists and a humourless barman," he nodded briefly at the bartender who was working diligently pouring further pints of stout, "all enjoying the craic together."

Anna smiled politely. "Craic?"

It was Sean who answered. "Yes, like having a good time. Enjoying fun together, that sort of thing."

"And is it spelled, c–r–a–i–c?" asked Anna.

"Well, yes it is! You know, I think there is something you're not letting on. You certainly have a bit more knowledge of this country than one might expect from the average Dutch visitor."

Anna smiled once more, but this time more inwardly as her memories now delved back to the summer day when Grietje pulled a crumpled note from her purse. Cees smiled too, a little in keeping with the jolly chat that continued unabated, but his thoughts were really directed at his wife. He could see a side of her now that he had not seen before. He could see a depth of understanding she had failed to advertise in their relationship, but nevertheless must have always existed. Pride was a feeling he had mostly reserved for his children but now he felt a warm admiration for Anna's academic knowledge, so far from the certainties of the science world he knew so well, but still so full of colour and intrigue.

The little international group chattered on for most of the night, enjoying each other's company and interacting with the various visitors to the bar who came to replenish their empty glasses from time to time. The atmosphere was relaxed and informal. Cees involved himself enthusiastically in the often boisterous conversation and Anna smiled, interjecting the occasional contribution that always engaged the group's attention. As the evening wore on, she felt relaxed and at ease. She looked around herself from time to time, absorbing the atmosphere. *Michael's home town*, she thought. She was glad they had come.

At last the elderly Englishman set his empty glass on the counter with a loud clunk as it absorbed the abrupt shock of its meeting with the hard marble of the surface. "Ah, time for me to go. My beer is rationed, my life is ordered from morning to night with pills and potions but I still feel like shite! Oh, excuse me Miss!"

Anna smiled. The Englishman held out his hand. "It's been a pleasure meeting with you both. I do hope you have a wonderful stay in our city. Maybe you'll have time to see the countryside a little before you go. You won't be disappointed. Weather's supposed to be better after the weekend. What did you say your names were again?"

Cees shook his hand warmly, "Cees Bouwmeester," he said, "and this is my wife, Anna."

"And you are?" she asked expectantly.

"My name is Bailey, Oliver Bailey."

Back at the hotel, a long day behind them, they settled down in bed. Anna dozed off quickly, not being accustomed to late nights, but Cees lay awake for a while, his thoughts engaging his brain in gentle discussion. It was rare that they would find themselves standing in a bar with unfamiliar company. Since marriage, their social lives had mostly centred on groups of friends with whom they were well acquainted. Then when the children came along, they quickly came to focus on their wants and needs and social lives became limited to the children's activities. However tonight, Cees, had watched his wife engage with complete strangers and he noted how her apparent shy disposition had found a new confidence. Maybe it was the opportunity to use the English language that was her passion. Maybe it was just the casual and jovial nature of the people with whom it seemed so effortless to interact, but she had shone in a way he hadn't seen for some years. He liked it.

The city too had already generated a warm feeling in his consciousness. There was a buzz of activity in the place, of placid excitement. People didn't take themselves too seriously. He liked that too. He wondered too about the young boy, Michael, who had so caught his wife's imagination all those years ago then lain dormant in her mind. He turned and looked across at Anna's sleeping figure, her hair strewn across the pillow and her eyes closed in peaceful slumber. He wondered what they would find out the next day and both optimism and apprehension mingled together in his thoughts as he dozed off to sleep.

CHAPTER 25

Sarah Thompson (Miss)

Like the English and the Scottish too, the Irish like their breakfasts, cooked, greasy and tasty and the offering at Cees and Anna's hotel was no exception. However, for visitors to Ireland, the usual offering of bacon and eggs is supplemented with the local specialities of potato and soda bread filling the breakfaster with a starchy meal of guilty delight. However, they declined to try the recommended English Breakfast tea, instead they washed it down with a rather disappointing weak coffee or *coffee for people who don't drink coffee* as Cees referred to it. When they were well filled, the couple set out for their appointment with Sarah Thompson at the offices of the 'Belfast Telegraph' in the city centre. The sky was overcast and a cool wind was blowing. A light drizzle filled the air.

Despite the weather they decided to walk, wishing to enjoy the atmosphere and perhaps look in one or two shops. The city offered an architectural mix from the grandeur of elaborate Victorian and Edwardian buildings, remnants of the city's heyday as an affluent commercial centre, to post war office blocks from the fifties and sixties. There were of course also the more recent shopping centres and department stores, a testimony to the post Troubles rebuilding programme with household names many of which were already familiar to the two visiting foreigners.

People went about their business, rushing around, takeaway coffees in hand, jumping on and off busses. Taxis stopped, setting down and picking up clients, shop girls gazed out towards the street, awaiting the day's customers. Despite the light rain, few wore coats and many were even dressed in short sleeves or loose summer clothing as if summer happened in Belfast whatever the weather and a positive expectation overruled reality.

A bicycle whooshed by, its bell ringing alerting the two visitors who had instinctively looked the wrong way before stepping on to the road. Anna's alarm turned to a giggle as Cees held her tightly and they retreated to the safety of the kerb before making a new more careful attempt. They passed by the grandeur of Belfast City Hall. Anna explained that it had been designed in a baroque style, similar to St Paul's Cathedral in London, but built more than two hundred years later as part of a revival movement.

Cees looked intently at his wife. She seemed to have a whole world of knowledge hidden away that he had never really noticed before. "How did you know that?"

"Michael wrote a poem about it." She paused, considering briefly if she should expand on the subject, but quickly concluded she should and engaged her memory, "it was called Durban's big brother, I think. Or else, Durban's half-brother, I'm not sure. Apparently, there is a building in South Africa which is almost an exact replica, but strangely designed by a different architect. He likened the relationship to two siblings who share only one parent."

They proceeded down the main thoroughfare, Donegall Place, leaving the City Hall behind them and gazed in the shop windows. Cees mused how his wife seemed somehow at ease in the city, like she knew it and understood it already. At last the bustle subsided a little as they followed the simple directions Sarah Thompson had supplied and arrived at their destination, a tall imposing building towards the Cathedral end of the city.

The Belfast Telegraph has a proud tradition of delivering the news throughout the various trials the city has experienced over many years. Outside the main entrance stood a bronze plaque above some superficial damage to the building's stonework which Cees and Anna stopped briefly to read:

The scars on this stone were caused in the German air raids of the Second World War. Despite severe damage to the building, the 'Belfast Telegraph' was published without interruption.

Inside, they were greeted by a smartly dressed receptionist with a tight fitting skirt and white blouse accessorised with a small silk scarf tied loosely around her neck. She smiled widely as she welcomed them and showed them into an oak-panelled room with high windows facing the main road outside.

"Please, sit down and make yourselves comfortable." Smiling politely, she stepped backwards from them towards the door and asked, "can I get you something to drink? Tea? Coffee, perhaps?"

They both declined the beverage and sat down in two large wooden armchairs positioned to one side of a huge desk topped in red leather that dominated the room. One wall was furnished floor to ceiling with bookcases of polished mahogany that bore the hallmarks of time gone by and contained a vast array of books, most of which looked as if they hadn't been opened for decades, centuries even. The two looked at each other, a little apprehensively, as they waited.

Presently they were joined by Sarah Thompson, whom

Cees had already spoken with on the telephone a few days earlier. She was an attractive woman, if a little plump, who despite being aged only in her thirties wore a set of old fashioned looking glasses on the end of her nose in the way those who develop long sight in later years do as the eye muscles lose flexibility.

She carried a suspension file which she set on the desk before launching into enthusiastic welcomes interspersed with questions which she quickly answered herself, followed by short reprimands and scolds as if there was a kind of jovial split in her personality.

"Did you fly in? Well of course you did, how else would you get here. We're an island after all. People hardly go on the boat any more, not unless they're transporting something large and you would have needed more than one boat, then trains and buses, or whatever. Where is it you're from again?

"Holland," said Cees in the shortest of intervals before the monologue continued.

"Yes, yes of course. Holland. So, thanks for your email. I understand you're interested in Michael Coglan." She stopped briefly for a smiling interlude. "We are the Belfast Telegraph, the historical record of the city, the province too. We have records downstairs going back to 1870. Since then, anything that's happened here, good or bad, we have recorded it."

Cees and Anna looked on intently, patiently.

"Well, Michael Coglan, a sad story, like them all back then, but of course, people forget that and nowadays everyone sees this with a much more positive outlook."

She paused again, her face suddenly poised in thought conveying, perhaps uncharacteristically for a journalist, her own intimate thoughts to the newcomers before her. "Forgiveness?"

Well, yes," she said briefly, answering her own rhetorical question, "people are trying you know," she affirmed. Her eyes met firstly with Anna's before moving to look at Cees intently. She went on, "we have had many dark years here, but yes, I do believe that today, people *are* trying, trying to forgive."

She nodded her head agreeing with herself, before her demeanour changed to a more cheerful disposition and she went on, "still the mystery remains. Can't shed too much light on that," she chuckled, "but look, I have what we have here."

Cees raised his eyebrows and looked over at Anna who shrugged, the two now a little vexed as they struggled to take in the confused monologue of disjointed information, thought and opinion their new acquaintance conveyed while Sarah quickly opened the file skipping from page to page nodding from time to time and muttering a more or less constant stream of acknowledgment and affirmation as if any silence or the prospect of anyone else speaking were to be avoided at all costs. Cees found himself wondering how she could ever have succeeded in any journalistic sense as her mind seemed so constantly occupied with her own forethoughts that the gathering of new information must be rendered all but impossible but quickly discarded the question as Sarah continued.

"Well, yes you see. There doesn't seem to be any family. Both his parents died in the same attack, so Michael was left alone. Also, there doesn't seem to be any Aunts or Uncles or anybody from what I can gather. Rather unusual for Ireland; people typically have large families here, well at least they used to, though younger couples seem to be more into family planning and that sort of thing nowadays. Anyway, it seems his father was an only child... No hold on, there were some brothers, estranged though and there is a sister, but none of them seemed to have had any involvement with the family at the time. His mother had also had no contact with her siblings for many years. Hold on, there is a pencil note, just added here," she pointed to a short paragraph scribbled on the side of the otherwise neatly typed page, "yes, mother's siblings live abroad. Oh, and I hadn't realised that, yes, look, it says here his parents were a mixed marriage."

"Mixed marriage?"

Sarah smiled sweetly. "Ah, yes, his father was a Catholic and his mother a Protestant. A mixed marriage. Sorry! That's what we call it here."

She shuffled some more papers, shaking her head from side to side. They both watched as she picked up the actual cutting from the newspaper of the article they had read on the internet only a few days earlier.

"Yes, and Michael was an only child himself, so really, it appears there was no one. Terribly sad. I guess that's why the nurse took such an interest, but we'll come to that in a minute."

She turned over a few more pages.

"The house is long since gone. Demolished to make way for the motorway to the North. You probably travelled on it when you came in from the airport, unless of course the driver took you on some needless tour of the area if he thought you were foreign and didn't know your way around." She chuckled. "You did take a taxi did you?"

She didn't wait for an answer.

"There is a bus too, but it just dumps you in the middle of town and it's not cheap either."

"So, the house is gone. Nothing there for you then. Not sure what happened to the furniture, or even the family's personal effects or any money there might have been. Someone must have it, but I can't see anything here. Must find that out really."

She paused, thinking for the briefest of moments. "Some solicitor in the city must know." She lifted a pencil and made some notes on one of the papers. "I'll call around and see what I can find out."

"So, like I said on the phone, this nurse, Bernadette O'Callaghan is her name, I'm sure I said already. She looks like your best source for information. She sort of adopted Michael during his last days when he was in hospital. Sat with him, talked to him and so on. A very nice lady."

She made a short, uncharacteristic pause before continuing.

"She's retired now of course. Seventy something years old I would say, but spritely, bright as a button really. You know what they say, 70 is the new 60! As I said, she's not on the phone, so I went around there again on Thursday and rang her door bell. She's still very happy to see you, so that's great. I said you would call and see her at about 3 o'clock this afternoon. I hope that is OK with you?"

She raised her eyebrows as she looked over the top of her reading glasses first to Cees, then to Anna. They both nodded.

"I suppose you could go earlier, but well better not to. She is quite old now, lives alone. Never married. It's *Miss* Bernadette O'Callaghan by the way. Call her Bernie though. I'm sure that will be fine. I called her Bernie anyway. She lives up near the hospital, off the Falls Road."

She pushed a note with the address across the desk which Cees lifted and inspected carefully.

"So, have you had a look around the city yet? Sorry about the weather, although they say it's going to be better after the weekend. Maybe you'll get a chance to go and see the countryside a bit. It can be beautiful when the sun shines. Are you staying long?"

"No, no, not long. Just a short trip for us. Thank you so much for your time Mrs Thompson."

"Oh please do call me Sarah. Actually, it's Miss. And if I can do anything more to help, please just let me know."

Cees nodded to Anna and they both got up from the table.

"I'll show you out myself. Where was it you said you came from again?"

"Holland."

"Yes, yes, yes, yes, yes," she said out loud reprimanding herself, "Oh, yes. The tulips."

She hummed briefly, *Tulips from Amsterdam* without realising it, then smiled as she opened the door.

"Thanks so much for taking the time to see us on a Saturday Miss Thompson, Sarah," said Cees, "It is most kind of you."

"Oh, we're always here. News happens twenty-four hours a day, seven days a week . There's always somebody here." She paused, "oh and Mr and Mrs Bowmeester," she leaned forward, "it really is so nice that people from Holland are showing an interest in Michael Coglan."

Cees raised his eyebrows and looked briefly at Anna who shrugged her shoulders. They walked out onto the street. Outside, the sky was overcast and a cool wind was blowing. A light drizzle filled the air.

"Jesus it's cold," said Cees.

"The coldest winter I ever spent was a summer in Belfast City," joked Anna, thinking of a novel she had read some years before.

They both laughed. Cees put his arm around her and pulled her close, "Let's see what this nurse has to say."

CHAPTER 26

A Trip up the Falls

They had a few hours to kill and spent some time walking around the city. After a while they stepped into a small pub, not far from St Anne's Cathedral. It was up an alleyway and as they approached, they hesitated for a moment, looking around at the damp walls above. A gutter had clearly become blocked a year or twenty ago and the drips had turned to a pale green slime that traced its way right down the wall to the alleyway below. A stout man walked by and burped as he passed, causing Anna to snigger childishly in a mixture of disgust and embarrassment.

Inside it was warm and cosy, with several small round tables sitting beside bench seating against the walls and topped in dark red velvet. Around the tables sat similarly covered stools. Anna sat on a bench in the corner. It was early for lunch, but some of the tables were already occupied with a few shoppers who had clearly sought refuge from the constant drizzle as well as a few regulars who stood, propping up the bar.

As Cees approached, he caught the gaze of two old men who were discussing a football match while enjoying their drinks, each expressing dissatisfaction with a collective, resigned acceptance.

"What'll it be," asked the barman?

"Are you serving food?" asked Cees, his foreign accent showing through. There weren't many people in the pub and looking around, he couldn't see anyone else eating.

"We certainly are," replied the barman and handed him a menu. Cees perused it thoughtfully but few of the dishes really caught his imagination and his breakfast hadn't quite digested sufficiently to instigate the pangs of hunger that simplify such choices.

"What would you recommend," he enquired at last,

The barman shrugged, but one of the men at the bar, turned around, "Oh, I'd go for the Irish stew," he said at once, smiling warmly, his yellow teeth showing between old lips that bore a tint of purple as they bordered the red of his face.

"Irish stew? What's that then?"

"*Stew from Ireland* said the man," his mouth breaking into a wide grin. His friend looked around from behind and laughed, raising his glass and nodding towards Cees as he caught his eye. Another man chuckled as he rose from his seat and joined them at the bar as he sought a refill.

"Oh, potatoes, some sort of meat, onions I suppose. Come to think of it, I've never really thought about it. Hey Sammy," he called to the barman who had gone off to serve another customer, "What's Irish stew then?"

Predictably, *stew from Ireland*, came the reply from the rather animated barman who clearly enjoyed the childish games that he must have played many times before. It amused the jovial group which Cees had now become a member of, the butt of a joke being more of an initiation process in Ireland than a humiliation. He smiled shyly, and stood awkwardly, the menu still in his hand as the patrons enjoyed the interlude of light entertainment he had unwittingly provided.

However, the casual banter had spread to the Dutchman and in a slightly uncharacteristic lapse from his normal, sedate manner, he looked over at Anna, and shouted to her in English,

"Hey Anna, do you fancy trying the Irish stew?"

Anna had been sitting quietly, her thoughts turning through memory and intrigue, sadness and apprehension. Nothing much about Michael seemed too positive. No family at all. Coming from the warm, close community she knew, she could hardly comprehend it. He must have died alone, all alone, she thought. Not for the first time, a tear welled in her eye.

"Anna, do you want the Irish stew?" Cees called out again.

She awoke from her thoughts and turned towards her husband. "Irish stew. What's that?"

"Stew from Ireland" he shouted back, the smile breaking on his lips. The small group burst into a minor fit of laughter, patting Cees on the back. Some others in the bar nodded with approval, smiling and raising their glasses towards him as he surveyed the small audience around the room.

Anna ignored the frolics and went back to her thoughts. Cees ordered two portions of the *Irish stew* and two glasses of mineral water and, excusing himself to his new friends, who immediately returned to their previous dialogues, joined Anna at the table.

The Irish stew was very hearty indeed, but Anna had little appetite. Her thoughts were dominant in her mind and the meeting scheduled for that afternoon concerned her. She didn't know what to expect. On the one hand, she reassured herself that the visit was simply an honouring or acknowledgement of her friend, her first love, who had died long, long ago. She had no agenda beyond that, but suddenly she felt close to him once more. Close and at one the way she had done all those years ago. She could still see him in her mind's eye, opposite her in the tent, his shy mannerisms amusing and attracting her at the same time. Now he was gone and although she hadn't known it at the time, she had been the young woman left to mourn, as so many before her had been left, as man's conflicts both great and small claim their young prizes.

Cees didn't fare much better with the stew, having rather over indulged with the breakfast and in time they set to leave. Outside, the sky was still overcast and a cool wind was still blowing. A light drizzle still filled the air. They made their way back to the main road and set about looking for a taxi to take them to Bernie's house. Quickly they came across a taxi rank with four or five black cabs sitting in a row in a side street, awaiting customers. They approached the foremost vehicle where the driver was standing, leaning on the open door nonchalantly smoking a cigarette. Cees approached him and finding the pronunciation of the address less than straightforward, handed him the paper that Sarah Thompson had provided. He seemed a little reluctant to take the note at first but on Cees's insistence, he glanced it over, reading the address.

"Are you takin' the piss?" retorted the driver and gave him the note back. Cees stood back looking stunned and inspecting the page as if Sarah had scribbled some vile insult on it as part of a sick joke, but it just looked like a regular address to him.

The driver took a last drag and got in his car. Some other people arrived and jumped happily into the back seat of the vehicle. They were engaged in a busy conversation and took little notice of the foreign couple standing nearby. Anna and Cees looked at each other. Presently they backed off a few yards and were set to go altogether when the driver called them back.

"Ha! You're not from around here, are you?" said the driver, having lost his scowl. Cees shook his head. The driver nodded over his shoulder. "Go back to the main road, turn right, then right again. You'll get a taxi there, for where you want to go."

The two loped off, still feeling a little put out by the poor reception, but did as he suggested and followed his directions. The next street looked just the same with a row of black cabs sitting one in front of the other. This time, Cees approached more cautiously and ventured to the driver, "Excuse me, we wish to go to… " Cees couldn't quite pronounce the name and hesitated a bit, his foreign accent now apparent, but the driver broke in; "If it's the tour you want, you won't get it from here."

"No, no, we want to go here." He held the paper so the driver could see the address. The driver took it cautiously from his hand, looked closely at it and nodded; "I can drop you close by. These are shared taxis though, are you OK with that?" Once again, the Dutch couple looked at each other in mild bemusement but nodded and got in.

During the troubles in Belfast, bus routes were often disrupted due to various disturbances in the city. Intimidation and a general sense of malice deterred transport employees from operating some routes, especially in the West and some parts of the North of the city. This problem was partially alleviated by the operation of 'black taxis'. These were traditional black Hackney carriages like those especially found in London, but were actually used as a shared transport service and operated in much the same way as buses, with each passenger paying individually. They followed basic routes similar to the bus routes, but the drivers would often deviate a little for your convenience and would usually pick up and drop off anywhere along the way.

Although, they all looked the same, those serving the Protestant areas collected at a specific location in the city centre, while those operating in the Catholic areas collected at another, though only a few streets away. Understanding of the system was therefore crucial to safe transport in these vehicles which were entirely unregulated and outside of any form of state authority or control. Today, regular transport services have resumed in all parts of the city and the black cabs can now more often be found offering novel tours of the city's more colourful historic districts to tourists seeking a more individual experience together with an often irreverent and entertaining cabbie.

However, the shared taxis do still operate and as chance would have it, Bernie's home was situated on a route still served by this alternative transport system. But it was also situated in an area where the two communities bordered each other, living side by side while seldom actually meeting. If tension was still to be found anywhere it would be found there and at the time of Cees and Anna's visit early in the summer marching season, while there was peace in the city, the city was not necessarily at peace.

The taxi sat in the rank for another few minutes without moving. Just as Cees was about to enquire about the lack of progress, a middle aged woman with three shopping bags came over, opened the door, folded down the seat opposite and got in, slumping herself in place with a loud sigh. She smiled at the two with a disarming grin.

"Thems is kicking off again," she said casually.

"I'm sorry?" replied Anna.

The woman scoughed. "Thems marches is goin' ahead after all."

Anna and Cees didn't ask for further expansion on the subject and quickly the driver engaged gear and the car took off, chugging its way through the city traffic. The woman seemed friendly enough and Anna found herself explaining that they were from Holland, about the pen pal she had written to many years ago, how the letters had suddenly stopped and how she had only just recently discovered that he had sadly died in the troubles. The woman smiled sympathetically interspersing her nods of acknowledgement with the occasional comment which Anna noted were tinged with a thinly veiled bitterness of her own. She wondered if she too had historic wounds, not yet completely healed.

"What brings yews up this way though?"

"Oh just to visit an old family friend," had been Anna's reply, now reticent to go further into too much personal detail. "The city seems really very attractive though and the people we have met have all been so very friendly. Indeed, everyone has made us feel really quite at home."

"Oh yes, sure you won't get a better welcome anywhere in the world than here." The woman grinned, her smile distracting from the grey stubble on her upper lip she had ceased to temper some years ago. "Not sure about the weather though," she said glancing out of the window, "supposed to get better tomorrow, but sure they're always wrong."

The three passengers sat politely looking at each other until the woman turned and muttered something to the driver causing him to nod before pulling quickly over to the side of the road.

"Are we there then?" asked Cees, looking at the driver in his mirror.

"No, yews are further up. I'll let you know."

The woman clutched her shopping once more and motioned to get out, but then paused and sat back in her seat, again with a loud sigh. She looked at them both closely, firstly at Anna, then at Cees, then back again to Anna again before narrowing her eyes a little. "See when you're up in these parts," she said beckoning towards Anna's husband, "better let him do the talking."

Anna looked back at her, bewildered. "But why?" she asked, slightly perturbed, her brow wrinkled at what she assumed was a slight on her command of the language. The woman made her cheeky grin once more, "*you* sound too *English*."

Anna was still vexed as the woman handed some money to the driver and sprang quickly from the seat causing it to emit a loud twang-oomph as it reverted to its upright position as she bade the Dutch visitors a good day.

It was only a few moments later when the driver pulled to the side of the street once more. "Yews are over there, down that street and turn left at the end," he said pointing. Cees and Anna got out and the car drove off, leaving them strolling down the street, note in hand to fulfil the appointment that Sarah had made with the last person to see Michael alive.

CHAPTER 27

A Message Sent

Much of the area had been re-developed in recent years and modern terraced houses, with attractive white rendered walls, lined the street. The basic designs were repetitious, but many bore the signs of individual ownership most usually with a new front door, often painted in a primary colour or fake Georgian windows that gave the houses a rather pleasant homely feel. On one side of the street, a number of satellite dishes hung from their high perches, all uniformly angled towards the broadcast signals that would beam the latest sporting events into the living rooms of the modern day residents of West Belfast.

Bernie's house had no satellite dish, but the door had certainly been changed from the original. It was of a deep stained wood, a little too grand for the residence, with a fan light window towards the top and a large brass knocker in the middle that shone brighter than the others in the street. Up on the wall, several hooks had been mounted with pots dangling, one on either side of the door and another two either side of the front window from which red geraniums trailed between pansies and begonias. The house fronted directly on to the street and passers by would certainly have enjoyed the mild scent of the flowers and even the occasional brush of foliage on their cheek as the cheerful summer blossoms of the well cared for plants bloomed copiously despite the dampness of the day. Anna inspected the blooms as Cees, hesitating momentarily, perhaps conscious that his finger prints may impair the sheen of the brass finish, lifted the knocker and rapped assertively three times on the back plate.

The door was answered by an elderly lady with short grey hair and small bright eyes that together with a shy smile bade a warm welcome to her visitors. Her furrowed skin bore the hallmarks of a tough life of service and dedication and her lips cracked allowing just the faintest creep of freshly applied lipstick to overrun the line of her pale red upper lip.

"Miss O'Callaghan?" enquired Cees expectantly.

Bernie's smile grew in confidence revealing small grey teeth that had enjoyed a lifetime of diligent attention, but lost their lustre only due to the years behind her. "Oh, please do call me Bernie," she answered stepping backwards into the hall and gesturing to her visitors to enter, "and you must be Mr and Mrs Bowmeester."

Inside, the house lost much of its modernity due to the more traditional tastes of the occupant. An old clock made of polished wood and brass ticked confidently in the hall, its pendulum marking the time rhythmically and a small table with Queen Anne legs supported a ceramic vase with a selection of freshly cut carnations and freesias. Carpet with brightly coloured flowery patterns extended through from the hall into the front room into which they were shown by their hostess.

The room itself was small and old fashioned in appearance, but spotless, and there lingered a feint smell of wood polish. Anna found herself imagining Bernie diligently cleaning in preparation for their visit. Bernie smiled once more. She seemed nice and Anna comforted herself that she had been there for Michael during his last days. Still her mind was rushing. Her thoughts were fearful as well as inquiring. Suddenly, her journey which had in reality only started a few days previously seemed like it had lasted the full twenty-seven years since she had last heard from Michael. *Was this the woman who had sat with Michael those last days?* She sighed, poor Michael, she thought again.

For a moment, the three of them stood awkwardly looking at each other. "Please do sit down. Make yourselves comfortable," said Bernie indicating a small settee covered in a loose cream cover of the removable type used to keep good furniture good for many years, despite the fact that it often looked like the decorators were expected in the meantime. Cees made himself comfortable while Anna, preferring a more upright posture sat on one of two more rigid dining type chairs that sat opposite. Bernie sat on the other and turned the seat a little towards Anna in order to address both visitors at once.

"Would you like a cup of tea?"

Coffee would have been quite welcome, but appeared not to be on the menu, so the couple declined being rather indisposed to try the English tea.

"I understand you are interested in Michael Coglan," said Bernie, breaking the silence, as she looked over the attractive foreign couple who had come to visit in search of information.

It was Cees who spoke first.

"Well, yes. I understand you spent some time with him during his last days in hospital. You see, my wife used to write to him many years ago when she was a child. She had met him on holiday and they became," he paused, "*pen pals*, I believe you say in English."

Bernie gazed over at Anna, the faint smile on her face now seeming quite permanent as she nodded her well-practised, sympathetic expression that had met the ill and injured at the hospital where she had spent her entire working life. Anna smiled back softly, her eyes engaging Bernie's as they each took the measure of the other.

"Well, the letters just stopped one day," Anna interjected, speaking for the first time, her studied Home Counties elocution contrasting with the staid tones of Cees's Dutch accent and the broadness of Bernie's local dialect.

"Of course, we were young and I just thought he had become bored with writing to me. It was only recently when I googled his name that I realised *why* he had stopped writing. It was a shock, I have to say, to have one's whole understanding of someone rewritten all in the flash of a moment. I don't know what I want really, or what I am looking for, just well, maybe to learn a little more about him. His last days perhaps"

Her voice tailed off as her thoughts invaded her speech.

Bernie explained that she had of course only known Michael for a very short period, less than four weeks, and knew little of his life before his admission to hospital, but she recounted what she knew. The story of the attack, his arrival at hospital, his grief at the loss of his parents, his apparent recovery and then of course his final demise.

"So, that's all really I can tell you," she went on. "He had no family remaining and I guess had been forgotten by just about everyone, although even today, in my mind's eye, I can still see his imploring eyes looking at me in those final hours as clearly as I did then."

She pouted slightly and stopped talking briefly, her mind wandering before resuming with a short sigh where she had left off.

"Then of course when the poem was published, people started to take much more of an interest in him, only there wasn't really anyone who could tell his story. No one around seemed to have known him closely."

"Poem?" asked Anna urgently, her eyes widening.

"Well, yes…"

She didn't get time to finish.

"He published a poem?" asked Anna, a look of astonishment now in her expression.

"Well, yes," replied Bernie. "Didn't you know that?"

Cees and Anna looked at each other, before turning once again to face Bernie, their heads shaking dismissively from side to side.

Bernie looked intently at the couple, confusion displayed on her face. "I thought that was why you had come."

Anna sat staring, her gaze flitting back and forward between Bernie and her husband.

"*Ahoy for Joy,* that's what it's called" added Bernie quickly. "Have you really never heard of it?"

Anna shook her head once more.

"But you must have, everyone knows *this* poem. The children study it at school."

"Children study it at school," exclaimed Anna, now conscious that she was repeating everything Bernie said. "Of course, we're not from here, you understand," said Anna at last, "we're from Holland."

Bernie nodded, a long slow nod, as some pieces of the jigsaw slowly fell into place in her mind.

"And Michael wrote it?" asked Anna.

"Yes, he wrote it, just before he died. Well, he dictated it and I wrote it down for him as best I could, but they are his words. It was quite near the end and I couldn't always understand exactly what he was saying, so there are a few bits we don't really understand, but I got most of it. It wasn't until twenty years later as the violence was dying down that the Belfast Telegraph, that's the local newspaper here, ran a feature asking people for short stories, recollections, poems, songs, articles etc., from or relating to folk who had perished in the Troubles. Well, at the time, I had placed the poem in an envelope which I sealed and kept ever since in my drawer. I always expected that one day someone would arrive to collect it, but no one ever did. So, I decided to open it."

"Of course, I already knew what was inside. I have to say, I felt uncomfortable about it. It wasn't my work and I felt I had no real authority to do anything with it, let alone publish it. Michael seemed a very private, deep person and the work, his poignant last words seemed somewhat personal, but there was no one else I could consult, he had no family as you know. So, I decided to send it to the editor. It turned out they were planning to publish a book entitled; *The Troubles in Poems and Prose*. They liked Michael's poem, but there were a few words especially towards the end where I couldn't quite read my own hand writing. I was quite emotional at the time and some discretion was required to complete the work but they agreed to include it."

"The book itself was full of various reports, articles, a few poems, some song lyrics; that sort of thing from a variety of sources. Some came from British soldiers injured or maimed in the conflict. Other pieces came from a variety of civilians caught up in the violence. Many were of course from relatives of the dead. There were even contributions from terrorists, ex terrorists, some reformed and some, rather evidently not so reformed, but the publication was diverse and open in its content."

"Actually, it was a great success. Many said they had found comfort in its contents. Some said they had found a greater understanding of their lives in the present day through it, but for most, it was about closure. Somehow the little collection of memoirs helped people close the book on the past and look forward to the future. As time passed, of course, it's influence faded, but one or two pieces found a longer term place in our culture. Michael's poem was one of these. Critics called it a passionate and balanced work that spoke for many and it had just enough intrigue to retain the public's imagination."

"Some teachers introduced the poem to their classes in school and it quickly became well-known in its own right. Then, when the power sharing government was formed in 2001, the education department agreed to make it a formal part of the school curriculum. It was one of the few things they *could* agree on. Today, in Northern Ireland, every child between the ages of fourteen and sixteen years *must* study this poem. Michael was still at school when he died, so the children of today could relate well to his internal conflict and mixed emotions. Have you really never heard of it?"

"No, sorry. I guess it just never travelled as far as Holland."

"Yes, of course. Now I see. Of course, I suppose it won't be known much outside of Ireland."

Bernie gazed closely at Anna and she could see the old woman was thinking. Suddenly as if a penny had dropped in her mind, she leaned forward, narrowed her eyes and asked, "What did you say your name was again?"

"Anna," was the reply. She smiled and nodded as she spoke.

Bernie looked stunned. "Oh, I hadn't realised. Of course, I had always hoped but I hadn't quite considered it might be you." She peered at Anna, intently now causing her some consternation, while the aged nurse assembled her thoughts.

At last, Bernie got up from her seat and walked over to a small mahogany dresser with highly polished woodwork that stood in the corner of the room. The top section displayed a variety of china cups, saucers and plates behind glass. From one of the drawers below, she pulled an envelope that had already been opened and handed it to Anna.

"I believe this is for you," she said

Anna's face took on a distinct air of intrigue as she removed the pages from the envelope, but looked quickly at them and handed them back to Bernie.

"This isn't Michael's handwriting," she said sharply.

Bernie placed the pages once more in Anna's hand and using her own hand carefully folded her fingers over them.

"Oh, no dearie. I told you already, that's my handwriting. You see, it was very near the end. Michael was too ill to write, you see. He dictated to me and I wrote down what he said, but they are his words."

Anna unfolded the pages realising her mistake and began to read.

Bernie looked for the first time at Cees who shuffled nervously in his seat while Anna read intently the several pages of rough handwriting. Meanwhile Bernie nervously pulled the curtain a little to one side and peered out. There was some activity on the street. Noisy youths. Every so often as a group would pass by, the noise of their steps and voices became loudly audible in the room.

"Is everything OK?" asked Cees nervously.

"Yes, yes, fine. It's the marching season. One lot marches. Sometimes the other lot turns up to show how much they don't like the marching. They generally try to aggravate each other.

Sometimes they succeed, usually they don't. Usually things just pass, but you can get trouble if spirits get too high. Not great really. I don't think we will ever be free of it. Each generation is replaced by a new one, but little really changes."

"But, I thought things were much better now."

"Yes, they are much, much better," she emphasised, but the old resentments are still there and there is always the occasional incident that brings it all to the surface again." She lifted the edge of the net curtain and looked once more out to the street.

Cees pondered a moment. His knowledge of the province, its problems and conflicts was really rather sparse. At last he looked back at Bernie and asked, "which are the ones who march?"

Bernie let the edge of the curtain fall once more and looked back across the room at her visitor, "does it really matter?"

Cees opened his mouth to speak but thought better of it and looked back over at Anna.

As she read the poem, despite the different handwriting, Anna recognised at once the style of his poetry that had so warmed her teenage years and she was now carted back to then in her mind. The words, from a mind not taught nor compromised by the experiences of the life she had lived since then or the life he might have lived, were as crisp and clean as they had ever been, only sadly, this was not just another poem, this was his last poem and he knew it.

As she read, Anna could see Bernie's handwriting become more and more inconsistent and scrawled in appearance as the poem progressed and this too accentuated the emotion of the words she was reading. Perhaps he might have been sorry for his fate, resentful of those who had taken everything he had, then come back for even his own life, but instead he had forgiven, just as she had asked him to. Perhaps he might have been sad for his loss, the years he would miss, the chance of a career, a family and a future, but instead he was grateful for just one thing. He was grateful for a chance meeting, a tiny moment that was now so very long ago but one that Anna too remembered as if it were yesterday. An encounter, a liaison and a relationship, now separated by time and mortality as well as distance that no one else knew about, nor understood, except as was now apparent to Anna herself. As the poem drew to a close and she read the final few lines, he expressed something he had never expressed before, but she now knew profoundly that it had always been so from the first and only time they had met. Despite the outscoring of letters and words and the several attempts Bernie had made to write down what he said. Despite them being misspelt and unclear and a mystery to everyone, they were as bold and clear to Anna and as welcome in their message as any she had ever heard uttered. The little nonsense line the publishers had thought they resembled, that had intrigued the Irish people for years and even given the poem its name, were in fact the declaration in her own language she had longed to hear so many years earlier.

At this the tear that had been swelling in her eye and remained under her usually calm control, defeated by the laws of surface tension burst forth and dropped to the page as a message sent twenty-seven years earlier finally found its recipient. The tears turned into a flood and she was left in Bernie's front room sobbing uncontrollably, clutching Michael's final poem in her hand.

Eventually, as perhaps dehydration settled in, she finally calmed and just sat staring at the pages.

"Are you OK?" asked Cees. She nodded.

245

It was Bernie who went over and stood by the sobbing woman, still clutching the papers in her hand. She slowly leaned over and pushing the damp hair from her face, kissed her softly on the forehead just as she had done with Michael, many years before. Bernie had worked in healthcare her entire life and seen many sorrows and tragedies over the years. She had comforted the bereaved and hugged the dying many times, but Michael and Anna would remain the only two she had ever kissed in this way.

Presently she left Anna with her thoughts and Cees with his and left the room. Moments later, she returned with a silver tray with a porcelain teapot and three cups and saucers decorated with gold rims and wild flower motifs. She laid out the cups and poured a little milk in each before filling them with fresh tea from the pot. Then she spooned a little sugar in one which she handed to Anna. Her little hand clasped the saucer and the cup shook as she sipped, seemingly not noticing the milk or sugar.

She handed another cup to Cees and took the last herself and sat once more, carefully watching Michael's muse, whom she had always known existed but had long since given up hope of ever meeting.

"It is a lovely poem," said Bernie finally. "Many people are struck by it emotionally."

Then she paused as Anna lifted her chin slowly, her bloodshot eyes focusing on Bernie's once more, "but I think it means perhaps more to you than it does to anyone else."

There were more noises and sounds from outside as a larger group of youths milled by, shouting, swearing and chanting some sort of slogan or rhyme, but Anna didn't notice.

"Maybe you know what that line there means, she said pointing to the untidy letters scrawled towards the bottom of the page. I had trouble knowing what he meant. I wrote it as best I could. He tried to spell it but he was really quite weak by then and I could hardly hear him, let alone understand what he was saying. Maybe you know?"

Anna felt the wave of emotion hit her once more, but there were no more tears and she quickly recovered her composure.

"I figured perhaps it wasn't English, but I didn't know what language. No one seemed to know. There was speculation that it might seem to be from many languages or even perhaps no language at all. Then a teacher at one of the schools suggested that its origin and meaning could only be identified if we discovered to whom it was written."

Anna nodded.

As her composure returned, Anna began to feel rather embarrassed by her actions. At once she stood up and forcing a smile, thanked Bernie for her hospitality and indeed for filling in the answers to questions that she had been asking herself for so very long. *Poor Michael* she thought once more, thinking of him now, again more rationally. She folded the pages and replaced them into the envelope before handing it to Bernie, but Bernie knew it was no longer hers to keep.

"You are now the rightful owner," she said. "This poem was written to you and for you. The people here have shared in it. They have known Michael through it and like you, today hold him close to their hearts, but it belongs to you. I know it to be so. You keep it."

Bernie thought briefly, then a little grin emerged, "Indeed, you are now the custodian of an important piece of Irish literary heritage!"

Anna looked at Cees who nodded. She slowly placed the envelope in her handbag.

"I think we'll be going now. Thank you so much for everything."

"Do you need to go upstairs before you go?" asked Bernie.

Bemused, Anna raised her eyebrows as her mind searched for the answer to the question that seemed so simple but whose meaning she couldn't identify.

"Do you need to go to the little girls' room? It's upstairs on the left."

The penny dropped and Anna laughed spontaneously as she realised the euphemistic term that was so confusing to the foreigner from a land where a single bathroom in the home is always situated on the ground floor. However, she accepted the offer and left Cees with her new friend alone in the room.

When Anna returned, she was looking much more like the wife Cees knew, with her face returned to her natural pale complexion and her hair brushed to her usual mop of curly locks. She looked at Bernie directly in the eyes, then leaned forward and paused briefly before kissing her first on the right cheek, then on the left as she would with family and close friends at home, but Bernie put her arms around her. She pulled the Dutch woman close to her as she confronted her own emotion which had been delayed due to her medical training and sensitivity to the challenges faced by others. Both women now realised that they were each for the other the only living connection they had with the seventeen year old boy who had so touched their lives. When the embrace broke, and their gazes met once more, it was Bernie whose eyes, glazed with emotion, betrayed her feelings. Each looked at the other, wanting to say something of meaning and sense, but neither finding the words. Instead, they each laughed once more at the teary eyes and swollen cheeks. A friendship was born that day.

"So, do you have a car? How did you get here?"

"By taxi. We came by taxi."

"What, a black taxi?"

"Well, yes. It was very nice. We talked to a lady during the trip, she was very friendly. Is there a taxi rank on the main road?"

"Oh dear. You won't get a regular taxi to come up here this afternoon. I don't know a number to call in any case. It's getting a little agitated out there. I don't want you getting caught up in anything."

She opened the front door and the three of them walked out on to the street. Outside, the sky was overcast and a cool wind was blowing. A light drizzle filled the air, but the little baskets hung patiently from their hooks, their bright blooms waving slowly in the wind, as they waited for the sun to shine, like holidaymakers at a washed out beach resort.

"Do you see that wall?"

Bernie pointed. Down at the bottom of the street was the highest wall Cees and Anna had ever seen. The lower section was solid concrete and decorated with graffiti, like the Berlin wall they had watched come down years earlier as the two great ideologies of East and West found common ground. Above the concrete were huge green corrugated panels that rose even above the houses nearby. Above these was a wire fence, so sheer that even the most ambitious climber could hardly scale its height. The whole structure rose over eight metres into the sky. In the distance they could hear the faint sounds of drums, marching songs and stamping feet amid sporadic shouts and chants. For the first time since their arrival, the two visitors felt an uneasy tension in the air.

"Find yourselves on one side of that wall and you're a

Catholic, on the other you're a Protestant," said Bernie. "That's how it is here."

The old woman looked longingly at the couple, like she expected them to say something that would make it OK, but neither spoke. She looked at them as if asking them to judge her and her people, like they had some right to do so, or like they could explain something she could not explain herself, but neither could. She looked at them, old as she was and with little time in front, like she was recording her wish and asking them to *do* something. The two just stared at the elderly woman, her face now a little greyer, her skin a little rougher, her stance a little shorter and her eyes a little sadder. They looked back at the wall, then to Bernie once more.

"I'll get you a taxi," she said at last. "Wait here."

She took off on foot towards the direction of the main road from where they had come, leaving Cees and Anna waiting by her open front door. Some more youths walked by, but took little notice of the two visitors now in their midst.

It wasn't long before she returned, still on foot, hurrying along the pavement, with a black cab driving beside her just at the pace of a fast walk, turning periodically to talk to the driver through the window of the car. When it reached her house, she stopped and slightly out of breath, gave directions to the driver.

"These people are not from here. They are visitors, friends of ours, friends of my family. They are from Holland."

The driver nodded.

"Please take them safely into town. Please don't pick up other passengers, just take them directly to their hotel."

The driver nodded once more. Anna and Bernie said their final goodbyes and the couple hopped into the back of the vehicle.

They sat in silence for the short trip to the hotel. Towards the city centre, some people milled in the streets, waving flags and emblems in the air, but they passed by without incident. In the city centre, the Saturday afternoon shoppers thronged, as they do in any affluent modern city, meeting the ever present needs of hungry consumers with money to spend.

Cees put his arm softly around his wife's shoulder as she sat beside him deep in thought. They had almost arrived at the hotel when he squeezed her arm gently to attract her attention. She looked up at him.

"You know, that tea was a lot better than I thought. I might try it again at breakfast."

CHAPTER 28

A Tour of the Irish Countryside

Anna slept well and the next morning when she awoke, Cees was nowhere to be seen.

Although the memory of sad events is always emotional and because tears are usually shed in sorrow, there is a temptation to assume that the tears of memory are a wretched reliving of that sadness. But it is not always so. It would have been easy for the couple to leave that morning. Easy to leave the sad end to Anna's first love behind and hurry to the airport, board a plane and never return. Easy to fly across the Irish Sea, gaze upon the Lancashire coast beneath, then across England and the winds of the North Sea to their home and the lives they knew. It would have been easy to return once again to that tranquillity, to a culture they understood and leave Michael Coglan, the city of Belfast, the Island of Ireland and its people behind forever.

But already a bond had developed. Anna had felt it from long ago but though she didn't know it, Cees now felt it too. Somehow their visit could not be considered as just another city break to see the sights or a short getaway to recharge the batteries. As she lay in bed, she realised entirely that a faint glow was emerging in her heart. She had felt it, even as she sat deep in thought in the taxi, on the way back to the hotel the previous evening. At first she resisted this uplifting sense, rejecting it like an imposter seeking to interfere with her melancholy state. But, as she lay in bed, it was not sadness that filled her heart but a joyous buzz, a zest for life. She had never before felt so alive. But where was Cees?

She got up and washed, cleaning her teeth and caught herself looking back in the mirror at her own image. Suddenly she found it amusing to see her with white foam bubbling from her mouth as the shape of her cheek expanded and contracted with each stroke of the brush. She washed a little and returned to the bedroom.

Then she noticed it. She had noticed it when she got up although it hadn't registered, but there was definitely something different about the room. It was the light. She went to the window and drew back the curtains. Her eyes widened in astonishment for the overcast drizzle that had been the weather since they arrived had withdrawn like the curtain of a theatre and the summer sun beamed like a spotlight on the city. She felt her heart flutter with excitement, like she was on the edge of a great discovery, as she looked outside at the buildings lit like sculptures in a gallery, casting shadows on the streets below.

She was still engrossed in the sight when she heard the lock buzz as an electronic key opened the door. Cees entered. She turned and beamed a smile at him, but it was no more than the smile he returned.

"Look Anna. I've been thinking. Why don't we stay here another day, hire a car, maybe drive around the countryside and visit some of the places that inspired Michael's poems."

She was at least a little surprised by his generous suggestion and showed the same hesitation she habitually did when offered something she truly wanted, but Cees, knew her well. He had already been down to the concierge to book a car. Indeed, even as he proposed the idea, it stood outside the foyer, tanked up and ready to go.

The winds blow from west to east and evaporating water condenses into clouds that retain much of their moisture until land disrupts their motion. To the west of Ireland there lie several thousand miles of sea over which such clouds can develop. These drift eastwards and constantly drench the island with rain. In terms of total volume of rainfall, it is not especially high, but it is very constant throughout the seasons. On average some rain falls on two hundred of the three hundred and sixty-five days of the year and many more days will be overcast. The result is that grassland grows with astonishing vigour and the dry earth of a European or even an English summer, seldom appears. Such a landscape is rather part of Irish heritage and the mixture of greens such weather encourages exists in the song, dance, folklore and romance of the Emerald Isle.

For the people, whether they are visitors or the local population, a day of glorious sunshine is therefore a little less common and a little more appreciated than it is elsewhere. For those with the time to venture into the countryside, the sunlit greens of meadows and distant hills of purples and greys contrasted against sky which somehow seems just a shade of blue, deeper than elsewhere, is almost psychedelic in nature. It was into this world that Anna and her husband ventured that day.

It took a while for Cees to master driving on the left side of the road and changing gear with his opposite hand, but besides a shaky start the pair quickly found their way through the city streets and headed north onto a large motorway. The vast road promised much but quickly diminished one lane at a time into a coastal road that wound around the bays and headlands of County Antrim.

As they motored on, they drank in the sights around them.

On the left, the land rose steeply with cattle grazing in luscious fields separated by stone walls with stiles that led to pathways up towards the hills beyond. The road ran by rocky faces that swept right down to the sea with occasional tunnels hewn roughly through the stone. Beyond, the sea crashed upon a varied coast where black granite mounds emerged between stretches of unbroken sand and little dunes speckled with tufts of hardy grass.

Before long, they arrived at a small bay where the water stood still and tranquil like it was a lake. They parked up and walked to the shore. A pair of colourfully painted wooden clinker boats sat slanted on their keels their hulls resting on one side on the sand. Tarpaulins had been tied loosely over and the last of the rain sat in little slowly evaporating puddles. Anna stopped by, leaning over to see her own reflection momentarily in the pool before Cees disturbed the puddle with a playful splash.

Along the beach, little waves washed slowly to shore, each emitting sustained whooshing sounds as timeless in their ebbs and flows as the sands beneath or the sky above. The two visitors held hands as they walked in silence taking care to maintain enough distance from the occasional errant wave that managed to avoid the counter flow of the previous one and run quickly and silently up the shallow beach. The sun shone hot, warming their faces and twinkling on the surface of the water. There was not a cloud in the sky.

At the end of the beach, little granite rocks peaked out from the sand, first one or two, but then joined together in raven clumps that extended out to sea like little natural piers. Cees climbed up atop one, then turned and held his hands out to his wife. Anna nervously grasped his wrists, then he pulled her firmly up, briefly hugging her as she balanced on the jagged points. Between the rocks, little pools of sea water had collected, leaving strings of black and brown seaweed with bubble flowers amid green sea moss, which was quickly drying in the sun emitting a salty, pungent odour. Limpets sucked hard on the smoothed surfaces sustaining themselves in wait for the next high tide that would once again link them with the vastness of the sea beyond.

They walked out upon the rocks, balancing carefully and taking care not to slip on the wet surfaces until water gathered around them on three sides. Anna jumped as a little crab with its eerie sideways movement lit across the rock causing her to lose balance and once again seek stability in the arms of her husband. Involuntarily, she giggled and their eyes met, her pupils dilating rapidly as her lashes flashed her message and her lips smiled as she spoke to him in silent language. He pulled her closer and she felt the warmth of his body against hers as he angled his mouth slowly towards her. Anna urgently flicked her eyes to either side in a futile effort to check no one was looking and might have even looked behind, but Cees gave her no more time. Their lips met.

It wasn't a long kiss or a slow kiss, but it was a lovers' kiss. In their busy lives it was rare for them to find the time to offer such a simple offering of love, each to the other. But this kiss was a little more special than most, for in the confusion of the last few days, there had been so much that each wanted to say to the other. Cees so wanted her to know that he too felt the loss of her friend, that he too felt her grief. He wanted her to know that those she loved, he loved too. He wanted her to know that Michael's memory was as welcome in their lives as any other memory they shared, but he had found few words that could properly convey his feelings.

And Anna too wanted her husband to know that she loved him more than ever, that no one could ever replace him in her heart. She wanted him to know that he was everything to her, that it was he who had been her strength as her past knocked urgently on her door, paying the present a visit. But the kiss spoke. In those few seconds outside in nature's wonderland, alone and at peace, in warm embrace as the sea rushed its rhythm against aged rocks and sandy shore they said everything they needed to each other without either uttering a word.

When they broke from embrace, the two skipped as children across the rocky outcrop, taking care to dodge the puddles making their way right to the end where the waves now broke with passionate vigour upon the rocks. Together they peered at the foaming sea beneath them washing in and out, the white foam on top, then out towards the horizon where the sunlight sparkled its diamond dance.

Once again, they set off in the car, singing a chorus of *drive on the left, drive on the left!* The road wound around bends towards grassy headlands, then eventually turned inland as they crossed over a little hump-backed bridge of stone under which a flood of water from the recent wet weather streamed in torrents towards the sea. For no other reason than the adventure that a day with no agenda can offer, they turned off the main road onto a narrow lane that ran quite straight up towards the hills. The car bounced up and down on the thin surface of a road that still registered every tiny undulation of the land as it rose higher and higher towards the sky. Cattle grazed lazily in the fields as if they too had turned out in number to catch the warmth of the summer sun. Gradually the salty smells of the coast gave way to the spicy odours of livestock farms, silage stocks and dampened meadows. They passed through tiny hamlets with little whitewashed cottages that looked like they hadn't changed in centuries amid modern homes with panoramic views across the wooded glens.

They drove higher and higher into the hills where the land became more barren with sheep restlessly grazing the shiny grass between white rocks that littered the landscape like a giant had hurled a huge pile of stones across the country. It seemed like they might be reaching a pass when Cees pulled the car over to a car park strategically placed with views over the hills beyond and out towards the sea, now in the distance. The sun was now high in the sky and beaming its warmth generously on the day trippers who willingly inhaled the clean, fresh air in the silence, only occasionally broken by a bleating sheep picking its grassy dinner.

They got out of the car once more and gazed across the land of God's own country. It seemed strange to think of the conflicts that had raged before amid such panoramic peace, where Anna could hardly think but to rejoice. Behind the car park on the other side of the road was a stile of silvered wood that bridged a hedgerow to the open lands of the plateau. They climbed over, jumping the small height onto the windblown grass that was normally used to living in a state of survival, but today drank the sunlight like a nomad at a desert oasis. A little track ran higher still beside a dry wall of grey white stones dappled with moss and lichen. Some of the rocks had fallen beside, perhaps dislodged by winter storms or impatient animals seeking greener grass on the others side.

Cees stopped to lift one or two, carefully fitting them in place on top, before standing back to survey his work, then placing a few more. As they walked on, the path left the wall behind and the grassland steepened into scree slopes of loose stones that rolled like marbles below their feet causing slips and trips. Anna ventured gingerly on helped by Cees who himself jigged and danced before her as the unpredictable surface slipped and tripped his feet beneath him.

The top was not a craggy peak, but an even mound that rose slowly and in the end imperceptibly to its summit which was only identifiable by an angled flat rock. Anna stood atop twirling around, her arms splayed catching the air while her mind recorded the three hundred and sixty degree view she would take home with her that day.

They spent some time on the hill, enjoying the peace of the day, lazing in the sun and watching the life around them. Hills extended in every direction like there was not a truly horizontal surface to be seen. It was mid-afternoon when they decided to return to the little car, parked far below. They drove around for the rest of the afternoon, never bored with the views that changed rapidly but also remained within a defined theme of colour and landscape that was reassuringly constant. They drove by handsome folk on ponies with rising trots to the sound of hooves clipping joyfully on the pavements. They passed farms where dirty dogs ran out to bark at the car in hostile welcome. They sat patiently as shepherds herded bleating sheep along narrow lanes flanked with varied hedgerows. As the afternoon faded and the expectation of summer evening rose to take its place, gentle pangs of hunger were sending messages to the travellers' brains and thoughts of hearty fare quickly became the subject of conversation.

"Do you want to find somewhere to eat here or head back and get something at the hotel?"

Anna didn't answer but shrugged, rather paining Cees who had to turn his eyes briefly from the road to see her response.

"I'm easy," she said at last. "We have passed a few places advertising food. Let's head back, but keeping to the country roads. If we see somewhere, then great, if not, then we can always eat at the hotel."

"Sounds like a plan."

It wasn't long before they entered a village. It was like many they had seen that day with a main road that ran from one end of the village to the other with a few shops and a post office providing life to the little hamlet. On one side of the road was a large whitewashed building dirtied by the passing traffic as it fronted the main street, set back only the width of the footpath. A white sign hung from a frame on the wall that advertised; *Parking first on left. Food served all day. Music now and again.*

The couple nodded agreement to each other and Cees, now having adapted his driving mind to think in opposites, took the first left turn which led to a narrow lane. This in turn led around to a car park at the back of the pub.

The entrance was through a black, latched door, one of the kind that split horizontally in the middle, like those found in a stable and inside there was indeed something of the farm about the smell. However, this was mingled with the familiar musky scents of alcohol and home cooking that always provided the warmest of welcomes to weary travellers. The inside was gloomy, but cosy all the same with aged black beams in the ceiling, between which dangled an eclectic mix of vintage farming utensils and household trinkets. Some dangled rather too low for the tall elegance of the protein filled Dutch visitors and Cees found himself ducking as he and Anna headed for the bar. The walls were filled with old photographs of bearded farmers posing with prize cattle or groups of smiling patrons with tankards in hand. To the left of the entrance door, tables and chairs were being moved, clearing a space in front of a small window that looked out onto the main street outside.

"Will you have the *Irish* burger?" asked Anna, carefully pondering the menu. Cees elbowed her softly in the ribs and she yelped mockingly and smiled, flicking her eyes to his returned gaze beside her.

"I'd recommend the steak." said the barman interrupting the foreign language he didn't understand, but figuring the inspection of the menus was a giveaway. "Cattle slaughtered locally. See yer man over there." He nodded towards three old men sitting playing cards at a small round table in the corner. "The one with the hat. He could probably tell you which steer it came from. Gives them all names he does!"

The couple looked over and watched the animated activity of cards being thrown on the table amid the laughs and tuts of the players.

"Go for the rump. It's tender like fillet, but with a much fuller taste."

Anna looked at Cees and shrugged. "I guess we'll have the rump steak then." Cees nodded approval.

You English?

Anna smiled disarmingly. "No, Dutch," she said.

"Ah," came the reply. There was a long pause while the slow wheels of thought processed in his mind. "Andre Rieu!" he said at last. "He's Dutch isn't he?"

"*Oh surely not!*" thought Anna, but said nothing, smiling politely.

"So what brings you to our little village?"

Cees broke in. "Well, we always wanted to visit Ireland, then my wife came across a poem by Michael Coglan and we wanted to try to find out a bit more, so we booked in for a long weekend."

"Ah," said the barman, "Ahoy for Joy. Nobody knows what it means, you know."

"Yes, quite a mystery," said Anna smiling more to herself than anyone else.

"Well, do stop with us a while. There's a wee band playing tonight and if I'm not very much mistaken, we will have another humble poet visiting us later on as well."

Anna raised her eyebrows.

"If I were you, I'd get settled at one of those tables over there for it'll fill up fast and you'll be left standing, eating your steak in your hands like a burger. I'll bring them over when they're ready."

The steaks were indeed very excellent and the pair chomped enthusiastically as they watched the activities develop around them. Before long, the door was wedged open and several rough looking men lugged microphones and amps into the small building and proceeded to set them up. In time, jackets were removed, revealing white shirts with jeans held up with colourful braces. Several violins were removed from cases, drums set at the back and a saxophone set on a stand to one side together with two flutes.

By the time Cees and Anna had finished their steaks, the little pub was filled with folk of every shape and size. At last the band were set and ready to go. Most of the five members looked to be in their fifties but the band leader who introduced himself simply as Paddy was much younger, maybe in his early thirties and clearly adept at keeping the crowd entertained. He beckoned for silence, then tapped his fiddle before the band sprang into song with a selection of Irish jigs and moody ballads. They played nothing that Cees and Anna recognised, but this did nothing to dampen their enjoyment for the spirit of Ireland lived there that night.

They had played for almost an hour when the main door opened and a young lad rushed in loudly whispering, "Jackie McDee's here. Jackie McDee's here." He waited a moment for the song to finish, then whispered in Paddy's ear. Moments later, Paddy beckoned with his hands, waving them slowly before the little crowd. The voices slowed and stopped and before long the entire bar was covered in an eerie silence. Anna hadn't noticed but all eyes were now fixed on the little window. At last there were three firm knocks on the glass. Paddy smiled, looking expectantly at the delighted crowd as he pushed the casement open to the street. Outside, Cees and Anna could just see a bearded figure with a rampant mop of unkempt hair, peering through from the shadows.

"I am a poor poet, weary with travel and hungry too," he said in a clear voice laced with mock sadness. "But, I have no money. Can I sing for my supper?"

Paddy, turned to the crowd, now stirring a little.

"Can he sing for his supper?" he cried. There was a cheer. "Can he sing for his supper?" he shouted now against the din of the crowd.

"Yes, yes, yes," was the reply mixed with comments like, *let the man sing* or *yes, let's hear him*.

With that, Paddy calmed the crowd once more to silence and at his nod, the first notes of *Che Gelida Manina*, Pucinni's haunting refrain from the opera *La Boheme* filled the room, the fiddlers having suddenly morphed into concert violinists. From outside, the voice rose of an accomplished tenor, broadcast through the window as the Italian words he sang told the story of the carefree poet, squandering rhymes and love songs and of dreams of castles that melt into the air.

Anna was transfixed, her astonishment only tempered by

delight. Cees, more the classical authority of the couple, strained his eyes to see the owner of such a remarkable voice, as his thoughts followed the song to completion. At last the final notes were struck and the crowd erupted in rapturous applause. The door swung open and a ragged man of sixty years or more walked through to pats and smiles and claps and whistles. He was barely five feet tall and nearly as wide. Despite the warm summer evening, albeit rare, he wore a three quarter length coat with a satchel over one shoulder, fastened tightly closed with two canvas straps. Cees wondered if he was dressed for the role or if he actually lived it.

He smiled faintly at the applause, as a table was quickly prepared for his supper by a smiling waitress who presently ushered him to his seat. Before long, the steak was served and a pint of Guinness settled in the glass as he tucked in to the hearty meal he had bought with his voice.

The second half was as exciting as the first and folk took to dancing and twirling around in front of the makeshift stage. The atmosphere was terrific and every age group was represented from old men and grannies through to scruffy youngsters, far too young to be in a bar.

At last, the band finished, but the crowd cried for more and the normally reserved Cees and Anna found themselves jumping up and down and cheering and shouting with the rest. Feet were stamped and eventually, grinning with delight, Paddy beckoned with his hands once more for hush.

"Ok, ok, ok. We'll do one more!"

The crowd cheered.

"Now, some will say that we Irish got nothing from the English."

Muted mutterings followed, together with sniggers and whistles.

"But, I beg to differ! For the most beautiful tune ever to lilt its melody on the ears of man, or woman," he paused for effect, "lay without a suitor of credible means for a century if not a day. It was not until 1913 that an Englishman called Frederic Weatherly bestowed on us poor Irish, the greatest of all gifts. He wrote the words, the Irish longed to speak, that of a ballad so haunting and beautiful it is sung the world over by people of every creed who wherever they roam are instantly whisked to this fair Isle in thought, in mind and in spirit."

"Ladies and gentlemen, you all know the words."

The cheers of the crowd grew once more.

"Jackie will you help us out with this one?"

"If I can have another beer!" croaked a voice to the laughter of the buoyant crowd, who had come to accept that the clarity of his spoken word starkly contrasted with the notes of his song.

Paddy opened with a solo on the flute and the fiddles built into a complex introductory arrangement, before the familiar lilt of the Londonderry Air broke through and Jackie McDee, who had not yet made his way through the crowd, opened with the familiar words;

Oh Danny Boy...

He sang both verses before the band returned to the beginning and the crowd joined in for a final refrain. It was after 11.00pm when Cees and Anna took their leave and set off for the drive to their hotel in Belfast. Anna curled up, relaxed, warm and satisfied. They had been fed, watered and entertained in a way she had never imagined. They had been welcomed openly without question or suspicion. Anna reflected once more and in pensive mood as the car sped along the narrow country roads of Michael's homeland. She looked across at Cees who was concentrating hard to keep the car on the left of the narrow road.

"So, which Irish do you think these ones were?"

"What?" replied Cees.

"You know, like Catholic or Protestant. Which do you think these ones were?"

"Does it really matter?" he replied, echoing Bernie's words of the day before.

Anna was silent and pondered his reply. Quietly to herself she blushed. It was a blush from a little shameful embarrassment and she reproached herself for it. It was a question she would never ask again, not even in her mind. As the busy day finally caught up with her, she drifted off to a gentle slumber.

CHAPTER 29

A Reluctant Scholar

The next morning they set off for the airport. The sun still shone. Anna sat back in the seat of the taxi, now at last relaxed. She was glad she had come. She had expected the trip to be sad and it was sad, it had been sad, but she did not *feel* sad. Instead she felt uplifted, elated even. *Michael would have loved this*, she thought, thinking of the little poem. He would have loved its notoriety, the unifying effect it had had on the community and its funny little controversy.

Ahoy for joy! She wondered if he was looking down on her, chuckling at the unintended little riddle. She felt close to him now, closer than at any time since events severed their contact. Now they were joined together in spirit, bound in the common knowledge they shared.

So, he *had* loved her then. She thought back once more to the young man she had met so very briefly who had wooed her with his letters and poems. Surely she had known that all along. Yes he did love her. Why was there ever any doubt? Maybe the doubt had been her only protection from the terrible truth. She thought again, *if she had known, she would have come at once. Of course she would have come at once.*

Cees looked over and smiled at her but could see she was deep in thought. He watched the city go by, the people milling around, going about their business. The traffic was slow and the taxi edged forward cautiously in the Monday morning congestion. He looked at the buildings, the bridges across the Lagan and the ships beyond in the estuary. *Belfast was famous for something else* he thought. The traffic was just easing a little and the car picking up pace when he leaned forward and asked the driver,

"Titanic was built here wasn't it?"

The driver glanced at him in his mirror, "yes, surely indeed it was. If you look over to the right there, that's the shipyard. Titanic was built over there. Indeed," he paused a moment, changing gear as the car swept around a long bend, "if you want to see the *exact* spot, we'll pass right by it in a minute. They're planning to build a visitor centre there to celebrate the centenary in 2012."

Cees gazed intently from the window, but Anna was still lost in her own thoughts. Then the driver spoke again. "There. If you look now. Do you see just this side of the great, big cranes; Samson and Goliath, Titanic was built right there. That's the dry dock where she was built, right there."

Cees gazed thoughtfully at the spot where the world's most famous ship had started its short life. Like so much else they had seen, the theme of the city seemed a constant paradox of beauty and tragedy, of majesty and disaster and yet the easy mirth of the people could surely warm the coldest soul.

He pointed. "That's the actual dry dock, just there," he pointed. "Greatest ship of her day, you know. We specialise in that sort of thing here."

"What, shipbuilding?" replied Cees.

"No, failure on a Titanic scale!" The driver chuckled, enjoying his little self-deprecating joke. "Only here do they celebrate that sort of thing!"

Suddenly, Anna stirred from her thoughts as a mighty din

invaded her mind as she heard the driver's voice. Louder and louder the names of the two Biblical giants, *Samson and Goliath* chimed like a mantra in the wind. "What are Samson and Goliath," she enquired urgently.

The driver, swerved a little and pulled out as the motorway traffic eased and they gathered pace.

"The big yellow cranes in the shipyard. Biggest in the world in their day. Look, you can still see them." He nodded over his shoulder.

Anna looked. She hadn't noticed them before, but there they stood, towering over the city; bright and yellow in the sun. Cadmium yellow!

She sat back in her seat again. *Oh Michael*, she thought once more. It was all in the words. *For tis not flower but plant I seek, man-made upon the earth.* Not a plant that *grows*, but *industrial* plant, big pieces of equipment for construction, road building or *ship* building! She knew the words so well, for she had spent hours contemplating them. On she thought, reciting the poem once more to herself.

Then off toward home and o'er a ridge I craned *my neck to see.* Oh it was there all along. He *craned* his neck. He was describing the huge shipyard *cranes*. The clues were all there. He was playing with the words. She scolded herself. They had *always* been there. Everyone in Belfast would know what Samson and Goliath were, but he knew she wouldn't. He had always reassured her, she would find out one day. He had always known she would come. Maybe she was late, very, very late. Twenty-seven years late, but she was here now and she was so glad, so very, *very* glad that she had come.

The car sped on, leaving the city a haze in the summer sun and the cranes faded into the distance. Anna turned for a final look. It seemed serene, the contrasts of heavy equipment silhouetted against the sea, then merging through the houses towards the overlooking hills, a rising permanence in a changing world and she felt a pang of sadness at her own departure. They had met the local people too. Where in the world was it quite as easy to meet people as here? Where in the world could you just walk into a bar and immediately be engaged in conversation, not just idle chat, but animated jokes and puns, fun and laughter. *Craic*! She had found out the meaning a long time ago, but this was a dictionary meaning. Now, she *really* knew what it meant.

But, it hadn't all been so relaxed. There had been some tension in the air when they visited Bernie as the old traditions of mistrust brushed against each other. There was that wall. She could still see it in her mind's eye, towering above them. A wall whose sole purpose was to keep people who hate each other apart. But what people? Which people were these? They hadn't met them. What was so different about these people? Maybe one day that wall too would fall, like the walls man has built since time immemorial. They all have their day, but their eras come to an end and that wall looked old, a wall of the past. Not a wall of today. It looked tired in its purpose. She satisfied herself that its days were indeed numbered.

Then they had seen the countryside whose peaceful glory her mind had recorded just the day before. There were indeed forty shades of green, but there were also tumbling streams of water, silent lakes, sand and rocks, forests and glens. The landscape was as varied as it was timeless.

She thought of Bernie, once more. She sighed. Bernie whose grace had held Michael's memory alive for twenty years, then modestly presented his work for publication. Bernie whose life of service and dedication had preserved his final little note that now rested in her purse, the final piece of the poetic jigsaw that would now join the others she held in her dresser at home.

They arrived rather early at the airport and the check in was not yet open, so they decided to have a cup of coffee. Finding a restaurant in the main terminal they settled down to wait. Just opposite, a smartly dressed lady wearing a black and silver dog tooth checked jacket and matching skirt sat together with her teenage son and a small daughter, aged about eight years old. The lady was reading a magazine, stopping and starting from time to time to engage with one or other of the children. The little girl had a freckled face and bright red hair tied with a green bow that matched her flowing dress that caught the air a little as she impatiently spun and twirled beside the table.

The boy wore a school uniform with a dark navy blazer, white shirt and a rather ruffled loose tie of dark blue with thin, red stripes. They appeared to be waiting for someone on an arriving flight. As they sat, the boy was fiddling awkwardly with a folded piece of paper, a photocopied sheet like one of those hand-outs often given to pupils in class.

The mother was pushing him to do his homework study as they sat. "You won't have time to do it tonight when we get home," she said, "not if you want to watch TV."

"Aw, but I don't want to read it" he retorted. "Sorry Mum but poetry's just not my thing."

"Come on Malcolm, it's a beautiful poem," said the mother encouragingly, "It was written by a boy, not much older than you who sadly died in the Troubles."

The boy sighed. "Yes, yes, I know."

The mother looked at him once more, then set her magazine aside.

"Look, here, give it to me. I'll read it."

The woman took the sheet, unfolded it and sat upright in her seat. Projecting her voice a little and taking care to enhance the words with her own expression, she began to read:

Ahoy for Joy

The doctor speaks with wicked mendacity and the nurse's eyes
    are black
Mum and Dad are gone and they won't be coming back
What wretched mark did seal my fate
What flag or politik
What tortured mind did nervous seek
This little life to take

But as time erodes, conviction ebbs, oh beware contrition's ridged
    grip
It shatters hatred, love and fear, engulfs the mind in vain regret
A shudder in the daytime
A terror in the night
A tacit realisation
A lonely mental fight

But relax my friend, I bear no slight let me help you with your
    pain
The aged winds of discontent are really all to blame
Let not remorse your heart endure
Nor idle reprimand
For pardon's unconditional
By Anna's blessed hand

Oh Anna, muse and confidante, your wonder woke my muted
    voice
And made me know the beauty and in the world rejoice
Then words and rhymes that filled my mind
Fluttered from above
To settle on my pages
In messages of love

But is an unrequited love just a love forlorn
And ardour penned in text and prose of intimacy shorn
No lingered gaze of wanton eye
Nor taste of that first kiss
No mingled scent of close embrace
Or sensual caress

Or can this love immaculate transcend these mortal days
And see you blossom as your life abounds in many ways
A husband and some children then?
Oh happiness bestow
Your life with every blessing
Where 'ere the winds may blow

Now as my mortal senses fade and life and death collide
All truth is known, all dies are cast, all doubts now brushed aside
I'm rising high no longer shy
And cry *Ahoy for Joy*
Ahoy for joy with angels sing
Eternal to avow

The boy sat slightly vexed, his head staring aimlessly at the
empty cups and saucers on the table, but the girl stopped her

spinning around and now stood listening attentively to her Mother's words. When the lady had finished, the boy got up. "I'm off to look in the shops" he said and with that he loped off alone, his loose shirt tail now visible beneath the hem of his jacket.

"Was the poem really written by a boy, just like Big Brn?" asked the girl.

The mother smiled. "Yes, it was. Look, see here at the bottom."

This poem was written by Michael Coglan, a 17 year old student as he lay dying in hospital in 1980. His words were recorded by Miss Bernadette O'Callaghan, a nurse at the Royal Victoria Hospital who sat with him for many of the last days of his life. Miss O'Callaghan states that while she recorded his words as best she could, she does not believe she caught everything absolutely accurately and in one or two areas some editorial discretion was required to complete the work. The penultimate lines, recorded here as "Ahoy for joy" remains the most controversial of these as Miss O'Callaghan claims that when she referred back to her notes many years later, she really couldn't properly read her handwriting. She maintains that she was quite sure Michael was trying to say something either, made up or perhaps in a foreign language. The girl, Anna to whom the latter verses appear to be addressed has also never been identified.

The mother handed the paper to the girl and smiled softly. "Maybe at least one of my children will grow to love poetry".

Anna had been watching the episode and at last caught the girl's eye. She beckoned her over.

"Oh, you have such lovely freckles," she said smiling.

The girl scowled a little and pouted, "the boys at school tease me about them."

"Oh but they shouldn't, they're beautiful. Look, I have them too."

Anna pointed briefly at her own face and leaned forward. The girl looked attentively at her. "You're very beautiful" she said.

"In my language, we call them kusjes van engelen"

"What language is that?"

"Ah, that's Dutch, I'm from Holland, you see. We speak Dutch there. It means kisses from Angels"

"Angel's kisses! Angel's kisses! That's what Mummy calls them," cried the girl now lighting up, her smile widening to reveal a row of little white teeth. Anna caught her eye once more and smiled. "Can I see your poem?"

The girl handed Anna the sheet and sat down beside her on the bench. The mother looked up and reviewed the scene briefly before going back to reading her magazine. Anna unfolded the paper and pushing her coffee cup to one side laid it flat on the table. She gazed avidly at the text. It was the first time she had seen it in print. "It's a lovely poem isn't it?" she said at last.

"Yes, it was written by a poor boy, just a little older than my brother. But he died".

"Yes, I know" said Anna, "Michael Coglan."

Suddenly the girl looked closely and for no other reason than some kind of sub-conscious, childhood intuition asked, "did you know Michael Coglan?"

"Yes, I did" said Anna at once. The girl's eyes widened and she drew a little breath, but Anna quickly caught herself and went on, "of course, in the way that we all do, through his wonderful poem." She paused, briefly raising her own eyes, "but, I think I can help with this."

She pointed to the penultimate lines of the poem, "I think Michael might have been trying to say something in my language here, in Dutch." She opened her handbag and took out a pencil. Carefully beside the text, she wrote the words; *Ik hou van Jou.*

"Look, here, you see. It looks quite similar doesn't it"

The girl looked sceptically at the neat writing on the page, then back again at Anna.

"Of course, we would say it phonetically a bit like you might say, well," she paused, "a bit like; *ik how fon yow.*" The girl didn't really know what phonetically meant, but she found herself shaping her lips to make the new little words.

"*Now*, wait till you see what happens," said Anna delightedly. She read the last few lines of the poem out loud, but this time with her own words inserted in place;

> I'm rising high, no longer shy
> And cry *Ik hou von Jou,*
> *Ik hou van Jou* with angels sing
> Eternal to avow

"Look, *now* it *rhymes!*" she exclaimed.

The girl's expression broke to a wide smile as she surveyed the sheet and listened to the funny Dutch words. Then she looked again at Anna and raised her eyebrows, "is that how you say it?"

"Yes. Ik hou van jou" said Anna slowly, "can *you* say it?"

The girl smiled and drew a small breath; "ik – hou – van –

jou," she said carefully watching her teacher's face for approval.

"Very good, very good" laughed Anna, "but you say it like *how now brown cow*," she said emphasising the rounded vowel sounds used in Dutch. "Say it again, say it again!"

The girl giggled at the funny words; "ik – *hou* – van – *jou*" she emphasised.

"That's much better. Now you're speaking Dutch. That's quite wonderful."

The girl beamed, her bright teeth sparkling as she engaged with her new friend, "ik-hou-van-jou," she said once more. "Yes, yes, yes, but what does it *mean*?"

"What does it mean?" exclaimed Anna, "what does it *mean*?" She paused, a moment, smiling, but the girls eyes never left hers, "Why it means *I love you* of course, what else *could* it mean?

The girl smiled, "Ik hou van jou, ik hou van jou" she said again, practising.

"Of course, you must keep it for someone very special indeed, don't you think?" interjected Anna cautiously.

The girl widened her eyes once more and nodded slowly, "oh yes, yes, of course."

With that the frosted glass doors of the arrivals lounge slid open and a man with a shock of bright red hair came through, towing a large suitcase. He wore brown leather shoes, a grey jacket and a white shirt. He also wore a grin from ear to ear.

The girl sprang to her feet and running towards the man, cried "Ik hou van jou Daddy, Ik hou van jou." She threw her arms around his neck and jumped into the air clutching him tightly, her face nuzzled against his cheek. "I love you Daddy," she said softly once more.